# The e

Anyway, three months ago I v                                     en
Franklin Middle School a free woman. New page. Clean slate.
How can I describe my feelings walking out of Ben Franklin?
You know when you do something that you don't want your
parents to know about but you think there's a good chance
they might find out and if they do, your life as you know it is
over? At first, you can't breathe, you're totally self-conscious,
and you're positive you'll be found out any second. But days
go by and it dawns on you that you pulled it off. Well, maybe
that hasn't happened to you, but that's how I felt when I
walked out of that school for the last time. I just kept thinking,
"I did it. I'm free."

## ALSO BY ROSALIND WISEMAN

### Queen Bees & Wannabes:
*Helping Your Daughter Survive Cliques, Gossip, Boyfriends,*
*& the New Realities of Girl World*

### Queen Bee Moms & Kingpin Dads:
*Dealing with the Difficult Parents in Your Child's Life*

### Owning up Curriculum:
*Empowering Adolescents to Confront Social Cruelty,*
*Bullying, and Injustice*

# Boys, Girls
# & Other
# Hazardous
# Materials

# Boys, Girls & Other Hazardous Materials

## Rosalind Wiseman

**speak**
An Imprint of Penguin Group (USA) Inc.

SPEAK
Published by the Penguin Group
Penguin Group (USA) Inc., 345 Hudson Street, New York, New York 10014, U.S.A.
Penguin Group (Canada), 90 Eglinton Avenue East, Suite 700, Toronto, Ontario, Canada M4P 2Y3
(a division of Pearson Penguin Canada Inc.)
Penguin Books Ltd, 80 Strand, London WC2R 0RL, England
Penguin Ireland, 25 St Stephen's Green, Dublin 2, Ireland (a division of Penguin Books Ltd)
Penguin Group (Australia), 250 Camberwell Road, Camberwell, Victoria 3124, Australia
(a division of Pearson Australia Group Pty Ltd)
Penguin Books India Pvt Ltd, 11 Community Centre,
Panchsheel Park, New Delhi - 110 017, India
Penguin Group (NZ), 67 Apollo Drive, Rosedale, North Shore 0632, New Zealand
(a division of Pearson New Zealand Ltd)
Penguin Books (South Africa) (Pty) Ltd, 24 Sturdee Avenue,
Rosebank, Johannesburg 2196, South Africa

Registered Offices: Penguin Books Ltd, 80 Strand, London WC2R 0RL, England

This book is published in partnership with Walden Media, LLC. Walden Media and the Walden
Media skipping stone logo are trademarks and registered trademarks of Walden Media, LLC,
17 New England Executive Park, Burlington, MA 01803.

First published in the United States of America by G. P. Putnam's Sons,
a division of Penguin Young Readers Group, 2010
Published by Speak, an imprint of Penguin Group (USA) Inc., 2011

1  3  5  7  9  10  8  6  4  2

THE LIBRARY OF CONGRESS HAS CATALOGED THE G. P. PUTNAM'S SONS EDITION AS FOLLOWS:
Wiseman, Rosalind, date.
Boys, girls and other hazardous materials / Rosalind Wiseman.   p.   cm.
Summary: Freshman Charlotte "Charlie" Healey's plan to shed her "mean girl" image at her new
high school hits a road block after meeting her former next-door neighbors and best friend, Will,
who is hanging out with a questionable crew.
ISBN 978-0-399-24796-5 (hc)
[1. High schools—Fiction. 2. Schools—Fiction. 3. Conduct of life—Fiction.] I. Title.
PZ7.W780315Bo 2010   [Fic]—dc22   2009018446

Speak ISBN 978-0-14-241819-2

Printed in the United States of America

Book design by Marikka Tamura
Text set in ITC Galliard

*To my mother, Kathy,*
*and my aunts Mary, Nancy, and Peggy—*
*you more than anyone have made me believe*
*that what I say matters.*

# Boys, Girls & Other Hazardous Materials

# PROLOGUE

Here's the deal. My name is Charlie—and, yes, I'm a girl. My full name is Charlotte Anne Healey. I'm about to start ninth grade, live in a fairly normal neighborhood, have a tolerable older brother, and my parents are usually sane. I'm about five feet five, have brown eyes, brownish blond hair that's okay, but I'm definitely not shampoo commercial girl, and I don't wake up at five A.M. every morning to blow-dry my hair. I'm not anorexic or bulimic and generally think my body isn't completely unfortunate. Which frankly, maintaining that perspective while I'm surrounded by skinny girls constantly complaining about how fat they are, is a serious accomplishment.

On the other hand, I can be slow to admit the obvious. Painfully slow. That, combined with my other major personal weakness of occasionally having no backbone with my friends, meant I had to get a grip and do two things: First, I finally admitted to myself that my best friends were actually my frenemies. (You know, girls I didn't trust 100 percent, but for some reason were my closest friends.) Second, when I graduated from eighth grade last year, I ran at the first opportunity, which in my case took the form of transferring to another high school so I could hopefully meet cool, interesting, nonevil, nonvindictive friends.

What was my middle school like? Ben Franklin Middle School was one of those renovated middle schools that look like a mall. Everything was a soothing shade of beige, strategically placed skylights gave us the illusion of access to the outside world, and it was way too big for any twelve-year-old kid to walk the halls alone. When I started there in sixth grade, I really began to doubt the sanity of adults. Seriously, who could possibly think it's a good idea to put 1,500 sixth-, seventh-, and eighth-graders together? I guess *they* never read *Lord of the Flies*—even though it's been on the summer eighth-grade reading list for the last thirty years.

Anyway, three months ago I walked out the front doors of Ben Franklin a free woman. New page. Clean slate. How can I describe my feelings walking out of Ben Franklin? You know when you do something that you don't want your parents to know about but you think there's a good chance they might find out and if they do, your life as you know it is over? At first, you can't breathe, you're totally self-conscious, and you're positive you'll be found out any second. But days go by and it dawns on you that you pulled it off. Well, maybe that hasn't happened to you, but that's how I felt when I walked out of that school for the last time. I just kept thinking, "I did it. I'm free."

## CHAPTER ONE

**I SHOULD HAVE BEEN CLEARER ABOUT MY MUSICAL DEMANDS** because I arrived at Harmony Falls High School in my dad and brother's pet project, a restored 1963 Ford Falcon, top down, with my dad blasting Styx's "Come Sail Away."

Why couldn't my brother Luke have driven me? When I begged him that morning he just shook his head and laughed. "Not happening, Charles. I'm not getting within a mile of that place."

I slid down in the seat so no one would see me. But that also meant I couldn't see exactly where we were going. Before I knew it, I saw a huge flagpole and multicolored brick walls. My dad had driven right up to the driveway of the school.

"Dad!" I hissed, "Seriously, please let me out of the car! You're killing me."

My dad turned off the music, not because I asked him to but because he couldn't hear me. "What, honey?" He looked around. "Seems like this is where I should drop you off, doesn't it?"

"I'm not sure. Maybe you could drive around a little more and completely humiliate me again before I get out of this car," I said, slowly sitting up and looking around to see if anyone noticed our arrival. Of course they had. There were hundreds of kids walking past me, and some of them were definitely looking in my direction.

Three boys looked up. They were dressed in khaki shorts, Rainbows, and T-shirts, as if there was a dress code. "Nice car. Is that a sixty-five?"

My dad grinned. "Almost! It's a sixty-three," he said, like a ten-year-old showing off his new bike.

"Dad," I whispered, "please try to restrain yourself."

Not a chance because a really hot brown-haired one asked, "Is it stock?"

My dad grinned even wider. "It's got a few tweaks. My son and I swapped in a 302 with a T-5 and a Hurst shifter. We're still sorting it out, but she'll do sixty in about six seconds, if you can get the traction."

The boy stepped back a few feet and looked at the car again. He crossed his arms. "Sweet," he said, nodding.

Then my dad did the worst thing possible. "Guys, this is my daughter, Charlie!"

All three did the "Hey, what's up?" boy grunt.

"Hi," I mumbled, bright red.

"Okay, Dad, you can go now!" I groaned, opening the car door.

My dad grimaced. "Oh, I guess that was sort of bad. Sorry about that. Maybe I'm a little nervous for you."

"I know."

He leaned over and kissed me on the cheek. "How about I make it up to you? Get takeout at Nam Viet? And feel free to tell those boys your dad's really lame."

"Don't worry about it. I'll definitely say something bad about you," I said, standing up.

My dad yelled behind me, "Bye, Charlie! Have a good day!" I waved to him without looking back and stepped into the next four years of my life.

**CHAPTER TWO**

**I IGNORED MY DAD DRIVING AWAY AND JOINED THE RIVER OF** kids streaming toward the front entrance. Ten doors side by side. Ben Franklin Middle School was big, but this was really big. For the first time in months, I missed Lauren and Ally. They might have been terrible friends, but at least I wouldn't have walked into my first day of high school alone. But I couldn't think about that—I'd made my decision, and there was no going back.

I walked into a huge open space as a sign above me scrolled WELCOME TO HARMONY FALLS! WE'RE GLAD YOU'RE HERE! Below the sign was a blond girl with freckles, wearing a black T-shirt that said HARMONY FALLS PRIDE!

"Welcome to Harmony Falls! Follow the paw prints to the gym for registration!" She repeated this over and over as new students poured into the school. The girl couldn't possibly smile any wider without her face splitting, and she'd written her name (Morgan) in bubble letters with an exclamation point at the end of her nametag. I know this is totally judgmental, but have you ever taken anyone seriously who writes in bubble letters? Maybe it'd be better to have bitter, angry people greet you instead. You know, set new students' expectations so low that any friendly person you'd meet later would seem even better.

Gigantic blue paws were taped to the floor leading out of the entranceway and down a long hall. But even without them it wouldn't have been hard to find the gym because everyone was going the same way.

Seventeen paws later, I arrived in front of another set of ten doors. But before I could enter the gym, I had to register. I went up to a plastic table where a woman wearing the HARMONY FALLS PRIDE T-shirt with mom jeans and blindingly white Keds sat smiling. I could hear hundreds of voices behind the door.

"Hi," I said nervously, "I'm here for the orientation."

"Welcome to Harmony Falls! What's your name?" she chirped.

"Charlotte, Charlotte Healey."

"Go down to the *E* through *J* table and we'll check you in!"

I walked down to the *E* through *J* table, where a woman wearing a long-sleeve shirt under a PRIDE T-shirt completely stretched out by her obviously fake boobs was checking kids in. Did moms get boob jobs? And she had Botoxed her face so much that it looked like she was standing in front of a large fan. Maybe she wasn't a mom. Or if she was, she was a different kind than I'd ever seen.

"Hi, I was told to come down here. My name is Charlotte Healey."

She studied a stack of papers in front of her. "I'm sorry. I don't seem to have you."

My heart raced and my stomach twisted into knots. Maybe I'd dreamed of getting into Harmony Falls and now I was about to be publicly humiliated. For the second time that morning, I ached for more familiar faces.

"Well, I don't think you're in here, but tell me your address," Ms. Big Boobs said, as if she was doing me a favor.

"Um . . . 4912 Sherwood Avenue. . . . It's in Greenspring," I said hopefully.

I got a totally vacant look. Greenspring was only ten minutes away, but this woman acted as though she had never left Harmony Falls' gated community in her life.

"On the other side of the lake?"

"Oh, right. . . . I think I know the problem. Check in with Ms. Wilkens. She's at the out-of-boundary table. Maybe you're there."

At the far end of the hall was a table with a sign that said OUT OF BOUNDARY REGISTER HERE. Nice. Orientation was not making me feel welcome or oriented. I tried to calm down. Under no circumstances was I allowed to lose it on my first day of school.

"Hi, I'm Charlotte Healey. I'm supposed to register here. My last name is Healey. . . ."

"Oh, I'm sure we'll find you. We've got everyone right here." Her nails clacked against the keyboard as she mumbled, "Let me see. . . . Hmm . . . Not finding you. Are you sure you're in the right school?"

I couldn't believe it. I had pored over every part of the application so I could avoid this precise moment. "I think so. . . . Could you please check again?" I pleaded.

"Maybe you should go to the office and see if they can help you. I'm sorry, I'm only a parent volunteer. Could you step aside, please?"

She waved me away and told the boy behind me to step forward. Once again, I was on my own. As I looked around to find where the office was, trying to ignore my growing stomach ulcer, a black woman in, you guessed it, the same PRIDE T-shirt approached me.

"Hey, I'm Ms. McBride. Are they having trouble finding you?"

"Yeah. I know I did all my paperwork, but they don't have my information," I said, my voice cracking a tiny bit.

"I'm sure this is the last thing you wanted at your freshman orientation," she said gently.

"Yeah," I admitted.

"Don't worry about it. The databases get confused all the time. Do you have a hyphenated name or a nickname?" she asked.

"Yeah. My name is Charlotte Healey, but I go by Charlie."

Ms. McBride walked over to another table and on the back of her T-shirt I read the slogan *Where excellence isn't a choice but a way of life!* Were they serious with that? Maybe Luke was right that this place was too full of itself. When she sat down at a computer, I read the front, PRIDE stood for Perseverance, Respect, Integrity, Diversity, and Ethics. What was it with schools that they were so into slogans like PRIDE? It's as if adults think if they didn't constantly throw stuff in our face all the time, every student would be completely psychotic.

Ms. McBride stood up. "Charlie, you're in here. Whoever input your information made a mistake and registered you under Charles Haley instead of Charlotte Healey. I'm really sorry about the confusion." She handed me some papers. "Here is your class schedule and information for the day."

"Thank you so much," I said. All I had to do now was actually enter the gym. I took a deep breath and followed a few students through the double doors.

The muffled sounds at registration were now a full surround-sound experience. There were people everywhere. Flags hung from every beam in the ceiling. Harmony Falls was the champion of every sport a high school could offer. Girls 1987 Basketball, Boys 1996 Tennis, Girls 2005 Soccer, Boys 2003 Lacrosse, Girls 1987 (and every year after that) Swimming, Girls 2006 Lacrosse, Boys 2007 Hockey, Girls and Boys 2008 Tennis, Boys 2009 Fencing. The school had a fencing team? Who had a fencing team? And did this school ever lose at anything?

I suddenly had a giant adrenaline rush. Spanning the entire length of the wall above my head was a huge panther painted in black, dark blue, and gray, mouth open, arms outstretched with huge silver claws looking as if he was leaping out to eat all of us. When I took my eyes off of him, they landed on the sea of students in front of me.

What if I got to this school I had waited to go to for months and somehow I ended up again being friends with girls I hated? What if I had lost my ability to know who was a genuinely decent human being and who was a nightmare? It can be hard to tell sometimes.

But here was my clean start. For a few minutes, all I did was watch everyone around me. Girls screamed hello and hugged like they hadn't seen each other in decades. Some kids sat on bleachers against the wall. Others huddled in different groups around the basketball court catching up from the summer. Two girls and two guys were kicking a Hacky Sack back and forth. To my right was a group of guys all wearing HARMONY FALLS SOCCER T-shirts.

I was debating whether to go up and introduce myself to someone when a cheerful voice broke through the chaos and snapped me out of my trance. "Good morning! Can everyone settle down, please?"

No one cared.

"All right, everyone, can you settle down and give your attention to the center of the room?"

That didn't work either.

Ms. McBride took the microphone from a woman with perfectly layered, straight, brown highlighted hair, and commanded, "IF YOU ARE AN INCOMING FRESHMAN, I NEED YOUR ATTENTION NOW!"

The roar immediately died down.

Someone tapped me on the shoulder. "I'm Sydney! What's your name?" she said.

"Oh, hey! I'm Charlie," I said, a little shocked at how outgoing this girl was.

"You want to sit with me?"

"Yeah! Sure!" I said, maybe too desperately.

I'll admit I was kind of embarrassed she could tell I wasn't fitting in, but who was I kidding? At least now I had a friend! As we walked up the bleacher steps and sat down about halfway up, I realized how pretty Sydney was—Amazon tall, strawberry blond, blue eyes, and thin. That look so many girls aimed for—where they pretend they're not trying too hard but really are—Sydney nailed it with just jeans, a T-shirt, and worn-out cowboy boots. I thought back to what I'd said to Luke that morning. Could girls this pretty be nice? Was that possible?

Ms. McBride continued, "Thank you, ladies and gentlemen. This is the Harmony Falls freshman orientation. If you aren't a freshman, now is the time for you to depart." She put down the microphone and scanned the crowd. Her eyes narrowed in on someone. She raised the microphone to her mouth again and said, "Jason Giogietta, you can leave now. I know you just came to drop off your brother, but he will be fine without you."

Laughter bounced around the room as a guy with a backward baseball hat raised his hand to acknowledge the crowd. "No problem, Ms. M! Leaving right now. You know I always do whatever you say." Laughter turned into applause as he walked out, smiling.

Ms. McBride waved good-bye to Jason and turned her attention to us. "Now that we're all settled, I'd like you to meet Ms. Fieldston, one of the ninth-grade coordinators. She'll take you through orientation today."

The same brown-haired woman Ms. McBride had taken the microphone from walked up the short flight of stairs to a raised platform in the middle of the gym. Now I could see she was also wearing the PRIDE T-shirt, but she looked too young to be a teacher.

With the microphone in her hand she said, "Good morning, students! Welcome to Harmony Falls! We're going to have a lot of fun today! So get excited!"

I leaned over and whispered to Sydney, "Wow. She doesn't look like a teacher at all!"

"Yeah, no kidding! Look at her jeans! They're the same as mine!"

"Seriously?" I said, laughing in disbelief. Then I realized I had the headband Ms. Fieldston was wearing.

In the back of the gym someone whistled and everyone laughed. Ms. Fieldston ignored it. "On behalf of Harmony Falls' Welcoming Action Committee, I'd like to welcome you to your freshman orientation. We want this to be an opportunity for you all to get acquainted so we can kick off the new school year in the right frame of mind. Now I'm going to introduce you to our principal, Mr. Wickam."

A man wearing black pants, a black turtleneck, and a sport coat with those patches on the elbows strode up to the stage and walked over to Ms. Fieldston. This apparently was our principal, even though he looked nothing like any principal I'd ever seen. I mean, he was old and had some gray hair, but he wasn't wearing a bad suit or an argyle sweater. He was the kind of guy my mom would think was good-looking.

Mr. Wickam raked his fingers through his hair, gazed around the room, and began, "I want to take a few moments to personally welcome you to Harmony Falls. It's good to see such promising young faces! I want you to think of me not just as your principal, but as your friend." He paused at the far end of the platform before continuing. "In the next four years the people in the gym will become your family."

Awkward silence filled the room.

"Your class will join Harmony Falls' proud legacy of achievement," he said, gesturing to the banners above our heads. Then Mr. Wickam's face became serious and still. "Now, you may have noticed some of us wearing shirts that say PRIDE. That stands for perseverance, respect, integrity, diversity, and ethics. These are the pillars of the Harmony Falls community. Every time you walk through these doors, I want you to remember that."

Sydney leaned over and whispered, "Does he really think we don't get it?" I glanced at the sea of bored faces, but Mr. Wickam continued.

"So I say to you, channel your energy in positive ways, challenge yourself to be the best you can be, never quit, and your years at Harmony Falls will reap great rewards."

Ms. Fieldston stepped back onto the stage and took the microphone. "Thank you, Mr. Wickam. Okay, everybody, members of WAC, our Welcoming Action Committee, are walking around the gym with boxes filled with little pieces of paper. Your job is to take one of those pieces of paper and go around the gym imitating the thing or person written on the paper and find the people who share your word. The goal is to get all the people with the same word in the same place. The first group to get all their people together will win a gift certificate to Rosa's Pizza on Central. Does that make sense?"

I had no idea what Ms. Fieldston was talking about, but I didn't want to look stupid, so, again, I pretended I knew what was going on. Sydney and I followed the mass of people down from the bleachers and stood in line in front of a WAC person to get our assignment. My paper read OSTRICH. She wanted me to run around the gym imitating a large, awkward bird? Why would anyone think this was a good idea?

"I got superhero!" Sydney exclaimed. I watched in horror as Sydney flew away, her arms stretched in front of her. I lost her as she dove into a crowd—except it wasn't superheroes. Judging from the growling and exaggerated clawing, she had just leapt into a group of tigers.

There went my only friend. She'd only been my friend for five minutes, but still. With Sydney gone, I was going to have to play this game. But the question loomed large, how does one imitate an ostrich?

More importantly, who was that really cute dirty-blond, green-eyed guy in front of me with the soccer boys? As I stared, he brushed the hair out of his eyes, a thin shell bracelet on his wrist.

"Who's that?" Sydney's voice came out of nowhere—she was standing next to me like she had never left.

"Will Edwards," I said, shocked at my own words because what I had just said was true. I knew him. My brain was immensely confused. I took a step closer. There was no doubt. Standing in front of me was Will. Will Edwards, my best friend and next-door neighbor until he moved away three years ago and apparently turned into a super-hot guy.

"Oh, you know him. That's why you're staring," Sydney said.

"Yeah . . . that's why." There was no way I was going to admit anything else. "How could he be here? Why didn't he tell me?" I said in disbelief.

Sydney shrugged, clearly confused at why I was completely freaking out.

I brushed by her and went over to him. I wasn't going to be immature about this. What had happened before he moved away was over. Finally, here was someone I knew, and of all people, it was Will!

"Will!" I yelled as I walked over to him.

Will looked at me in total shock. "Charlie?" he said.

The guys surrounding us backed away and stared.

"Will, I can't believe you're here!" I said, throwing my arms around his neck. I definitely didn't remember him being this tall.

He hugged me back. I mean, it was one of those pathetic one-armed guy hugs, but I didn't care.

"What are you doing here?" I asked.

He hesitated. "Um . . . my dad got a job in Harmony Falls. I meant to call you, but I didn't have your cell."

"That's okay," I rushed. "Don't worry about it. It's so great to see you! I can't believe it. How's your family?"

Before he could answer, Ms. Fieldston interrupted. "Okay, everyone, looks like we have our winners!"

Will ignored her. "Umm . . . they're fine. David just left for college, and my dad's getting settled in his new job."

"Where do you live?"

"Right around here. Close to my dad's new church, Holy Trinity. It's that big church on Carlyle Boulevard. So why are you at Harmony Falls?" he asked. "I thought you'd be at Greenspring."

"I was going to, but I got into this program here for kids who live nearby. It's sort of like a rescue program for smart kids. . . ."

"Hey, Edwards! Stop talking to your new girlfriend and get over here!" yelled one of his friends.

"I'm coming!" Will said, taking a step back. "Charlie, I've got to go, but I'm sure I'll run into you later. It's really good to see you." He grinned.

"Good to see you too," I said, but he was already walking away.

"So . . . what's up with that?" Sydney asked.

I shook my head. "It's nothing, just a little weird. I used to live next to him."

"And you didn't know he was going to be here?"

Before I could answer her, we were interrupted by Ms. Fieldston's explanation of our next activity. "Okay! I need everyone to sit back down so we can watch a short film about the history of Harmony Falls High School!"

Everyone corralled into the bleachers again. The lights dimmed and a perky girl came on the screen to tell us about when the school began (1927), the number of students in the first class (32), and the current percentage of students who go to college after graduation (92). I zoned out and found myself thinking about the last time I'd seen Will. . . .

It was the night before he left and we were hanging out in his backyard, sitting on some old plastic lawn chairs. Finally I heard him mumble "I'm going to miss you." It was good to hear him admit it, but I also wanted to hear him say something like "I'm also really sorry for being such a jerk and making you feel like our friendship meant nothing to me all year." All I said was "I know." A few minutes later I went home. The next morning he was gone.

The crowd clapping and whistling snapped me back to reality.

"Okay, everybody," said Ms. Fieldston, "we're going to rotate you all through a couple of activities by bleacher sections. Section one, the farthest to my left and your right, will go to a sports presentation with Coach Mason. Section two"—that was us—"will go on a tour of the school with the WAC student leaders." Morgan, the bubble-letter girl from when I walked in, started frantically waving her hand. "Section three will go to the administrative office to get your school handbook. Finally, section four will stay here with me to play some more get-to-know-you games! Okay, now everyone break into your groups!"

I looked for Will again and saw him in the corner with the soccer guys. I caught his eye and he smiled. I couldn't help thinking, What was he like now? How well do you know someone when you haven't seen him in three years? I was a completely different person back then. Was he?

I followed Sydney over to a group of girls and introduced myself. Not one of them gave me a mean-girl look. This was good, I thought, and walked with the girls out of the gym to see the rest of Harmony Falls.

## CHAPTER THREE

**"COME ON IN! WE'RE ABOUT TO GET STARTED!"**

A few days later, I took a step into the classroom and recognized Ms. Fieldston from orientation. "Is this Advisory 9G? I'm sort of lost."

"You've come to the right place! Just find a seat!"

I scanned the room and noticed that I was one of the last students to arrive.

She looked down at the piece of paper in front of her. "You're Charlotte Healey? And you prefer Charlie, right?" she asked.

"Uh-huh." I nodded, wondering how she knew that and thinking that I'd never had a teacher who wore wrap dresses and high-heeled boots.

I moved toward the nearest empty chair, but just as I was about to sit down I stopped, because in the next seat was Paul Nelson, from my elementary school. I don't care if it's mean, but the only two things I remember about Paul Nelson from third grade are that he ate crayons and picked his nose. I smiled weakly at him, ready to be more mature, but I just couldn't do it. I quickly looked around for another chair. There was one wedged against the wall behind a preppy-looking black guy, but I couldn't get to it without tripping over him.

He stood up, tall and skinny, wearing Polo from head to toe, leaned over, picked up the chair, and put it next to him. "Here you go," he said, smiling.

"Thanks," I said. Polo guy was now my new best friend, even if he didn't know it.

Ms. Fieldston leaned forward in her chair, gripping both hands to the desk and said, "Welcome to Advisory, everyone! As one of the advisory counselors at Harmony Falls, it's my job to watch out for you. If you're having a problem in school, you can come to me. No problem is too big or too small."

Ms. Fieldston ended every sentence as if she was asking a question.

As she talked, I checked out the other students and was happy to see that Sydney, the really nice girl from orientation, was in the class.

"Advisory will be a chance throughout the year for us to discuss important topics like alcohol abuse, drug abuse, drinking and driving, bullying, and any other topic you think is important. But I want you to think of me more as a friend than a teacher."

She leaned down and took out a shoe box covered in dark blue construction paper with cut-out silver-glitter question marks and put it in front of her. "I was thinking that maybe it'd be a good idea to begin every Advisory with this question box. You can ask whatever you want." She smiled at all of us expectantly.

A short red-haired boy nervously raised his hand and said, "Do we have to put our name on the question?"

Ms. Fieldston shook her head. "You don't have to put your name on it unless you want to."

The boy raised his hand again. "Are we being graded on this?"

She laughed. "No, honey, you aren't being graded, so don't worry about asking the 'right' question. If it's important to you, it's important to me. Sound good?"

Even though Ms. Fieldston's voice was a little too enthusiastic, there was something about her that made me suddenly imagine her as my cool older sister.

A brown-haired boy with freckles leaned into his chair, grinning. "I have a question."

"Great!" Ms. Fieldston said.

"So if we're having girl problems, can we go to you for advice?" he asked.

She laughed again. "Of course. That's what I'm here for."

Then Ms. Fieldston handed out tons of brochures and didn't stop until she'd gone through every possible disease and problem. Anorexia, bulimia, obesity, steroid use, alcoholism, cyber-bullying, cyber-stalking, depression, suicide—she had it all. She'd just finished giving them all out when the bell rang.

Sydney came right up to me, stuffing the brochures into her shoulder bag. "Hey, Charlie! Let's see if we have any other classes together because I think having Advisory puts us on the same track."

She put her bag on the chair and rifled through it until she found her schedule.

"I've got mine right here," I said taking it out of my pocket. "Look, we have American Government together sixth period."

"Cool! That means you must have your lunch period now too, right?"

"Yeah, I think so."

"I've got to go to the office to pick up my new ID, but save me a seat so we can eat together?"

I'm sorry, I know there are bigger issues in the world, but having someone like Sydney wanting to eat with you the first week of school made the world feel like a good place to be. Because the feeling of standing in the lunch line by yourself . . . really, there's nothing like it to make you feel totally insecure. You try to convince yourself that no one notices you have no friends. You try to look like you're too busy to talk to anyone because you're on your way to something much more important. But you can't help it, you're crushed with self-consciousness.

When I got to lunch, I moved through the line as quickly as I could, hoping Sydney would show up soon. I tried to look interested in my choice of grilled chicken and French fries or spaghetti and meatballs but found myself wondering why adults love to schedule things so the only way you can be on time is if you wear a digital watch. For some reason, our lunch periods were scheduled between 10:26 and 11:03 or 11:08 and 11:41. I mean what's so offensive about scheduling things between 10:25 and 11:00?

Anyway, I chose the chicken, got some carrots at the salad

bar, and moved over to the drinks, where I ran into my Polo guy from Advisory.

"Hey, thanks again for getting that seat for me!" I said, grabbing a plastic cup and placing it below the iced tea dispenser.

"No problem. Charlie, right?" he asked.

I nodded. "I didn't get your name in class. . . ."

"Michael Taylor." He reached up, got four cups, and put them on his tray, which was already weighed down by two plates full of food.

"You're really going to eat all of that?" I asked.

"This? This isn't that much. I'm carbo-loading for soccer."

"Right, of course," I said.

We both picked up our trays and walked through the double doors that led out to the long rows of lunch tables. Michael motioned forward, so I followed him. Finally, he found a table that was half empty and sat down.

"So what middle school did you go to last year?"

"Ben Franklin. It's in the next town over, in Greenspring."

He nodded, inhaling the spaghetti in front of him. "Cool. I went to Westminster, but I've heard of your school. Do you know Anthony Maderal? I played select soccer with him last year."

"Yeah, he was amazing! I wrote about him for my school newspaper last year. There was this big controversy because he was playing for some special team so he couldn't play for the school too. He's a really nice guy. So, do you play basketball too?"

Michael rolled his eyes and laughed. "No. Just because I'm tall and black doesn't mean I play basketball."

Insert foot in mouth. "Okay, that sounded really stupid," I said apologetically.

He shrugged and smiled. "Really, don't worry about it. Happens all the time."

Someone tall and blondish caught my eye. "Oh, there's Sydney!" I said, waving, so relieved to change the subject.

"Hey, Charlie!" Sydney said, putting her tray down. "You're in Advisory, right?" she asked Michael.

He nodded, taking a huge gulp of milk.

"Michael, Sydney. Sydney, Michael," I said, feeling great to know two people and be able to introduce them.

"So what do you think of Ms. Fieldston?" Sydney asked us, putting three packets of Equal in her iced tea. "Doesn't it seem like she's trying a little too hard?"

Michael laughed. "Whatever. She's still hot. Last year, one of the guys in my brother's senior class asked her to go to prom."

"Seriously? Did she go?" I asked.

"Oh, absolutely," Michael said and then laughed as I looked at him in shock. "No, I'm just playing with you. I think they have rules about that sort of thing. But after she turned him down, he asked if she had a younger sister, but she doesn't."

Sydney stopped eating her French fry midway. "I'm not saying the woman isn't pretty, and she seems nice. Maybe I'm not used to a teacher who is so enthusiastic about helping us."

"Where are you from?" Michael asked Sydney.

"Denver, mostly. I've moved around a lot for my mom's job. I'm a huge Broncos fan."

"You can't be serious." Michael looked down at his plate and shook his head. "This may be a deal breaker. I'm really not sure I can hang out with you."

Sydney's mouth dropped open. "Please, don't tell me you're a Raiders fan."

Michael leaned away from the table. "Of course not. Chiefs all the way. My parents are from Kansas City."

"Okay. Because this is the first week of school and I need to make friends, I'm going to let it go. But on the weeks that they play each other, it's better if we don't speak."

Michael laughed. "Sounds good."

The bell rang. I stood up with my tray. "Looks like we have to go to class. Sydney and I have American Government. What do you have?"

"I've got Physics," Michael said.

"Physics? I thought freshmen could only take Bio?" I asked.

"I got sort of a special pass."

Sydney and I both looked at him closely because he suddenly seemed shy.

He shrugged. "It's not a big deal. I took a lot of science classes last year, so they let me take that instead of repeating things. I'll see you around!"

As I walked to American Government with Sydney, I realized that Lauren and Ally seemed a million miles away. It was easy to forget all about them as I navigated my way through the hallways filled with kids. I survived, pretending I knew what was going on, but paranoid that I'd do something that would show how clueless I actually was at Harmony Falls.

It wasn't that I'd never heard of Harmony Falls before I got here, it's just that most of the information I got was from my brother, Luke, telling me about how stuck-up the kids were. And even though he had made up his mind that he hated Harmony Falls, I can't tell you how many times I wished Luke was here with me. I mean, unless you have an older brother or sister at the same school, pretty much everyone gets to high school not having a clue.

I'm not talking about the information I got in my orientation packet. I'm talking about the unwritten rules between the students. Everyone assumes that the freshmen should just know this stuff, and when you don't, you're an open target for ridicule. Or worse, if you think the rules are stupid and you don't want to go along with them, people get mad at you.

Like in the library, freshmen can only sit at the first set of eight tables to the right, nearest to the librarian. Or if you're white, you don't sit on the bench to the left of the administrative offices because that's where the nonpreppy black students hang out. Or, don't talk to seniors unless they speak to you first. It's endless. Don't you think that would be incredibly helpful information to include in the orientation packet?

But even with all that, I already loved a lot about Harmony Falls. I didn't have to be embarrassed about being smart, and there were so many things going on all the time. The halls were filled with signs to join Model UN, a Chinese language club, a literary journal, a diversity club called Spectrum, a TV station, a film festival, and the *Prowler*, the student newspaper— which I really wanted to write for. There was even a place called the Good Karma Café where students performed live music.

I walked to class knowing I made the right decision to be here.

"Welcome to American Government. I'm Tom Jaquette," he said as he looked around the room smiling. He had big brown curly hair and small black rectangular glasses. "Before I delve into the Articles of Confederation, let's get to know each other a little better. Raise your hand if you've heard that I'm a really hard teacher, that it's almost impossible to get an A from me, or you're already trying to switch out so you don't jeopardize your GPA."

I knew nothing about the man, but apparently other people did because a few people's hands went up hesitantly.

"Thanks for your honesty. I know I have a reputation for being one of the hardest, if not strangest, teachers at Harmony Falls."

A few uncomfortable laughs ricocheted around the room.

Mr. Jaquette arched his eyebrows, and it honestly seemed like his eyes were twinkling.

"I won't lie to you, this class can be challenging, but I hope by the end you'll get something out of it."

A girl in front of me raised her hand. "How much reading are we going to get every night?"

"What an excellent first question. I'd say a minimum of ten hours. And I'll assign two papers each week—"

Complaints erupted around me.

"People, relax. I'm joking. I'll let you know all of that later. First, we need to set the guidelines for the class."

Someone in the back raised his hand immediately. "You mean, like, raise your hand when you want to speak?" Clearly whoever that person was planned to be the class suck-up.

Mr. Jaquette shook his head. "Nope. I want you to tell me what kind of teacher you want me to be."

We all stared at him blankly.

"Think of it this way: What kind of teacher do you want so this class won't be a waste of your time?"

Silence.

He walked from behind his desk and sat on it. He laughed. "I don't think you all believe me. Come on, I really want to know."

A guy shouted from the back, "Don't give homework or tests!" Hopeful laughter bounced across the room. I turned around to see the cutest, tannest brown-haired, blue-eyed guy ever.

Sydney leaned over and whispered, "You're staring."

"Shut up," I whispered back and turned around as fast as I could.

Mr. Jaquette said, "Unfortunately, Tyler, that's a request I can't fulfill. But I'll try not to waste your time with worthless assignments and tests, and I'll check in with the other teachers to coordinate test dates and deadlines for projects so they all won't be due on the same day. But please tell me you have other demands beyond no homework?"

Kids started yelling out all at once while Mr. Jaquette wrote our answers on the board.

"Don't lecture all the time."

"Don't yell."

"Don't talk in a monotone voice."

"Don't tell stupid jokes."

"Don't treat us like we're five."

"Don't call on me if my hand isn't raised."

"Don't tell us weird personal stories."

"Don't laugh at us."

Once we got started, we couldn't shut up. It was like we'd been storing up all the bad experiences with all the teachers we'd ever had.

Eventually, Mr. Jaquette stopped us. "Now tell me what you *do* want."

There was silence, but it was the thinking kind. Slowly people started raising their hands again.

"Make it relevant."

"Do stuff with us so we aren't sitting in our chairs all the time."

"Let us argue with you."

Mr. Jaquette put the marker down and turned around. "Excellent! Now you're thinking like the students I need in this class. There're two things I want you to remember. You're here to learn American government, but that doesn't mean I want you to memorize a bunch of dates and names. You're here to challenge yourself and each other. Challenge me. Tell me when you think I'm wrong. Just be prepared to back it up. Sometimes we may need to raise hands, sometimes we won't have to, but I'm not going to scream at you to be quiet, and I'm also not going to beg. So as long as you all don't act like you're five, I won't treat you like you're five. Are we in agreement?"

Everyone nodded.

"And the last thing about being in this class is about grades. I do grade hard, and if you're unsatisfied with what you get and want a chance of changing my mind, the single worst thing you can do is run to your parents and complain. If you think I've graded you unfairly, then set up a time to meet with me and state your case."

Nobody said a word because we all knew exactly what he was talking about. I mean, if I got a bad grade my parents would have told me I had to deal with it, but I knew a lot of parents who demand a grade change even if their kid didn't deserve it.

"All right, now that we have established where we stand, let's get to why we're here. The first thing we'll be reading is *Founding Brothers* by Joseph Ellis."

Mr. Jaquette started handing out copies from a stack of books on his desk. "We will begin this class, as Mr. Ellis does in his book, with the duel between Alexander Hamilton, aide-de-camp to General Washington and the first US treasury secretary, and Aaron Burr, the vice president under Thomas Jefferson. The duel occurred on a cliff near today's Lincoln Tunnel in New York. Although Mr. Hamilton died the next morning from his gunshot wound, Mr. Burr's political career was over the moment the bullet hit Hamilton. . . ."

The next forty minutes flew by. I didn't even think about the guy in the back the whole time, which really tells you how amazing Mr. Jaquette was. At least until the bell rang, when I slowly packed up my bag so I had a chance of walking out with the hot guy.

"Hey," he said as he passed me and stopped, "you're the one with the car."

"What?" I had no idea what he was talking about, but that was fine by me. I could pretend I had a car.

"Your dad has that car. My friend talked to him the first day of school when he dropped you off."

My cheeks burned. He was one of the boys I'd rushed by on my way to the orientation.

"Nicely done."

I had no idea what he meant. "Thanks?" I said nervously and then realized that was a totally stupid thing to say. Why was I saying thanks?

While I was obsessing on how much I'd just embarrassed

myself, the love of my life had already turned and walked out of the classroom, but not before I noticed a smell. It wasn't bad; like soap and spice and something else, but I couldn't place it.

Sydney was waiting outside of the class for me.

"Did you get a whiff of the Axe on that guy?" she said, fake coughing. I seriously think it's the chocolate one.

"I smelled something, but it didn't really bother me. What's Axe?"

"You have to know what Axe is," she said as she waved her hand in front of her face. "It's that cologne guys use before they graduate to Armani or something."

"Oh! I think my brother got it in his stocking for Christmas last year."

"Well, that boy's got a gallon of it on."

"I guess I didn't really mind."

"Really?" she said playfully, bumping into me on purpose as we walked down the hall. "I couldn't tell."

"Shut up, Sydney," I said laughing.

"Guess who his dad is?"

"Who?"

"The principal. Mr. Wickam. That's why Mr. Jaquette knew that his name was Tyler." Sydney stopped and put her hair back into a half ponytail so it was spraying out in all directions.

"Seriously? That's weird."

"Exactly. Can you imagine going to school where your dad is the principal? I'd feel like everyone was watching me all the time. And he's supposed to be an insane soccer and lacrosse player."

I stopped walking. "How do you know all of this?" I asked.

She smiled. "Easy. I noticed his last name on the class list posted on the door, and I heard people talking about it in the office." She raised one eyebrow. "So you want to check out soccer practice after school today? Just happen to do our homework on the bleachers?"

Will was on the soccer team. And if he was on the team, then he'd know Tyler.

"That's not too obvious?" I asked, sarcastically.

Sydney shrugged and grinned. "Charlie, there's nothing wrong with being obvious sometimes—especially when guys are involved."

# CHAPTER FOUR

**WHEN SYDNEY AND I ARRIVED AT THE FIELD, THERE WAS NO** sign of any soccer practice. The only practice I could see was the football team doing drills on the next field over. I reluctantly followed Sydney as she climbed up the metal bleachers, wondering if she had gotten her information wrong.

"Are you sure about this? Maybe their practice is somewhere else or they have a game," I said, sitting down and immediately feeling the metal through my jeans. I mean, if I was going to stalk someone, I wanted it to be worth it.

"I'm sure," she said, sitting down next to me. Right then, the back door to the gym opened and a group of guys walked out carrying net bags with soccer balls inside.

My heart jumped. As they got closer, I cringed, thinking how obvious we looked sitting there on the bleachers. I might as well have yelled, "Hello, soccer team! Yes, I'm a creeper freshman waiting for this boy who barely knows me to see if I can come up with an excuse to talk to him. But it's cool. I don't mind. Laugh all you want."

As I was freaking out and coming up with more excuses, Sydney was definitely not experiencing a crisis of any kind. She slouched on the bleachers, legs stretched out.

Michael came over kicking a soccer ball. "Hey, Charlie! Hey, Sydney!"

"Hey, Michael!" Sydney called out, not moving.

"What are you guys doing here?"

I got up and walked closer. "Oh, nothing, Just looking for a friend. His name is Will Edwards. Do you know him?"

Michael nodded. "Sure, he's a forward."

"I just need to talk to him for a minute," I said, wondering if Michael could see how nervous I was.

"He'll be out soon. I'll tell him when I see him."

I sat back down on the bleachers and reached for my Spanish book so I could read a fascinating conversation between Marta and Jaime enjoying chorizo and queso on their vacation in Sevilla.

A few minutes later (okay, maybe I was looking every ten seconds, but whatever), Will came out with Tyler. I panicked because this was not the plan. My plan was to see Will, talk to Will, casually ask him if he knew Tyler, and then maybe figure out a way to talk to Tyler later. Instead I had to deal with the possibility of Will watching me be nervous around Tyler and then teasing me relentlessly. I knew three years had passed, but some things don't change.

Sydney looked up from the book she was pretending to read. "See how a little bit of stalking pays off?"

"Yeah," I said, wanting to throw up. I couldn't believe how nervous I was. These were just freshman guys, one of whom I'd seen naked in a kiddie pool when we were five. What was the big deal?

"Will!" I called out when he was about fifty feet away.

He looked surprised as he walked over to the bleachers with Tyler.

"Hey, Charlie, how'd you know I was here?" Will asked as Tyler stood next to him in his soccer shorts and sweatshirt and a big bag slung over his shoulder. For the record, I want to say that I am an immense fan of cute boys in soccer shorts.

"I just guessed," I said casually, trying not to stare at Tyler.

The thing about excuses is that they should be controlled. Ideally, you should stay on script so things don't get complicated, but sometimes I don't follow my own rules and things come out of my mouth that I don't plan. "I told my mom and dad your family was back, and my mom totally freaked out about it. So I'm supposed to get your new phone number. She wants to invite you all to dinner."

Will put his bag down. "Sure, I'll tell them. Do you have a pen or your phone?"

"For what?" I asked.

"Um . . . so I can give you the number?" he said laughing.

"Right. . . ." I was sure my face had gone from red to purple.

Sydney stood up and said, "Hey, I'm Sydney. We met during orientation."

Will nodded. "Sure. I remember you."

"And your name's Tyler?" Sydney asked casually. "I think you have American Government with me and Charlie."

"Yeah. Jaquette. I was totally bummed I got him. The man makes you do insane amounts of work," Tyler said.

"But he seems pretty cool," I said, immediately questioning myself. What if my voice sounds really squeaky? What if I'm the most annoyingly obvious person in the world?

"Charlie, here's the number. I put my email on, too," Will said, handing back my phone.

We all heard a whistle. "Will! Tyler! Get over here for drills!"

Will turned back to us and said, "Got to go or else Coach will make us run twice as much."

With that, Tyler and Will picked up their bags and were gone.

I sat back down and breathed. Mission accomplished.

Sydney made me stay there so we could really finish our homework. But she was also determined to stay until practice was over and she could make me talk to Tyler again.

A whistle sounded and the boys huddled together for a moment, then broke apart.

My heart lurched as Tyler and Will walked back over to us. I tried to look very busy, but I was having a heart attack. I was sure of it.

"When did it get so cold? I'm freezing!" I said, trying to hide my nerves.

Tyler dropped the huge duffel he was carrying and asked, "You want my sweatshirt?"

I stopped myself from jumping up and down.

"Really? Are you sure?" I said lightly.

He shrugged. "Don't worry about it." He opened his bag and took out a black sweatshirt. As I put it on, I read HAR-MONY FALLS VARSITY SOCCER on the back. It was slightly big on me, and by slightly, I mean anyone would know if they saw it on me that it wasn't mine. And if they didn't know, I could tell them exactly who it belonged to.

"Fits you perfectly, Charlie. You should wear it to school tomorrow," Will teased.

"You're on varsity?" I asked, ignoring Will. My mind was racing. What did it mean that Tyler gave me his sweatshirt? Was it, Here's a sweatshirt, Charlie, because I have ten just like it, or, Here's a sweatshirt because I want you to have it?

Will answered, nodding over in the direction where Michael stood talking to the coach, "All three of us made varsity."

"Michael?" But then I remembered he'd said he had played select soccer last year.

The coach waved Will and Tyler over.

Tyler hoisted his bag over his shoulder. "See you in class."

"Hey, Charlie, just email me tonight, okay? If my dad sees me on my phone he'll freak. He's already on my case about work," said Will.

"Sure, okay. See you later." My head was buzzing as they walked away.

"That seemed worth it to me," Sydney said. She glanced at

the sweatshirt I was now wearing and laughed. "You planning to sleep in that tonight?"

"No! I'll give it back to him tomorrow," I said, breathing the vaguely chocolatey spicy smell. Even as I said that, I knew that wasn't happening. I was keeping it for at least a couple of days or the rest of my life.

# CHAPTER FIVE

**"MY MOM'S PICKING ME UP IN A FEW MINUTES."** SYDNEY took out her phone and looked at the screen. "If you want, you can come over, or she can give you a ride home."

"That'd be great. My brother is supposed to pick me up, but he won't mind if I tell him he doesn't have to get me."

We walked past the field and followed the path to the front of the school.

"You have an older brother?" Sydney asked.

"He's sixteen. His name's Luke."

"Does he go to Harmony Falls?"

I shook my head. "He goes to Greenspring. So I'm a traitor for coming here."

She flipped her phone shut. "Oh, right. Greenspring's the other big high school around here. Well, I always wanted brothers or sisters, but my dad left when I was two and my mom has never even been on a date since their divorce. I've gone to three schools in the last six years," she said.

"Three schools? Why do you move around so much?

"It's my mom's work. She's kind of like an accountant for big companies."

"Is that hard?"

"What? Which part?"

"I guess not having a dad around?"

She shrugged. "I don't really know anything different. It's always been my mom and me." She paused. "If my mom got married now, that'd be weird, so I'm fine with how things are. But it would have been cool to have a brother."

"Yeah, well, he's usually fine, but he hates having to pick me up after school. He complains about it all the time and makes me wait forever. . . . Like it's my fault that I'm not old enough to drive."

"That's my mom now." A burgundy Camry had pulled up to the school entrance. "Hey, Mom!" Sydney said, opening the car door. "This is Charlie. Can she come over?"

"Of course! Hey, Charlie!" said an older version of Sydney in a dark blue business suit.

"Thanks for picking me up, Ms. Collins."

"Don't worry about it. And call me Heidi."

"Okay." I smiled, feeling a little self-conscious. "Thanks, Heidi."

Sydney and her mom lived in a new town house not far from the school. I walked up the four stairs that opened into her living room and immediately felt comfortable. Heidi walked in behind us, and said, "Okay, girls, I have a little more work to do before dinner." She handed Sydney a bag. "I got a rotisserie chicken, so if you could heat it up and make a salad that'd be great. Eat in about an hour? Thanks, sweetie!" she said, as she walked down the short flight of stairs. "And, Charlie, feel free to stay for dinner!"

"Want some hot tea? I always like to make some when I come home after school. It's a little ritual I have," Sydney said.

"Sure," I said.

A few minutes later, we were sitting at her small kitchen table with the best cup of tea I'd ever had. I knew I was just sitting in someone's kitchen drinking tea, but being there made me feel older.

"So I know we stalked Tyler at practice, but what's the deal with Will?" Sydney asked, settling into her chair.

"What do you mean?"

"Come on. You have to admit when you saw Will at orientation you were definitely into him, and not like just because he was an old friend."

"Okay, fine! When I first saw him, I thought he was cute, but . . . no way. He's like my brother. But if you think he's so hot, why don't you do something about it? I'm sure he'd go for it."

"He's cute. But he's not really my type. Way too preppy. Plus, I really think he's into you."

"Sydney, you're insane!"

"I am not! You obviously aren't noticing how he looks at you."

"If he's doing that—which I'm not saying he is—it's probably because we haven't seen each other in so long and we went through a lot together," I said, staring at the steam rising from my teacup.

"That sounds juicy! Like what?"

"I told you that Will and I were next-door neighbors, right? When we were little, we did everything together. Even though he was a boy, I guess he was my best friend, which was weird because we were so different."

"Like how?" Sydney asked.

"I know he's not acting like this now, but Will was so shy when we were little. I mean, he wouldn't talk to anyone unless he had to. And he was such a worrier. You know that character in *Winnie-the-Pooh,* Eeyore?"

"The donkey? The complaining one with the pinned-on tail?"

"He was just like that! And nothing we did was all that bad. I mean . . . we did break a window throwing a frozen candy bar between his room and mine. But I was the one who got in trouble. And we threw eggs at this kid's house. We both got into huge trouble for that one. But mostly we just hung out in Will's room and I'd read and he'd draw. Or we'd go hang out with Will's grandmother, who lived in an apartment in their basement."

"You wanted to hang out with her? God, she must be different from my grandma. I swear, you can't touch anything in that woman's house without her freaking out."

I looked over at the window and noticed that the sun was going down. I hadn't talked about this for years and never with someone I didn't know that well.

"No, it wasn't like that at all. Her name was Amelia. When I was really little, I was convinced she was a witch. I mean a good one, but I was sure she had magical powers. She had really long white hair always pulled back in a bun and wore these bright green or orange dresses with gold designs. She spent most of her time in a big antique red armchair reading, and she had a long gold necklace with a magnifying glass on the end. She'd sit there smoking these long colored cigarettes, telling us crazy stories about growing up all over the world with her missionary parents. Seriously, all of her stories began in some weird country with a poisonous snake in a bed or a huge spider in a shoe and ended with someone's finger or toe falling off."

"Really? I sort of assumed those religious people would be really boring."

"Not her. And she was the one person, besides me, I guess, who Will would open up to."

"What about the rest of his family? Are they that bad?"

"No, I always liked them, but sometimes I thought they were more like an advertisement for a family. Like, if you saw a billboard on the highway trying to sell you a family, they would be the picture."

"People may look like that, but . . ."

"Exactly," I agreed.

We sat there in silence for a minute.

"So what happened?" Sydney asked.

"I think it was a couple of weeks before we started sixth grade. Will was on vacation. Will, David, his older brother, and their mom left a few days earlier because his dad had to finish something at the church. One night I woke up to sirens and lights bouncing off the walls of my room. Two fire trucks were outside Will's house and smoke was pouring out of his basement. I raced outside, and before I knew what was happening, the firefighters gave me Will's two dogs."

"What happened to Will's dad and Amelia?" Sydney whispered as she leaned closer.

"Will's dad was fine, but Amelia died from breathing smoke during the fire. She'd fallen asleep with a cigarette in her hand."

"No way! That's so horrible."

I nodded. "Nothing bad like that had ever happened to any of us before. I mean when I was five, my mom's dad died, but I barely knew him. Amelia was way different."

"How did Will take it?" Sydney asked.

"It was so strange. At first he wouldn't even see me. I was totally devastated. It felt like I'd done something wrong, but I didn't know what it was."

Sydney got up to put the chicken in the oven. "How old were you? Twelve?"

I nodded.

"That's so awful!"

"He finally came over a few days later to tell me he found the magnifying glass necklace. But he was so mad at his dad."

"Why?"

"Because his parents just kept saying over and over again that Amelia was in a better place now that she was with God."

"Why would that make him mad?"

"Because Will didn't want her in heaven. He wanted her back. And it totally bothered him because Amelia didn't think about religion like his parents, and they refused to admit it. She'd always say things like, 'Even if there's a heaven, there's time enough for that later. He'd probably throw me back on Earth because I was arguing too much. I'm not even sure God's a man.' After she died, it was like his parents forgot who she really was."

"She sounds pretty amazing! But Will eventually talked about it with you, right?"

I shook my head. "No—not quite. Two weeks later, we started school and Will acted like it'd never happened. And then a friend of mine fell in love with him. . . ." I paused and Sydney leaned in, knowing she was going to hear something good. "Actually, this is the most annoying part of the story. This girl named Lauren became friends with me so she could get closer to Will. The next thing I know, Lauren and Ally are over in Will's backyard giggling at everything he's saying or screaming if they see an insect."

"I hate when girls do that! Doesn't that make you want to drop the spider on their head or something?" Sydney asked, laughing.

"Totally, but Will loved it. Then Lauren announced that she and Will were now going out, and I had to pretend to be excited about it because if I didn't people would think I was jealous. Which I wasn't, by the way."

"Really? Because you sort of sound jealous right now."

"No! It was just annoying. And there was no way I was talking to Will about it because his fat head would have gotten even bigger than it already was. Then Will's father got a promotion in another church the next state over and he moved."

"What happened between you and those girls when Will left?"

"Nothing. For some reason we stayed friends until last year. But that's not a very interesting story. We just went our separate ways."

Sydney looked at me suspiciously. "I sort of doubt that."

"Seriously. It was just your basic horrible middle-school-girl friendship. They put me down all the time, I put up with it like a total tool. It's one of the reasons I came to Harmony Falls instead of Greenspring with them."

Sydney got up and started putting placemats on the table. "Well, their loss," she said, grinning.

CHAPTER
SIX

## DO YOU HAVE THE WRITE STUFF?

Do you know who Maureen Dowd, George Will,
Anna Quindlen, Judith Warner, Ray Suarez,
Hendrik Hertzberg, Michelle Malkin, Gwen Ifill, David Ignatius,
Malcolm Fleschner, or Bob Woodward are?

Do you care?

If you answered yes to any of these questions and are
interested in writing for the school newspaper, come to
room 2367 at 3:15 on Tuesday, September 25.

"Um, hello? I'm here about the newspaper meeting?" I said, hovering at the door of Room 2367. Right in front of me I could see two guys. One was skinny with perfectly messy brown hair and black rectangular glasses. The other was Asian, huge, and wearing a Panthers' varsity football jacket. I blinked. I'd never seen two opposite stereotypes—the edgy newspaper writer and jock—in such close proximity.

No response. They were both hunched over a book and laughing.

"Excuse me, I'm here for the *Prowler* meeting?" I said.

They both looked up. The skinny one adjusted his glasses and slowly measured me from head to toe while I stood there withering under his gaze. I tried to meet his eyes, but who was I kidding? I looked away, reminding myself that I loved writing and I really wanted this opportunity.

"Sorry, didn't see you standing there. Come in. I'm Josh."

I hesitantly sat on one of the stools near him. "I wrote for my paper in middle school. I brought a couple of writing samples if you want to see them," I said, fumbling through my bag.

The Asian guy sitting across from me continued to read the paper. "Nice, the girl comes prepared. You'll be Ashleigh's little minion in no time."

Josh extended his arms and rolled back the sleeves of his crisp white button-down shirt onto his navy blue sweater. "I haven't introduced Gwo. He writes our comic strip, thereby filling our smart-jock quota on staff."

Gwo ignored him.

"So what's your comic strip about?" I asked.

"I write whatever comes to me. It's mostly about the school. I like to skewer Wickam whenever possible. I guess you could say it's my hobby."

"What's your name, freshman?" asked Josh.

"Charlie," I said.

"Hmmm . . . I like it. Hey, Ashleigh, come meet your new best friend!" Josh called out to a girl across the room.

"Look, you'll love her. She brought writing samples from the paper she wrote for last year," Gwo said.

"Great! I can't wait to read them! Josh, maybe we can do that right after the meeting?" said a pale, long-haired blond girl with obvious highlights.

"Sure. After we square away the fall sports calendar with Raj, ask Antony how many ads he's sold, and look at the layout, we can definitely look at Charlie's writing samples," Josh said sarcastically.

"Don't worry about me," I said, overwhelmed by all these people. "I'm not really expecting to get to write. Honestly, I just want to work on the paper."

Josh squinted his eyes, inspecting me. "Did you just say that to kiss up to us? Just so we're clear, I fully encourage that whenever possible."

Ashleigh took a sip from a Diet Coke can she was holding and then smiled. "Charlie, why don't you get started reading some back issues before the meeting? I'll show you where they are."

"Thanks," I said, grateful to have something else to do.

"All the senior staff put their articles up behind their computers," said Ashleigh as we walked to the back of the room.

"That's cool. Only senior staff?"

"It's a tradition around here," she said like a judge handing down a sentence.

"Oh," I said without taking my eyes off the wall. I felt her sizing me up.

"Being a freshman and all, you probably won't get to do a lot, but if you wait, you'll maybe get something good next year."

"What do freshmen get to do?" I asked, trying to keep my enthusiasm up.

"You know, hand out the newspapers, go to the copier, that kind of stuff. You'll see, but if you need any help with anything, let me know," Ashleigh chirped.

"Of course," I said, taking the back issues out of her hand, trying to ignore her fake tone of voice. The last thing that girl wanted to do was help me out.

Reading through back issues of the *Prowler*, I was pretty impressed. It was like the *New York Times* but with reports on cafeteria food and field trips. The cover stories were about the death penalty and a supreme court case and recent wildfires in the West and environmental policy. As I flipped through the pages, I read film, music, and book reviews, and editorials on national political candidates. This paper was no joke.

My reading was interrupted by voices from outside the hall and a second later, Ms. McBride, the teacher who saved me at registration, came in with two students behind her. When she saw me, her face lit up. "Wait a minute, I know you. You're the girl from orientation! What's your name again?" she asked.

"Charlotte but I go by Charlie; that was the problem."

"Of course," she said now, walking over to me. "I'm the faculty adviser for the *Prowler*. We don't get too many freshmen wanting to write for the newspaper, so it's really good to see you here. I'm hoping for one more freshman to show up this afternoon, a girl in my English class."

I immediately got nervous, positive that this girl was going to be a way better writer than me. I pushed the feeling away, and I had returned to my reading when I heard someone else come into the room. I raised my head to see who it was and almost fell off my chair.

It was Nidhi Patel.

*Damn it,* I thought. Would it have been so horrible if I'd successfully been able to outrun my past?

## CHAPTER SEVEN

**OKAY, UP TO NOW I HAVE TRIED MY BEST TO AVOID THINKING** about the exact reason I was at Harmony Falls. But once Nidhi walked in the door, there was no choice.

By eighth grade, my two closest friends were Lauren Crittiden and Ally Simpson.

You know the cute girl who can be the nicest person in the world until she gets mad at you but won't tell you why? Who loves to say, "I'm sorry but I'm just a really honest person"— and then rip you apart? Who is such a good liar that you believe her even when you know what she's saying is completely untrue? That was Lauren.

Ally was the first girl in our class who needed a bra, and she didn't exactly hide herself under big sweatshirts. She was completely obsessed with her looks and getting all the boys in the school to do whatever she wanted.

It's not like you can go up to your best friends and say,

"You know, I've been meaning to tell you for a while that I really don't like either one of you. Lauren, you're a controlling, vindictive bitch. Ally, you're entirely self-absorbed, fake, and boy-crazy. And by the way, I am unbelievably sick of both you treating me like dirt and then blowing me off by saying 'I'm just joking and don't be so uptight.'" But I kept it inside and stupidly hoped it would get better.

The beginning of the end was the school's annual eighth-grade spring trip to Colonial Williamsburg and Washington, D.C. Only thirty students got to go, so you had to register quickly and sign a behavior contract that promised you wouldn't breathe the wrong way. And for some reason, like I had temporarily lost my sanity, I thought it'd be a good idea to get Lauren and Ally to come with me.

From an eighth-grader's perspective, the perfect chaperone's most key qualities are that they're too nice and easily distracted. On this trip, two of the three fit perfectly. Mr. Slader was a really fat, like one-Big-Mac-away-from-a-heart-attack fat, math teacher. Ms. Galloway, the chorus teacher, had a helmet of thin, dry, straw-blond hair and an unwavering commitment to bright orange lipstick, making it impossible to take the woman seriously. The third was Ms. Morefield, one of the vice principals. She was nice, but she could easily stare down a girl like Lauren without flinching.

The coach bus had almost arrived at the hotel when Lauren, in her favorite skin-tight dark jeans, sat down next to me, took out my earplugs, and smugly said, "Hey, loser, you can thank me now."

"Why?" I said cautiously. I could see the look in Lauren's eyes, and she was way too satisfied with herself.

"I got the rooms switched so now Ally and I are with you."

"How did you do that?" No switching was rule #27 in our contract, and not to my surprise, Ally, Lauren, and I were all in separate rooms.

"It was easy. I found out who was in your room and told two of them that Ally had just broken up with her boyfriend, she was devastated, and we really needed to be there for her." She could tell I wasn't buying it. "Ugh! You're so annoying! I wasn't mean about it!"

"Was Nidhi one of the girls?" I asked.

Lauren frowned. She always had a hard time remembering people's names unless they were in her direct circle of friends, she needed something from them, or she was plotting their destruction.

"Indian-looking girl . . . ," I prompted.

"No. Both girls were white. Oh, you're talking about your little newspaper friend? Don't worry. I didn't talk to her."

I was now rooming with Nidhi, Lauren, and Ally. I knew mixing Lauren and Ally with other people was risky. But like I said in the beginning, one of my worst qualities is that I can be painfully slow to admit the obvious. This is an excellent example. So those little pebbles of nervousness in my stomach? I ignored them.

All it took for Lauren and Ally to switch rooms was to stay in the back of the check-in line and walk a little slower so they could exchange keys with the other girls.

Nidhi and I opened the door to our colonial-themed room. I threw my bag on the four-poster bed, sat down at the desk, and started spinning around in the chair.

"Hey, by the way, Lauren and Ally switched into our room," I said casually, trying to mask the dread I was actually feeling.

"What?" Nidhi said as she hung something up in the closet.

"Umm . . . LaurenandAllyarestayingoverhere." I may have said that a little fast.

Nidhi turned around. I kept spinning.

"Why?" she asked.

"I don't really know. On the bus, Lauren told me she'd gotten Maya and Emily to switch with them."

"Really? They're okay with it?" Nidhi asked doubtfully.

"I think so. Are you cool with it?"

She didn't answer.

"If you want, I can get them to switch it back," I said, knowing full well that was never going to happen.

She laughed. "Right."

I changed the subject by flopping down on the bed and saying, "So, which bed do you want?"

Before Nidhi could answer, Lauren and Ally barged through the door and the pebbles in my stomach turned into something like along the lines of boulders. Ally dropped her huge bag and equally large backpack in the middle of the room.

"FINALLY!" Ally said as she pulled out her iPod and speakers and put them on the desk while Lauren went straight to the bathroom to check her makeup.

For a few minutes, Nidhi and I watched as Ally spread her stuff around the room, oblivious to the fact that she was supposed to share the space with us. And then Lauren reappeared, scanned the room, and declared with her hands on her hips, "Don't you think it'd be better if Ally and I slept in this bed together? Nidhi, no offense, but since we don't know you that well and Charlie does, it just seems easier."

Nidhi briefly looked up from her computer. "It's fine," she said coldly.

*Great, this is working out well,* I thought. One minute together and they're already on their way to hating each other.

By lunch the next day, we'd already visited the blacksmith, the silversmith, the wig store, the apothecary, and the first public hospital for "Persons of Insane and Disordered Minds." Then we were off to the governor's palace and the maze. All of a sudden, I noticed that Ally was talking louder—a sure sign there was a hot guy around. I looked over. I was wrong: There were two guys. One was blond; the other had dark hair and blue eyes—and both boys were Ally's favorite kind. She called them Brads because they all had the same look so they all needed the same name. How could you tell a Brad? Rainbows, khaki shorts, cool T-shirts (in this case the blond one had MAKE PIZZA NOT WAR and the other, darker haired one, had a faded Abercrombie). But the most important part of being a Brad was the guy's hair. It had to be long but not too long, and shaggy.

Ally took off the rubber band she was wearing on her wrist. "Excuse me, do you know where the maze is?"

The blond Pizza boy one looked above her head, where there was a sign that read THE MAZE. "I'm fairly sure that if you keep walking you'll run right into it," he said, grinning.

He had a Southern accent. For Ally, finding Brads with a Southern accent was like a hungry lion finding a lone gazelle.

Her eyes focused on her prey through her fake Gucci sunglasses. She smiled. Her hands flew up to her hair as she effortlessly put it into a ponytail while her short T-shirt simultaneously rose up to show her perfectly flat stomach.

Ally smiled again. "You have such cute accents! Where are you from?"

"We're from Mission Academy in Columbia, South Carolina. Sophomore class trip. We've been on a hiking trip for the last week. We're just here for the night," said the brown-haired Brad, looking right at me. My heart jumped. I stared at the ground.

Without hesitation, Ally said, "Well, come with us to the maze so you can help us out if we get lost." She then turned around, giving them opportunity to stare at the rhinestone heart BeDazzled on the butt of her dark blue Juicy sweatpants.

"So where are you staying?" she asked.

Blond Brad said, "I think it's called the Patrick Henry Inn."

This was too easy. "Really! That's where we're staying! Wait, we never said our names. I'm Ally, and this is Charlie. We have another friend, Lauren, but don't worry, she's cute too."

The blond one laughed. "I'm not worried. I'm Jackson, and this is Tucker."

Jackson leaned against the wall and took out his cell. "We can't go with you right now because we have to meet our class, but you should give us your number and maybe we can hang out later."

Ally said casually, "Yeah, that'd be cool."

"We should definitely hang out," said Tucker, again looking right at me.

Of course I wanted to say "YES!" but I managed to not make a complete fool of myself. "Yeah, sure, that'd be great," I said, as Ally was pulling me away.

As soon as they were gone, Ally whispered, "You're so in love with Tucker! As soon as I saw them I knew it because you always love dark-haired, blue-eyed boys." She giggled. "Okay—you can have him, so don't ever say I'm not a good friend."

"Ally, I don't love him. I just think he's cute."

"Whatever, you love him. I can tell." She drew in her breath quickly. She was having an adrenaline rush. "Well, this trip just got a lot less boring."

Five minutes later, I was having a huge insecurity attack. Maybe I'd read too much into what Tucker said. Why would Tucker like me when perfect-looking Ally was standing right next to me the whole time? I mean, usually I was absolutely fine with being way less hot than Ally and Lauren. But this time I really wanted Tucker to ignore them.

"Ally, do you think they'll call?" I asked.

Ally looked at me like I was five. "Don't be stupid. Of course they'll call. I'm cute. You're cute. Of course they will. And don't worry. Tucker liked you. I could tell."

It was moments like these that I loved being friends with Ally.

That night at 9:50 P.M. Ally texted Jackson.

Heyyy, sooo bored Come over!!!
Room 311 and bring friend. Come after 11
Teachers roaming hallways.

At 10 P.M. lights were supposed to be out.

At 10:05 P.M. I put a towel under the door so none of the teachers would see light coming from our room. Then we watched *Mean Girls* on cable.

At 11:30 P.M. Tucker and Jackson still hadn't responded and I'd given up. Then Ally's phone vibrated. "Told you so," she giggled.

As Ally walked to the door I said to Nidhi casually, "By the way, Ally and I ran into these guys at the governor's mansion and she invited them over."

Nidhi's face fell. "You can't be serious."

"It just sort of happened. Ally and I met them at the maze, and she gave them her number. I didn't think they'd actually call. They're from some school in South Carolina."

"Charlie, this may be cool for you all, but my parents would kill me if they knew there were boys in my room," she hissed.

Lauren turned away from the mirror where she was putting on her Victoria's Secret "I Want Candy" lip gloss and faced Nidhi. "Nidhi, your parents aren't here. They'll stay for five minutes, be really boring, and we'll kick them out."

There was a soft knock on the door.

Ally shook her hair out and grinned while she pulled her sweatpants down another inch. "Well they're here now, so there's nothing we can do about it," she trilled and opened the door.

"Hey, what's up?" was said simultaneously in six directions. Six because Nidhi said nothing and was now reading a book in the chair farthest from the door.

"How come you didn't tell us to bring somebody else for

your friend? We only brought Haines," Jackson said, gesturing to the new blond freckly boy in the room.

Lauren and Ally looked at each other with eyebrows furrowed, confused.

Nidhi rolled her eyes. "That's okay. You really don't need to worry about me."

Jackson picked up the remote. Without even asking, he flipped through the channels until he suddenly stopped. I'm sorry, but coming into a room where you don't know anyone and changing their show is a clear violation of remote rules.

"Excellent! Haines, this is *True Lies,* right?"

Haines turned to Nidhi. "I'm really into movies. I've probably seen every Schwarzenegger movie at least thirty times. Minimum. This is a total classic. He takes on about a million Arab terrorists. The fight scenes are old school, but they're pretty sick."

Nidhi responded by looking up once and going back to her book, but he wouldn't stop asking her questions. She gave him the standard girls' I'm-not-interested-in-you one-word answers, but Haines wasn't getting it. If he had, he'd have also noticed Lauren shooting sideways glares at Nidhi when she wasn't pretending to text someone.

Suddenly Nidhi put the book down. "Do we have to watch this?"

Jackson kept his eyes on the TV. "Why? Do you have a problem with it?

"Actually, I do."

In that one sentence, Nidhi became the uptight girl I was never willing to be.

Haines cocked his head. "Are you, like, from there or something?"

Nidhi put the book down and smiled. "Where, exactly?"

Lauren put her phone down and said, "You know, a Muslim country."

Nidhi looked at her for about one second too long. "I was born in India. My parents came here when I was five."

Haines laughed nervously. "Whoa, that's crazy. I've never met an actual Muslim before."

Nidhi smiled sarcastically. "Well, then, this would have been a big day for you, except I'm not Muslim, I'm Hindu."

Haines looked a little relieved and grinned. "Well, I've never met one of those either." He wasn't getting this at all. Nidhi wasn't into him. Lauren was. He was ignoring Lauren. Boys are idiots.

Ally, attempting to stun everyone with her cultural knowledge, joined the conversation. "Wait, Lauren, do you remember how many times we had to listen to *Ray of Light* going back and forth in your mom's car from ballet practice? That was Hindu? I always thought it was Muslim. I really wanted to get that henna stuff on my hands, but my mom wouldn't let me because she thought it looked dirty. So, Nidhi, is that Hindu or Muslim?"

"That's Hindu," she said, like Ally had won a prize.

"Whatever. It's all the same," Lauren said dismissively and stretched like a cat across the bed.

"Actually it's really not," said Nidhi.

Meanwhile, Haines continued his cluelessness by throwing a pillow at Nidhi and saying, "I can't believe you don't like this movie. It's classic Arnold!"

She dodged the pillow. "If you're really asking me, it's because it's totally racist," she said matter-of-factly.

Haines froze.

Jackson turned around so he was facing Nidhi. "Relax. It's just a movie. I've watched it tons of times, and I'm not racist."

Lauren turned onto her side so now she also faced Nidhi. "If you don't like it, why don't you just read your book?"

For two very long seconds, Nidhi just stared at her and then slowly closed her book, got her pajamas and toothbrush, and walked to the bathroom.

The bathroom door shut. Jackson turned to Lauren. "What's wrong with your friend?"

Lauren groaned. "I don't know. She's Charlie's friend. I had no idea she was so intense."

"Isn't India where all the women go around in those capes and scarves on their heads?" Ally asked, chiming in again as our multicultural expert.

I tried not to sound annoyed, but it was so hard. "No, that's called a hijab." I knew that because I did a report on it in seventh grade. "It's something some Muslim women wear," I said, praying Nidhi would stay in the bathroom, but naturally she chose that moment to come back in the room.

"Look, it's late and I'm getting really tired."

Lauren stared at Nidhi like she was dirt. "Look, Nid-hi"—pronouncing it Nid-hee instead of Nidhi like the *d* was a *th*—"no offense, but you're making way too much of this. Why don't you relax a little, or were you in the bathroom strapping on some suicide bomb?"

Everyone laughed. Except me. I died.

"What did you say?" Nidhi said, her voice trembling with anger.

Lauren smiled. "You heard me. All I'm saying is you need to relax a little. You really don't need to be so annoying."

Nidhi grabbed her pillow and walked toward the door. "You all do whatever you need to do. I'm out of here." The door slammed behind her.

"Whatever," Lauren said smugly.

"That girl needs to go back to wherever she's from," Jackson said, laughing.

"I'm going to go check on her and see if she's okay," I said. I could feel Lauren rolling her eyes and laughing at me as I left the room.

I desperately searched for Nidhi because I wanted her to know that I didn't agree with anything that had just happened in that room. But she was nowhere to be found. After ten minutes of looking up and down the halls and in the stairwells, I gave up and went back to the room.

When I opened the door, I realized things had taken a turn for the seriously, painfully awkward. Ally and Jackson were all over each other; Lauren and Haines were also going in that direction. That left Tucker—who was on the bed closest to the door watching TV and texting someone—and me. Up to this point I'd kissed boys, but I hadn't really hooked up with anyone, especially not someone in tenth grade who looked like Tucker. So I was faced with a very difficult question: Was I really going to hook up with someone for the first time in my life while my other two friends did the same thing in the same room?

Tucker asked quietly, "Is she okay?"

"I don't know. I couldn't find her," I said, too nervous to look at him.

"Well, when you see her, tell her don't worry about Haines and Jackson. They didn't mean it."

Maybe it was his accent, but he seemed sincere. "Thanks," I said, concentrating on the comforter pattern.

As I talked, his face seemed to be getting closer to mine. "That's amazing. Did you do that?" I blurted, pointing to a drawing on his jeans.

"Yeah, I draw a lot. You want me to draw you something?"

He reached around me, got a pen out of the drawer, and took my arm. Although I could barely breath as an image of a dragon formed on my skin, I do remember one thing clearly. I decided then and there I would make out with him even if there were a thousand people in the room.

But then there was a knock on the door.

"Girls, it's Ms. Morefield. Would you please open the door?"

Lauren whispered, "Shit! Nidhi's such a bitch!"

All three boys jumped up.

Haines whispered, "No way! How do we get out of here?"

As Tucker ran to hide in the shower and Jackson hid under the bed, Haines opened the window but changed his mind and hid in the closest instead.

I got off the bed and opened the door to my biggest nightmare in the form of Ms. Morefield in navy blue sweats. Her dark brown eyes swept the room and then slowly landed on each of us.

"Where are the girls who are supposed to be in this room?"

Lauren spoke for us. "We switched. It was a last-minute thing because we weren't tired and the other girls were, so we thought it'd be easier this way."

"That's so considerate of you, Lauren," Ms. Morefield said sarcastically as her eyes scanned the room. "Is there any possibility you have boys in here?" she asked, staring at me.

Lauren answered for me. "I think it was the TV."

"Then you wouldn't mind if I look around your room a bit?"

All I kept thinking was why couldn't she have waited for just fifteen more minutes before she ruined my night. But that didn't matter. She went right to the bathroom and pulled the shower curtain back to find Tucker.

"Hi, there!" Ms. Morefield said as if she had run into an old friend. "I don't think I know you! You don't go to Ben Franklin Middle School."

Tucker's eyes bulged. "Middle school? Did you say middle school? What grade are they in?"

Ms. Morefield answered even more brightly, "These girls? Eighth grade. You didn't know that?"

Twelve hours later, we met our parents at the airport. Ally's and Lauren's parents hugged them as if they had suffered some huge tragedy and wouldn't stop talking about how the school was overreacting. My parents' idea of welcoming me home was limited to glaring. What was Ally and Lauren's punishment? Their parents thought Lauren and Ally were punished enough because they had to come home early. Oh, wait, Lauren's dad got her an iPhone because he wanted to make sure if she were ever in a "bad" situation with boys again, she could call or email him.

What was my punishment? I had to be my parents' slave until I worked off the money my parents paid for the trip.

And then things got seriously out of hand. Within days, Lauren and Ally had convinced almost the entire school that Nidhi was a snitch. Then they left anonymous voice mails (blocked the caller ID) and sent emails (with a fake name) calling her a fat, hairy, ugly terrorist. After the emails, I couldn't take it anymore.

CHealeyPepper324: don't u think the emails r a little harsh?

SweetNLo: y? u didn't think so when we called her. u were laughing just as much as we were!!!!!!!!!

CHealeyPepper324: i just think youve made your point

SweetNLo: that girl has 2 learn her lesson. if she hadnt gone to ms morefield none of this would b happening

CHealeyPepper324: but u dont know she did it

SweetNLo: dont b stupid. u kno she did

CHealeyPepper324: i just don't think this is really necessary

SweetNLo: c—stop complaining, absooooluuuutely necessary. u know were rite

CHealeyPepper324: fine. gtg

All that time I knew I should have confronted them. I kept going over the perfect thing to say so Lauren would finally shut up or stop. But I couldn't. I'd stare at my ceiling wondering when I had turned into someone who was so afraid to stand up to people. I knew I hadn't always been like this. If my ten-year-old self could have seen me, she would have been completely disgusted.

A week later things got even worse.

"Carlota, necesitas reportar a la oficina, por favor."

I woke from my haze of conjugating *estar* in Señora Fletcher's Spanish class.

My brain refused to understand what I was hearing.

"Carlota, necesitas reportar a la oficina inmediatamente, por favor."

"What?" I said coming out of my stupor.

Señora Fletcher gave up on me. "Charlie, please report to the office."

Even if you're completely innocent (or in my case, have no idea what you've done), you freak out when you're called to the office. And of course everyone stares at you while you're putting your books in your bag, imagining all your crimes. I walked to the office, my shoes slowly scraping against the floor, trying to think of anything I could have done wrong, when I ran into Lauren going in the same direction.

"Charlie, did you tell anyone about the Nidhi thing?" she asked urgently.

"What are you talking about?"

"Don't be stupid!" she hissed.

We walked a few steps in silence, but I could see Lauren scheming.

"This has to be about something else. But if we're in trouble we have to prepare. . . . Okay, Charlie, you can't look guilty when we walk in there."

"But I didn't do anything!"

Lauren just rolled her eyes at me and kept walking.

We got to the main office and Ally was already waiting, hands under her butt, staring straight ahead. Then we were ushered into the office.

Mr. Moossy was at the head of a huge conference table in his office sitting next to Ms. Morefield *and all of our parents.*

"I have asked you here because we have a problem in this school that we're going to fix. Young ladies, do any of you know what I am talking about?" asked Mr. Moossy.

I couldn't speak, and I definitely couldn't look at my parents.

"I have just finished explaining to your parents about the harassing videos and voice mails sent by you to another student in this school. And we know that many of them are of a racist nature."

"I for one, am having a very hard time believing this. We didn't raise Allison to be racist, and we've never had one complaint from this school. So if you're going to accuse these girls of something so serious, I'd like to think you have proof to back this up," Mr. Simpson said, smugly.

"Well, in cases like this we work with the telephone company to get a record of the voice mails. I have them here if you'd like to listen to them," Mr. Moossy said, gravely.

"I didn't do it," I whispered to my mom as tears uncontrollably fell down my face.

"Don't pretend you didn't know what was going on," Lauren hissed.

I was speechless with hatred.

Five minutes later, we left Mr. Moossy's office with a two-day suspension and the record of what we had done placed in our permanent file. Oh, and I was kicked off the newspaper for the rest of the year.

My parents were less than pleased.

Six weeks later, I was summoned to the principal's office again. As I waited outside his office, I was terrified that I had done something else wrong, but I couldn't remember what it was. I almost died when I saw Ms. Morefield sitting next to Mr. Moossy.

Mr. Moossy waved at me to sit down.

I kept standing. My feet couldn't move.

"Charlie, sit down. How's everything?" he asked like I just happened to be walking by his office and decided to drop in.

I hate when adults play games with you. I forced my feet to move toward the table and tried to keep my voice steady. "I'm fine."

He sat back in his chair. "There's something Ms. Morefield and I would like to discuss with you," he said.

Again, I desperately thought of what I could have done. Nothing came to my mind.

Mr. Moossy continued, "Let me get straight to the point. Do you remember the last time you were here?"

No, I completely forgot how you told me I was a huge disappointment to you.

I looked down at the table. "Yeah," I mumbled.

"Well, we're very happy with the changes we've seen in you. We know it was hard to lose your position on the newspaper, but you took responsibility for your actions. That's the kind of behavior we were hoping we'd see from you, Charlotte," Ms. Morefield said.

I exhaled and looked up for the first time since entering the room.

She leaned forward. "Charlie, you're not here because you're in trouble. We would like to discuss an opportunity with you."

Mr. Moossy handed me a brochure about an honors program at Harmony Falls—the high school the next town over. Ms. Morefield smiled at me. "Each year, Harmony Falls High School accepts a few outstanding students from middle schools outside its jurisdiction. We've nominated you as a candidate."

A way out of my social wasteland and nightmare had just fallen into my lap.

"Thank you so much! I'll fill out the application tonight." And I ran out of the room.

I waited until dinner that night to tell my parents. I had to explain it to them about fifteen times before they believed it. Unlike two months before, when they were ready to disown me, my parents were so proud of me that for about a week I could do nothing wrong. Eighteen days later, an envelope came in the mail. It was thin, as in "thanks for trying but we are rejecting you."

I really didn't want to open it, but I knew I had to get it over with.

>*Dear Charlotte,*
>*We are pleased to inform you of your acceptance to*
>*Harmony Falls! We believe you will make an outstanding*

*contribution to our community and look forward to
having you among us. In a few weeks you will receive
information about your freshman orientation and other
exciting activities . . .*

Who cared about the rest? I know I didn't. I was leaving
Lauren and Ally and the whole mess with Nidhi behind.
That is, until Nidhi walked into that room.

## CHAPTER EIGHT

**SEEING NIDHI AGAIN WAS, TO SAY THE LEAST, A SHOCK. MY** basic plan of avoiding her for the rest of my life had just miserably failed.

Nidhi looked at me like she wasn't too sure I was really there either. "Hi, Charlie—"

Ashleigh walked over to us. "You all know each other?" she asked excitedly.

"We both went to Franklin last year. . . . We worked on the paper together," Nidhi said flatly.

"Okay, everyone, we have a couple of new faces here, so let's start with introductions. Raj, let's start with you and then go around the table," Ms. McBride said.

"I'm Raj," said a cute black-haired Indian guy, who crumpled up a piece of paper and threw it in a perfect arc over Gwo's head and into the trash can. "I'm the sportswriter. And even though everyone's going to shoot me down, I'm seriously in need of assistance here. The fall schedule is completely out of control. Between varsity and JV, there are sixty-three games, so there's no way I can cover it all. So if there's anyone interested in helping me out, talk to me after the meeting."

Ashleigh smiled at me and Nidhi, Diet Coke again in hand, and said, "You can skip me, we already met."

"Josh, editor. Film and book reviews."

"Tony, sophomore, business editor," said a brown-haired freckly boy being swallowed by a huge Harmony Falls wrestling jacket.

The door opened and in strolled a really skinny tall guy with shoulder-length jet-black hair, wearing a Ramones T-shirt over a white long-sleeve shirt, black jeans, and red Converse. "I thought the meeting started at four," he mumbled.

Ashleigh smiled tightly. "Owen, that's why I sent you twenty emails today."

"Why don't you say hi to the freshmen," Josh said to Owen.

"I'm Owen. I do the editorials," he said like he could barely be bothered, and folded one long leg underneath him on a stool.

"Owen, are you covering the student elections again this year?" Josh asked.

"Are they going to be less pathetic?" he said, shaking his hair out of his eyes.

"Do you have to be so negative all the time, Owen? This year's candidates aren't that bad," Ashleigh said.

"Have you seen the posters? I'm ready to give up on democracy entirely."

"Just tell us if you want to do it because I'll do it if you won't," Ashleigh said.

Owen cringed and ran both hands through his hair. "God, please spare me. I'll do it. I just hope the speeches are better this year. Last year was a travesty."

"Owen, I really don't know where we'd be without you as our beacon of light," Gwo said.

Ms. McBride smiled widely. "Good, I can see we've all missed each other over the summer. Before we adjourn to do our separate things, I just want to say I have absolute confidence that you all will do an outstanding job this year. Nidhi and Charlie, my job is mostly stopping in from time to time, but feel free to come to me if you need anything."

Ashleigh beamed. "It's going to be great! With any luck, we'll stir things up a little this year. So remember deadlines for submissions are Tuesdays. Nidhi and Charlie, we'll see where's the best place to fit you in. In the meantime, you can organize last year's issues. Okay?"

Both Nidhi and I nodded, the picture of freshman compliance.

Later that night after dinner, I waited until my parents were downstairs watching TV, then I knocked on Luke's door.

"Can I come in?" I asked.

"Okay," Luke said robotically as he played his air-combat game on his computer.

"So I had an interesting surprise at school today," I said, flopping onto Luke's bed.

"Uh-huh," he said, not listening.

"Luke, I need you to pay attention."

"Okay. Okay," he said, finally spinning around. He put his feet up on the bed next to me.

"Luke, you're killing me. You've got to put those things away," I gasped.

"You're on my bed in my room and these are my feet."

"I swear I'm going to throw up. And it won't be pretty because I've been inhaling Oreos and chips all afternoon."

Luke shook his head. "Eating your feelings already? I thought you had too much self-esteem for that. I'll go into Mom and Dad's room and see if they have a book to make it all better."

"Could you possibly be more irritating?"

"Then why did you come into my room and bother me?"

I gave up and moved away from his feet. "Okay, you're never going to believe this, but Nidhi's at Harmony Falls."

Luke smirked. "Wow . . . that sucks!"

"I know, and she wants to work on the newspaper too," I groaned. "What am I going to do?"

"What do you mean? Just deal."

"Luke, don't you think it's a little awkward? What if she tells people what happened? They'll never let me write for the *Prowler*. . . . Maybe I should drop out," I said, getting up and pacing around his room. "I guess I can always write for the literary journal. Or maybe I'll try something totally different, like cross-country."

"Right. Cross-country. I'm seeing it now," Luke said, mockingly.

"I'm glad this is so amusing for you, but my life is over!"

He put up his hands, and leaned back, his green eyes all happy because he could make fun of me. "Come on, Charlie, the idea of you doing cross-country is pretty funny. You've never run more than a half mile in your life." He laughed.

"So?"

"Don't you think you're being a little dramatic about this? Nidhi probably doesn't want to bring it up any more than you."

I shook my head. "Luke, you're not a girl, so you can't understand this. Girls never, ever truly forgive each other for anything. Even if they say they do, they don't."

"If I can't understand, Charles, then why are you asking for my advice?"

"I don't know. I'm insane?"

"No, you came to me because you know I'm right."

I sat back down on the bed and put my hands over my eyes. "I really thought I'd put this behind me."

Luke swiveled his chair back to the computer screen and started playing his video game again. "Just get over yourself and talk to her. It's really not that big a deal."

"Fine. Thank you for being completely useless."

"Anytime," he called out to me as I walked back to my room. Of course I knew that was the right thing to do but it's way easier to confront imaginary people in a video game than do it in real life.

Two days later, I was doing homework in the library during my free period when I saw Nidhi sitting at a computer across the room. I tried to convince myself that seeing her was a good sign and now I had to force myself to do the right thing. But truthfully, if I hadn't really wanted to work on the *Prowler*, I would have run.

"Hey, Nidhi. Can I sit down?"

"Sure," she said, indifferently. Her eyes stayed on the monitor.

I dropped my book bag on the floor and sat down across from her. "Um . . . could we talk for a second?"

Her eyes left the screen and met mine.

My heart raced. I swallowed the basketball in my throat.

"Well . . . I know things got pretty bad between us last year. I actually switched schools so I could put all that stuff behind me. So . . . seeing you was . . . weird."

Nidhi's brown eyes glanced across the room and then back at me. "Charlie, I'm not going to lie to you. It wasn't like I was overjoyed to see you in that room either."

I inhaled deeply. "I'll try to stay out of your way as much as possible. I'll even drop out of the newspaper if you want."

She leaned back in her chair. "Thanks for the offer, but that's kind of stupid, don't you think? We both really want to work on the *Prowler*." She paused. "I just need to tell you one thing."

"Sure, of course," I said.

"Last year, I never got the chance to tell you what it was like for me."

"Go ahead," I stammered, dreading what she was about to say.

"So when we were working on the *Town Crier*, I thought you were my friend. Not one of my closest friends, but I really liked working with you. And I never thought you'd stand by and do nothing while your friends were so incredibly evil."

Slowly the words left me. "Nidhi . . . I just want to say how sorry I am . . . for everything. I should have backed you up in the hotel and stopped Lauren and Ally from all the stuff they did after. You have no idea how bad I felt. I guess I avoided you because I was so ashamed, and I didn't know how to fix it."

I waited for her to say something to make me feel even worse.

"It was like you were a different person around them. . . . It was really hard, Charlie. Putting up with those girls was a nightmare. You have no idea. I didn't want to go to school for a long time after that. My parents wanted to move or send me to live with my grandparents in India. All I kept thinking was, Why? I didn't do anything but walk out of that room, so why are these girls so obsessed with making me miserable? What gives them the right to do the things they did to me?"

"I'm so sorry. I wish there was a way I could take it back. I mean I know I can't, but I'm really sorry."

She watched something behind me but didn't answer for many uncomfortable moments. "Thanks for that," Nidhi said returning her gaze to me.

"For what?" I asked

"For saying sorry and meaning it."

"No problem." I exhaled in relief.

I waited for a few more moments, gathering my courage. "So, Nidhi, would you maybe want to write something together?"

"Maybe," she said, her eyes still doubtful.

Okay, it wasn't like she threw her arms around me and said all was forgiven, but she didn't want to kill me, so it was a start.

"I completely get it if you don't . . . ," I said.

"Well . . . what do you have in mind?"

# CHAPTER NINE

**A WEEK LATER, THINGS WERE GOING WELL. NIDHI AND I HAD** established a truce. Nothing momentus was happening with Tyler but he hadn't asked for his sweatshirt back and we were definitely talking before and after Mr. Jaquette's class. Of course Sydney loved teasing me about Tyler but she didn't do it in front of him. So all in all things did not suck.

By our next *Prowler* meeting Nidhi and I had come up with an idea. Since school began, people were obsessed with Spirit Week. So Nidhi and I wanted to find out as much as we could and cover it for the freshmen.

"Hey, Josh, can we talk to you about something?" Nidhi said nervously, a few seconds after we walked through the *Prowler* door.

"Just the people I wanted to see! I've been thinking about how best to exploit you. Right now it's a toss-up between making you get the printed copies with Owen or making you both Ashleigh's official assistants."

My heart sank. "Great," I said, weakly.

"Okay," said Nidhi also.

Josh rolled his eyes. "Actually, I have come up with a brilliant idea that you totally don't deserve but I'm going to give you anyway. . . ."

We both said nothing, waiting.

"Okay, how would you like to write a column once in a while? For freshmen by freshmen?"

"What?" we both said simultaneously.

"We need new features, and something like this hasn't ever been done before. But you can't screw up. You'll do it like once a quarter and come to me first if you have any problems or questions."

Nidhi's eyes were huge. "Thank you so much! This is amazing!"

I nodded in agreement. "I promise we'll do a good job!"

Out of nowhere I heard Gwo's voice from behind me. "You need to come up with a name." He'd been in the corner drawing the whole time.

"No problem," Nidhi said like she had a hundred possibilities already picked out. "Charlie and I will come up with something right away."

"Just don't do something that makes me look bad. I want this to be something good, where you are giving the freshman spin on things. Why don't you get started on the name and the first topics you want to cover? We'll let the staff know at the meeting, and if you have any ideas by then, you can tell us about them," Josh said.

Nidhi and I got up and walked over to one of the tables in the corner, sat down, and stared at each other. This was the moment of truth. Could we really put last year behind us?

I started awkwardly. "I can't believe Josh is letting us do this!"

"I know," Nidhi whispered. "But now I'm terrified we'll mess it up!"

"No we won't. We can totally do this." I said, clicking my pen back and forth.

Nidhi looked down at her notebook and whispered, "Yeah, now I'm not so sure."

"Don't worry about it. And if we mess up, I'll take the blame. It's the least I can do."

"Good point," Nidhi said nodding.

And with that, it really seemed like we were okay. By the time Josh started the staff meeting, Nidhi and I had agreed on a name and decided we would pitch the Spirit Week idea for the first column.

As we sat around that table listening to everyone's status reports, I could barely wait until it was our turn.

Finally, Josh said, "As you all know, I want to add some new features to the paper this year, so I have decided to let Nidhi and Charlie write a column just for the freshmen."

Ashleigh's head shot up. "They're getting their own column?"

"That's the initial plan. We have to see how it goes."

"How often?" she said tightly.

Josh smiled. "Not sure. I was thinking once a quarter to start off. Nothing Charlie and Nidhi can't handle."

"No offense, but what if they don't do a good job? That's

just going to give me a lot more work." She looked over at me and Nidhi, smiling thinly. "I mean, no offense, but it's true. Your writing is okay, but it needs a lot of work."

"Easy, Ash, I've seen their writing. They'll be fine. And this is on a trial basis. If they suck, we'll pull it."

"But what happened to seniority?" Ashleigh said indignantly.

Owen muttered, "Ashleigh, think about it. A freshman column can't be based on seniority. The only people who can do it are freshmen."

"Thanks, Owen. I get it," Ashleigh said sarcastically. "I'm not an idiot."

Everyone around the table saw Owen roll his eyes.

"We already have the name. We want to call it the 'Fresh View,'" Nidhi said brightly.

Gwo nodded. "Not bad. Could be worse. What do you want to write about?"

I looked over at Nidhi to see if I should answer, and she nodded. "Spirit Week," I said cautiously.

"Spirit Week?" Owen said with complete disdain. I got the distinct impression we couldn't have said anything worse.

"Yeah," I said hesitantly. "It won't just be a schedule of events. We'll embed ourselves in as many activities as possible and then report back."

Owen tapped his pencil on the table. "Okay, fine. But please tell me you're also going to interview people who despise the whole thing. Or are you only going to interview the people who buy into all this crap?"

Nidhi and I looked at each other.

"Of course we'll get both sides," I said.

"It's just that all the upperclassmen talk about it and we don't think the freshmen have a clue," Nidhi said.

"Owen, could you put us in contact with people like you're talking about?" I asked. "That way we can be sure to get the other perspective."

"I guess," Owen said, doodling on the paper in front of him.

"Ashleigh, you should have them talk to Matt," Gwo suggested.

"Well . . . he would be perfect for it. But I have no idea when he's going to be around," Ashleigh said.

"Just call him and tell him two freshman girls want to pay attention to him. He'll be over here in a second," Owen said.

"Very funny, Owen," Ashleigh said curtly.

"I wasn't aware that I was making a joke."

"All right, you two, relax," Josh said interrupting them. "And it is a good idea. Between Owen's friends and Matt, they'll get different opinions—and that is the point of journalism, right, people?" Josh said.

I needed to do some reconnaissance.

"Gwo, why do we need to interview this Matt guy?" I said, sitting next to him on the couch.

Gwo straightened up and looked across the room. Ashleigh was engrossed in something on the computer with Ms. McBride.

"Matt is Ashleigh's boyfriend. He's your basic high school cocky douche-bag jock. Mostly plays lacrosse."

"What? Lacrosse? I don't get it. Are lacrosse players that bad?"

"Not always, but they definitely have a reputation here for being arrogant and doing whatever the hell they want. Way worse than the football team."

"But you're biased. You're on the football team!"

"Trust me. Lacrosse is worse. Anyway, they have a new coach this year, so we'll see. Maybe he'll make it better, but then again, he has to go up against the parents and that'll be useless. I thought football parents were insane—"

"Gwo, Gwo, can you slow down a minute? What do they do that's so bad?"

"Charlie, you've been here for like a month, right?"

"And . . . ?"

"Haven't you noticed that if you're good at something here, really good, you don't really have to abide by the rules?"

"Uh . . . no. Can't say that's been a problem for me so far."

"Well, you'll see it soon enough. Anyway, you really should talk to Matt because he totally buys all the tradition stuff. And if you talk to Owen or any of his friends, you'll get the people who hate it."

"Owen doesn't really seem to like anyone," I observed.

"That's not true. He just thinks most people are mindless hypocrites. But he does hate Matt and a couple of other guys on the lacrosse team."

"Why?"

"Because Owen played lacrosse freshman year with Matt and something went down. Don't ask because I'm not really sure what it was—not that I want to know. The only thing I do know is that Owen was really good and then he dropped out. I think he even made varsity as a freshman."

"Wait, I'm confused. It's good to make varsity for a ninth grader," I said, worried. I couldn't help thinking about Will, Tyler, and Michael.

"Depends. It's good if you're willing to do what it takes to be on the team. If you're not, then it can get a little rough."

"But what do you have to do that would be so bad?"

He shrugged. "Let's just say that when I was in ninth grade, I spent as little time in the locker room as possible."

"But you just said football was easy."

"Compared to lacrosse it is."

A little later a guy with spiked blond hair, small slitty eyes, and pink skin strolled into the room.

Gwo leaned over and whispered, "There's your boy."

"Never would have guessed," I whispered back.

I scanned the room for Owen because I was really curious to see his sarcasm directed at Matt. But strangely, he wasn't around. I wondered if he had left to avoid him.

"Hey, Ashleigh, introduce your boyfriend to Charlie and Nidhi so they can interview him," Gwo called out.

"What's he talking about, babe?" Matt said.

"These are the new freshmen. They want to write something about Spirit Week," Ashleigh said brightly, as he hugged her from behind.

Nidhi and I weakly waved. In a second, he was sitting in front of us with his arms spread out along the back of the couch. "So, freshmeat. . . . What can I do for you?"

Freshmeat? Seriously?

Ashleigh followed close behind, like Nidhi and I would try to steal her boyfriend the second we got the chance.

We both ignored the greeting and grabbed our note-books. Nidhi sat up straight, pen in hand. The image of serious journalism.

"Okay, I'm Nidhi. Our column is going to be about Spirit Week, and we were told you'd be a good person to interview for it."

"For girls as hot as you two, I'll do whatever you want," he said, grinning.

I smiled weakly. "So what do you like about Spirit Week?" I asked, wondering how a person got so incredibly arrogant. Honestly, he wasn't that good-looking, and he didn't seem that smart, so how had he convinced himself otherwise?

Matt laughed. "Let's see. . . . You have the competitions during lunch. The root-beer chugging is the best. People compete to see who can drink a pint of root beer the fastest. Mr. Wickam is always the judge for that. Last year, Wes Thompson upchucked everywhere. It was classic. But then there's the bon-fire, the homecoming games, and the dance. There's just tons of stuff. It's a time when the whole school comes together."

"What do you remember best from your freshman year?" Nidhi asked.

He laughed. "Oh, man! What I remember best was the juniors waking some of us up at four in the morning to help them get the pallets for the bonfire. But then there are the little traditions the senior players hand down."

"Like what?" I asked.

"Ohhhh, I can't tell you that. Team secrets," he laughed.

"What do you want freshmen to know about Spirit Week?" I asked.

"That's easy. Harmony Falls is a great school because of the traditions. I know some people when they get here don't understand that, but they need to. Lots of people complain about it at first, but then you get used to it and when you're upperclassmen, it'll be your turn and you'll understand. Recently some people have wanted to change things around. I even heard that some parents want to stop us from doing the rootbeer chugging contest—which is completely retarded. People just need to calm down and not make such a big deal out of things."

It seemed to me that Matt needed to follow his own advice. But I didn't say that. We just smiled, thanked him, and gave him back to Ashleigh.

"Nidhi," I whispered as he walked away, "if I ever end up liking a guy like that, shoot me."

CHAPTER
TEN

**"THIS ROOM IS EXACTLY THE SAME! YOU STILL HAVE THAT** foosball table," Will said, shoveling chocolate cake into his mouth.

Will's family had come over for dinner. We had just left our parents in the dining room and had come down to the rec room.

"You want to play?" Luke asked.

"Sure, but it's been a while."

"Already making excuses?" I teased. "I'll play winner!"

"Like you have a chance of beating me?" Will asked skeptically.

"Will, do I need to remind you that I totally owned you in this game the last time we played?" I said, flopping down onto the couch.

"Right . . . I forgot. I never told you this, but I always let you win."

"You did not, you big liar!"

"Fine, we'll play after I play Luke. But I'm showing no mercy this time, even though you're a girl."

I groaned. "Why is it that boys always think they are so much better than girls at everything? It's so annoying! And you're wrong, by the way!"

Luke dropped the ball into play. "Can you all stop arguing? And anyways, Will, you need to tell me how my sister is dealing at the Death Star."

"The Death Star?"

"It's what Luke calls Harmony Falls," I said, rolling my eyes.

"So is she doing anything totally embarrassing that I should know about? Joined any secret Harmony Falls cults?"

"Cults? Not that I've seen. But she does hang out with this totally hot girl. Charlie, what's her name again?"

"Sydney? Why, do you like her?" I asked, my heart pressing against my chest. *Damn it,* I thought. I couldn't believe I hadn't seen it coming. I was friends with the girl everyone wanted.

"No, I mean she's hot, but I don't even know her," Will said.

"So?" I said.

"Charlie, she's fine, but I barely know the girl. She just seems like one of those girls who only goes out with seniors," Will said, grabbing the ball that had flown off the table.

"Great. Maybe I should meet her," Luke joked. "What about Charlie? Has she thrown herself on any guys yet?"

"Ohmygod, Luke! Shut up!" This whole situation was getting worse by the second.

Even from the couch I could see Will's smirk, and I knew I was in trouble.

"Well, Charlie dropped by my soccer practice—"

"So? That was to invite you to this dinner!" I insisted.

"That's what I thought until I noticed she had all these big red splotches all over her neck when she was talking to a friend of mine," Will said, grinning.

I hate that about myself. It always gives me away.

"Ewww, that's so cute!" Luke teased.

"You should have seen her when he let her borrow his sweatshirt. I thought she was going to pass out," Will said.

"Charles, your first high school crush!" Luke said.

I sat up and threw a pillow at each of them, but I couldn't help laughing. "For the record, I hate both of you right now! And I don't like Tyler. I was cold! And can I just say how much I've missed you, Will?" I said.

"No, but I can tell. If you want my sweatshirt, you can have it anytime."

"You really can stop now, Will!"

Luke laughed and shot a goal past Will. "Game! Will, I have to say, it's good to have you back. You're the only person, besides me, that can irritate her like this. Look, her ears are turning red!"

"Oh, this is great! I'm so glad you guys can be best friends. Should I talk to our moms and schedule another playdate for you?" I said.

"Sure! But I'm getting more cake," Luke said, walking up the stairs.

• • •

It was one thing to be all sarcastic and put each other down when Luke was there, but as soon as he was gone, it couldn't have been more awkward. So for two minutes Will and I sat there looking at each other, alone for the first time in three years.

Will grabbed the pillow and put it behind his back. "So are you really into Tyler?"

Wow—I was wrong. It was now way more awkward.

"I don't even know him," I said dismissively, thinking about what he'd said about Sydney. Maybe he liked Sydney like I liked Tyler? God, please don't make that true. That would be so incredibly uncomfortable.

"You know, Tyler's dad isn't exactly how he seems. I've heard him say some pretty messed-up things to Tyler."

"Like what?" I asked.

"Do you remember how intense my parents can be about sports?"

I nodded.

"Well, compared to Wickam, they're lightweights. One time after practice, I heard Wickam yelling at Tyler about how stupid and weak he was. It was completely out of control."

"That's awful!" I said, feeling sorry for Tyler. "And on top of that, it must be really weird having your dad be the principal."

"I can sort of relate to that part. It's always strange when people find out my dad's a minister. Everyone either expects you to be a total suck-up or a douche."

"Like you're trapped being one extreme or the other?"

He nodded.

"Which one's Tyler?" I asked.

"I'm not telling," he said, laughing.

"Why not?"

"Guy code of honor. Can't tell those things to a girl."

"But I'm not like a girl girl."

"Yes you are!" Will said incredulously.

"I'm not! Not with you anyway!"

His eyebrows lifted.

"Whatever. Don't be weird."

Why was everything about this situation so strange? I decided I was imagining it.

"So, do you miss your old friends?"

"Like who?" I asked, hoping he wasn't talking about who I thought he was.

"I don't know. . . . Like Lauren and Ally."

I hated hearing him say their names, particularly Lauren's.

"Not really. We sort of went separate ways. By the end of last year, we weren't exactly close. I was really into writing for the newspaper, and they . . . weren't," I said, needing to change the subject quickly. "But what about you? When I first saw you at orientation, I couldn't figure out why you seemed to know so many people if you just moved back. But I guess playing soccer explains it."

"Sort of. I wasn't put on varsity until right before school started, but I had to show up early for preseason."

"Really? So when did you get back here?" I asked.

"Um . . . I don't know. I guess a couple of weeks before classes started."

I hit him with a pillow. "Why didn't you call me when you got here? You're such a loser!"

"I knew you were going to be mad!" he said, throwing the pillow back at me.

"I'm not mad!"

"Yes you are."

"I just would have been less nervous about going."

"Why? You seem to be doing fine. You have tons of friends."

"I do?" I asked, surprised he'd say that. But when I thought about Sydney and Michael and even sort of Nidhi, I realized maybe Will was right.

A voice called down from above. "Will! Time to go!"

Will stood up and stretched. "I'll see you in school," he said.

"Yeah, we should hang out again soon," I said, hands in my back pockets, and followed behind him to say good-bye to his parents.

Later that night, as I was in bed reading *Rebecca* for my English class, my phone vibrated. It was a text from Will:

> **charlie, good seeing u tonight. first time it really felt good to be back. see u soon.**

I stared at the screen and thought about it. I wasn't blind. I was sure a lot of girls already liked him. Then my mind jumped to Sydney. Did he like her? What did I care? Sydney wasn't Lauren. Even if they got together, that should be good, right? I gazed at the ceiling. I was being stupid. It wasn't as if

I liked Will—not like I liked Tyler, anyway. And what Will said about Tyler's dad was intense. I wondered if Tyler ever talked about it. The next moment Will had evaporated from my mind as I imagined Tyler falling in love with me and confiding all his problems. And while everyone would think he was this cocky, hot, amazing guy, I would be the only one who really knew him.

I must have gone down that road for ten minutes or an hour. I'm not sure because I lost all track of time. I shook myself out of my Tyler haze, totally embarrassed that I had just had a typical girly-girl fantasy. I put the covers over my head, trying to regain my self-respect. It was time to go to bed.

# CHAPTER ELEVEN

"CHARLIE, TYLER JUST WALKED BY AND YOU SAID NOTHING. This is completely unacceptable behavior. And by the way, what happened to his sweatshirt? Have you given it back yet?" Sydney said, opening her locker. Two books fell to the floor and papers scattered around her feet.

"No, I asked him if he wanted it and he told me to keep it."

"See, he totally loves you—he's just too shy to make the first move. Lots of guys are like that. So . . . we have to make the first move for him."

"Is there any possible way you're going to stop bothering me about this?" I said, leaning into my locker.

She pretended to ponder the question. "Ummmm . . . no. Not a chance. It's been weeks since you saw him on the soccer field, and you have done nothing. You obviously need help to push things in the right direction," Sydney said.

"Okay. Like what?" I said, wishing I had her confidence. But then again, it's easy to be confident when you're not the one up for total humiliation.

Sydney's blue eyes sparkled in excitement. "This is what I think we should do. Since you and Will are friends, you should get him to invite Tyler out with us this weekend. We'll keep it simple, like go to a movie and get something to eat after. And let's invite Michael from our advisory too, and your friend from the newspaper."

"What is this, a triple date?" I asked, all of a sudden wondering if I wanted Sydney and Will in the same place like that. Maybe Sydney liked Will? Maybe this whole thing about going out together was really a way for Sydney to get closer to Will? And maybe I was having a paranoid delusion. Why was this whole thing about Sydney and Will confusing me so much?

"A date? No . . . that would be weird. This is just a way for us to get to know people better. And if you happen to hook up with Tyler, that's just an added benefit," she giggled.

"Okay. I'll talk to Will, but I'm only agreeing because I know you won't stop until you get your way," I said.

"You're such a liar, Charlie. You totally want to do this."

"But what if Will figures out what we're trying to do and won't go along with it?"

She rolled her eyes. "Charlie, he's a guy so he'll be completely clueless. You could flat-out tell him and he still wouldn't get it. Just ask him. It's not that big a deal."

"I know, I know. I'm just being stupidly nervous about the whole thing."

"That's why you need me to force you to do it. Plus, I have nothing to do this weekend."

"I'm so glad I can be your entertainment," I said.

"Just wait, you'll so thank me later."

"Fine. But I'm not doing it face to face at school. I'll wait until I can IM tonight so I can avoid any potentially awkward moments."

"I don't care how you do it. Just get it done and let me know," Sydney said, laughing.

CHealeyPepper324: hows it going?

FCBarcafan18: fine . . . back from practice totally wiped

CHealeyPepper324: have a game this weekend?

FCBarcafan18: friday night. off saturday

CHealeyPepper324: thinking of going to a movie
Want to go?

FCBarcafan18: maybe i can, need check tho

CHealeyPepper324: my friends Sydney and Nidhi kind of want to come too. can u handle going with three girls?

I paused and then my fingers flew through the words.

or if not u could always bring some guy. like Michael or Tyler.

FCBarcafan18: yeah maybe. i'll see.

CHealeyPepper324: don't worry about it if doesn't work out.

I looked at the words. Did I achieve the perfect balance of it-would-be-cool-if-it-worked-out-but-it-is-fine-if-it-doesn't that I was striving for?

FCBarcafan18: sure, but i'm not sitting next to u if ur planning on shoving ur tongue down his throat

CHealeyPepper324: shut up!!!!

FCBarcafan18: i don't care what u do as long as i don't have to see it. i'll ask them tomorrow at practice.

Sydney was wrong. Boys weren't clueless. Or at least Will wasn't. But I guess it didn't matter—I had accomplished the mission.

It was only after I made the plan with Will that I realized I had put myself into a high-stakes situation. I don't mean with Will teasing me or whatever would happen with Tyler. And I wasn't worried about Michael either. But I had serious concerns about Nidhi. I had just gotten the girl to stop hating me. Would she want to hang out with me outside of working with me on the *Prowler*?

But what was the right way to go about this? It wasn't like I was going to stop her in the hallway and say, "Would you be friends with me?" How pathetic would that be? But it was also a little weak to be too scared to do it in person. I pulled out my phone. No contest. At least with texting there was less pressure and potential for rejection.

**Want to go to a movie sat with me and some other ppl?**

I had to wait until lunch to get the answer.

**sure . . . just one thing . . .**

**sure what?**

**no Schwarzenegger**

**OMG . . . I promise!!!!!!!**

**C—just joking. Couldn't help myself.**

Six days later, the six of us arrived at the twenty-screen multiplex, along with what seemed like every other kid our age in the state.

"Mike, switch with Nidhi, Charlie, or Sydney! I'm not sitting next to your ugly ass," Tyler said, standing at the edge of our row, holding his popcorn and soda.

"But you make such a cute couple!" Will called out from the other end.

"Shut up, Edwards. If anyone's going in that direction, it's you, my friend."

"I'll move," I said, shrugging like I didn't care at all. As I slumped into the seat between Michael and Tyler, noticing the faint smell of Axe again, I felt like I'd won the lottery.

"Happy?" Sydney said, leaning over to me and hiding her grin behind a huge Coke.

Nidhi and Sydney both knew I'd been trying to figure out how to sit next to Tyler ever since we walked into the movie theater—without looking too obvious. I'd tried walking close to him so I would "have" to sit next to him when we sat down, but that didn't work when he bolted to get food. If I didn't like him so much I would have hit him for being so stupid. But just when I'd given up, it landed in my lap.

"Just trying to be cooperative," I giggled.

We had fifteen minutes before the movie started. Fifteen minutes to sit next to Tyler and get him to think I was the most fascinating, beautiful, sexy, not-desperate, cool, smart girl he had ever met.

"So, what do you do besides soccer at school?" Clearly not the most brilliant conversation opener, but I had to start somewhere.

He shrugged. "Like what?"

"I don't know. I'm working for the student newspaper. Things like that."

"You mean the *Prowler*?" Tyler asked skeptically. "I'll do lacrosse after soccer, but you should be careful if you're hanging out with those newspaper people. Especially what's his name the editor. The guy's such a fag."

"Who, Josh?" I asked.

"Yeah, that's his name. Don't get me wrong, the guy can do whatever he wants, even though it's disgusting, but he doesn't have to flaunt it so much. The guy's so flaming he lights things on fire when he walks by."

Before I realized what I was doing, I laughed but then was

completely irritated at myself. Josh was a good guy. He was smart and had given me a big break. What the hell was I doing laughing at that?

"He would have gotten a complete beat-down last week by some guys I know, but that big Asian friend of his had to save his ass."

Wow—Tyler was talking about Gwo. That was interesting. Way more interesting than this nagging feeling that Tyler was showing some serious toolish qualities. And he couldn't be serious about Josh getting beat up. But when you like someone and that someone happens to be gorgeous, you tend to overlook glaring examples of their personality deficits.

"So what's it like being a freshman on the soccer team?" I asked, trying to get back to a safe topic.

Before Tyler could respond, a Mike and Ike candy sailed through the air and pegged him on the head.

He jerked forward in his chair and stared at Will, but Will was fully engrossed in a conversation with Nidhi.

Reaching into his pocket, Tyler pulled out a Skittle—a candy I personally detest. I'm much more a Sour Patch girl but I was willing to overlook it at the time.

He quickly threw the Skittle at Will but missed. Instead it hit the chair and bounced onto the person behind Will. She was an unfortunate woman I'd seen earlier when we were getting tickets. It wasn't that she was unfortunate-looking. It was that she was very obviously on a date with a guy sitting next to her wearing too-tight, blindingly white jeans, a tucked-in Hawaiian shirt, and a gold chain. And I don't care who it is, that is a look no one should wear, ever.

Another Mike and Ike projectile flew through the air.

The piercing stare of adult hatred hit me so hard I looked around to see if anyone else in the group felt it.

Nidhi was trying to ignore it. Sydney was oblivious, trying to figure out the answers to the dumb trivia questions on the screen.

Another Skittle launched, this time in combination with a piece of Twizzler. I tried not to laugh, but the boys were being so stupid that it was funny. At least I thought so, but the couple didn't agree. This is why adults should just DVR it and stay home.

"Hey . . ." came from behind us. None of us paid attention.

White Jeans leaned forward. I could smell his cologne. "Hey . . . cut it out!" he barked.

Again none of us acknowledged him. We all stared at the screen and tried not to laugh. We were unsuccessful.

"What? You think this is funny?"

Michael turned around in his seat. "Sir, are you talking to us?" he asked politely.

"Who else would I be talking to?"

Michael smiled. "Sir, you're totally right. Ma'am, please accept my apologies. My friends are being totally, totally immature."

"Are you being smart with me?" said White Jeans, crossing his arms.

"No, sir."

White Jeans stared at Michael trying to figure out if he was making fun of him or not.

"All right, then, tell your friends I understand they want to have a good time, but they need to learn some respect," White Jeans grunted.

Michael turned back around. Only then could I see the huge grin on his face as he quickly chucked a Mike and Ike back in our direction so White Jeans wouldn't see.

I don't know what exactly was so funny about that, but I burst out laughing and couldn't stop.

"You gonna make it?" Tyler's hand was on my back. Now I couldn't breath.

"Sure," I said, trying to control myself.

My phone vibrated.

How's it going over there?

Great. Now Will was texting me.

I leaned forward and looked down the row. Will was staring at the screen, but I could see a small grin on his face.

u can shut up now

u going to jump him?

not paying attention

let me know if you two need some privacy after . . .

YOU ARE SO ANNOYING!

"Who are you texting?" Tyler whispered, grabbing for my phone.

"It's nothing!" I whispered back, pulling my phone out of his reach. "Will's just asking me a question. It's nothing."

"It'd better be about me."

Total adrenaline rush. This was the first evidence that Tyler liked me.

"He's just saying stupid stuff because we're sitting next to each other."

He leaned in even closer so our arms touched and whispered into my ear, "Good."

I didn't answer. I was too busy having a heart attack.


"The special effects were incredible!" Michael said, sliding into our booth at Chili's.

"But why did they have what's her name? She's not that hot. I can think of a million girls who would have been better," said Tyler, sitting down next to me.

"She's totally beautiful!" Nidhi said. "What did you want, some boring blond *Maxim* cover instead?"

"Well . . . now that you say it like that . . . yeah, exactly," Michael said, laughing.

"Okay, people, can we please discuss hot girls after we order?" Sydney said, waving to the waitress. "Because I'm starving and if I don't get something to eat in like five seconds, I'm not going to be responsible for my actions."

"Not to be weird, but for a comic book movie it was sort of deep," I said.

"Here we go. Charlie is now going to analyze this movie to death. Can't you just watch a movie?" Will asked.

"What's so wrong with analyzing something? The whole thing on anarchy and chaos was really interesting. And how cool was it that the bad guy was, like, the truth teller?"

Michael nodded. "You know what I think is the most

creepy, though? That guy is supposed to be an evil, violent lunatic. But little kids get plastic toys of him in their cereal boxes, and the parents are clueless that their kids are walking around with a toy psychopath. There's something so wrong about that, but so funny," Michael said.

"You're totally right! I hadn't thought of that before," said Nidhi.

"You people really need to rest. It was a movie!" Tyler said.

"Clearly I'm going to have to take control here!" Sydney complained, waving with both hands toward two waitresses.

"Hey, guys! Sorry about the wait! Do you know what you want?" said Cheryl! our waitress, who leaned over just enough so we could see down her shirt.

Tyler said something under his breath to Will, who immediately turned away laughing.

"Cheryl, please ignore them. They're ten and they're in love with your breasts. But I'm ready to order," Sydney said.

Nidhi and I burst out laughing.

So did Cheryl! but not exactly in the same way.

"Damn, Sydney!" Michael said.

Will turned bright red, Tyler didn't flinch.

Ten minutes later, our drinks and three orders of fries had calmed Sydney down.

"So, Charlie, how long have you known Will?" Michael asked.

"Let me see. . . . Since I was four or five. The first time I ever saw Will he was riding a tricycle outside of my house naked, wearing a cowboy hat and boots."

"Five? Weren't you a little old for that, Will?" Michael asked.

"Not Will. He was naked all the time, and he'd walk around shaking his butt. I swear, totally true. My mom thought it was so cute," I said quickly, noticing that Tyler had just put his hand on my knee. "I think I have some pictures somewhere."

"HA-HA! Charlie, very funny but that's enough," Will said.

"Oh, come on, but you were adorable!" I teased, trying very hard to pay attention to what I was saying and not the hand on my knee.

"Hey, if you want to trade stories, you're on," he said, as Cheryl! placed the rest of the food on our table and ran away before Sydney could embarrass her again.

"I'm so glad no one I grew up with is sitting at this table," Nidhi said. "But, Will, definitely tell some stories about Charlie!"

"Thanks so much for backing me up, Nidhi," I said.

"Okay, let's see, which should I tell? Oh, wait, this is easy. Okay, I may have gone through a little naked phase, but Charlie went through a belly-dancing phase."

"Will, don't you dare!"

"Shut up, Charlie. Let the man speak!" Michael said.

"When Charlie was ten, she got this belly-dancing costume and told everyone she was a professional belly dancer and she was going to have to leave school because she was going on tour."

"Will! I swear if you don't shut up, I will kill you!"

"Charlie, don't worry about it. Every girl goes through a belly-dancing phase," said Nidhi.

"Oh, definitely! Mine lasted for three years," Sydney said seriously.

"Okay! Okay! I'll just tell one more thing. In third grade, she was totally in love with me."

"I WAS NOT!" I said, jumping up so that Tyler's hand fell off my knee.

"You don't have to be embarrassed about it. I was a very cute eight-year-old. Lots of girls were in love with me. You said it yourself."

"Oh, my God, Will, you're completely out of your mind."

"You don't remember the valentine you gave me?"

"That's so cute!" Sydney said, bouncing up and down in the booth.

"Sydney, be quiet so we can hear him!" Michael said.

"I didn't give you a valentine," I insisted, but as soon as I said it I realized I was wrong. The memory of a huge red cut-out heart leapt in front of me.

"What did it say?" Nidhi and Sydney asked simultaneously.

"Okay, girls are insane. Who cares what Charlie wrote Will in third grade?" Tyler said.

"Shut up, Tyler!" Sydney said, laughing.

"Well . . ." Will was dragging this out way more than necessary. "It was a huge red heart with white decorations on it, and inside she wrote, *Dear Will, you are the most handsomest boy in our class. I love you. Will you marry me? XOXOXOXO charlie.* I didn't know what the 'XO' meant so I had to ask my mom."

"You showed your mom! Now I'm totally humiliated," I said.

"Oh, yeah, I think she may still have it somewhere. I could find it for you, if you want."

"You saved it all those years?" Sydney squealed.

"Okay, you all can shut up now! Can we please talk about something else?" I begged.

Tyler took a sip of Coke and burp-talked. "Okay."

"You want to see who can burp the loudest?" Nidhi asked sweetly.

"Really?" Tyler burped in response.

"Sure," Nidhi said, sitting up primly.

"You're on."

"I'm reffing," said Michael, rolling up his sleeves. "On the count of three. Loser buys a side of fries. Ready?"

Nidhi nodded her head gravely and settled into her seat.

Tyler nodded back.

"One, two, three. Go!" Michael ordered as his hand came down and hit the table.

Tyler grabbed his drink and gulped while Nidhi slowly and methodically sipped from her straw.

They eyed each other. The table waited in anticipation.

Tyler leaned his forearms on the table. *Buuurrp*! It lasted about five seconds. It was impressive but nothing monumental.

"Nidhi?" Michael asked.

There's no other way to put it. The girl erupted.

"Damn, girl!" Sydney said, laughing so hard she knocked the dessert card off the table.

"Sorry, Tyler, she kicked your ass," Will said.

"How about a rematch? I was just getting warmed up," Tyler insisted.

"Maybe some other time, but right now you need to be getting me another order of fries," Nidhi said, grinning.

• • •

"He totally likes you! It's so obvious!" Sydney said as she dragged out the air mattress from my closet.

"How do you know?" I asked, desperate for confirmation.

"Charlie, he sat next to you at the movie *and* the restaurant," said Nidhi.

"But he could have switched just because he didn't want to sit next to Michael."

"Right and that's why he sat next to you at dinner and put his arm around you, too," Nidhi said, getting her toothbrush and pajamas out of her bag. "I'm changing. Don't say anything interesting until I come back."

"You know what? I bet he's going to ask you to the homecoming dance. You guys would make such a cute couple!" Sydney said.

"The homecoming dance? That's, like, months away."

"Actually it's in a month," Nidhi called from the bathroom.

"You could put a note in Tyler's locker that says, *Do you like Charlie? Yes or No*. No, wait, one of us could do it for you!" giggled Nidhi.

"Oh, my God, could that be more seventh grade? No way."

"I don't know, it'd be pretty funny, I mean at your expense, but it's still funny," said Nidhi, brushing her hair.

"It's not happening. I'm not going to stress about it."

Nidhi and Sydney looked at each other and then looked at me. We all broke out laughing knowing I was going to obsess about getting Tyler to ask me.

But seriously, how do you know when a guy likes you? I know there're more important problems in the world like starving children, homelessness, earthquakes, global warming, and wars, but you have to admit life would be so much easier if someone could just sit you down and explain relationships. Yes, Tyler likes you. No, he doesn't.

"Hey, Charlie," Sydney said, interrupting my thoughts.

"Yeah?"

"Don't you need to tell me something?"

"What?"

"I'm not letting you go to sleep until you admit that I was completely, one hundred percent right to make you go out tonight. I will now wait until you say it." I could see Sydney fold her arms in the dark.

"She's right, Charlie. And you know she really won't let us go to bed until you do," Nidhi said sleepily.

"Fine. I admit it. You were right. I was wrong. I will always do what you say."

"I'm sensing a little sarcasm in your tone but I'll accept it for now."

"Sydney, go to bed, I'm begging you. You were right about tonight. Is that better?"

"Much!" Sydney said and rolled over.

## CHAPTER TWELVE

**"WHY DO ALL THESE PENGUINS NEED EYES AND BEAKS?**
No one's going to be able to see them up close anyway," I
whined, dropping my paintbrush into a plastic cup.

"How can you even ask that question? We have a vision
here," said Sydney.

"You may have a vision, but it's freezing and I think the
paint fumes are getting to me," I said. I was sitting on
Michael's garage floor.

The vision Sydney was talking about was a recreation of the
final scene of *Happy Feet* for the homecoming parade float. Ac-
cording to the ninth-grade float-making committee, it was absolutely imperative that we make a million papier-mâché penguins
dancing around a mountain range of papier-mâché chicken-wire
icebergs.

It was our class's interpretation of "Chillin' in the Arctic,"
this year's homecoming theme.

"Sydney, I'm not sure we should be stressing so much about this. We're not going to win. I've heard the other classes start working on these things over the summer. It's the end of October, and we're just getting started," said Nidhi.

"So? If we work hard enough, we can still totally beat them!"

"Sydney, relax. We don't have a chance. Nidhi's right. No freshman class has won the competition . . . ever," Michael said.

"Exactly! That's why we have to win! And if we can just get the iceberg right, I think we have a chance." Sydney surveyed the garage like she was a general overseeing a battle. "Charlie and Michael, can you help Jen and Patrick finish up those igloos? I need to look at the diagram to figure out where we can put the aluminum foil for the frozen water."

"Are you this intense about everything, Sydney? Because you're really scaring me," Michael said.

"Of course! Now come on and help me!" she replied.

With Sydney not hovering over us, Nidhi lowered her voice as she grabbed a Styrofoam snowball. "So I have a question for you."

"What?"

"Have you thought about the homecoming dance at all?"

"What do you mean?"

Nidhi looked at me skeptically. "You know what I mean."

"I don't know! He hasn't asked me. For all I know I could be the last person he wants to go with. What am I supposed to do, go up to him and tell him he should invite me?"

"Hey, that's a good idea for a column—girls asking guys on

dates. What do you think?" asked Nidhi, her eyes widening with excitement.

"Sure, but that doesn't help me right now," I said bitterly.

Sydney yelled across the garage. "What are you guys talking about?"

"Nothing!" I called out, turning back to Nidhi.

"Then keep painting!" Sydney ordered.

Nidhi and I looked at each other and laughed. We had never seen this side of Sydney before. There was no way we were taking her or these stupid penguins seriously.

"Why are girls still so weird about asking a guy to a dance? We're not this pathetic about anything else, are we?" Nidhi asked.

"I don't know. It's just so incredibly awkward," I said.

"Well, not that it matters to me. My mom is threatening to make me go with my cousin," Nidhi said, picking up a penguin and taking it over to the truck.

"Your cousin? That sucks. Why would she make you go with a cousin?"

"Ever since one of my other cousins dropped out of MIT to live with a white guy, I'm on total lockdown."

Michael turned around from stapling cotton batting to the flatbed and asked, "What do your parents think is worse, dropping out of MIT or dating a white guy?"

Nidhi frowned and thought about it for a second. "Not sure. Both? I know my parents automatically don't trust any guy that isn't from our culture."

"Why? That's like racism!" I said.

Nidhi nodded in agreement. "It's because they think white

parents let their kids get away with everything. Which, compared to my parents, is totally true."

"My parents think the same thing!" Michael said, grabbing one of the finished igloos and setting it on the flatbed to see how it would look. "But no matter who you go with, if you're a guy, you have to start thinking about it now because timing is critical."

"Why?" Nidhi asked.

"See, this is the thing about girls. You don't know how hard it is to be a guy. Guys can't ask too early because that looks desperate, but if you wait, then you run the risk of some other guy asking the same girl. Of course, the other problem with asking too soon is you have to be careful not to set up expectations."

"What are you talking about?" I asked.

"Think about it. If you ask a girl early and she says yes, then you probably have to hang out with her a lot before. You're looking for a date, not a relationship. So however you look at it, it's a narrow margin of error."

"God, I never thought about it like that. I'm actually feeling sorry for guys right now," said Sydney.

"By the way, gotten any invitations recently to homecoming?" Michael said to Sydney.

Sydney's eyes widened.

"What guy?" Nidhi and I asked simultaneously.

"You don't know?" Michael asked.

"Shut up, Michael. It's nobody," Sydney said distractedly. She began rifling through a pile of old newspapers behind the flatbed as if she were looking for something. "Just this lame guy from my art class." She stood up. "I have an idea. How about we girls just go together? That way we don't have to stress about it."

"Not so fast, Sydney! Who's the guy?" I asked. There was no way she was getting away with not telling us.

"You don't know him. Actually, I don't even know him. He's just some guy who stares at me while I'm trying to draw. It's totally not worth talking about."

"But how come Michael knows and we don't?" Nidhi asked.

"Because I ran into Michael right after the guy asked me. Right, Michael?"

"Yeah, pretty much." Michael said, bent over, staple gunning.

"Anyway, I'm serious about going to the dance together. If we don't have dates by the end of the week, we should really do it."

"Actually, I like it! Maybe if I go with you guys my parents will back off," Nidhi said.

Later that night, I realized I had completely overlooked my most obvious source regarding Tyler's date status for homecoming.

CHealeyPepper324: u there?

FCBarcafan18: yeah

CHealeyPepper324: r u going to homecoming?

FCBarcafan18: the game?

CHealeyPepper324: no loser, the dance

FCBarcafan18: idk. . . . might have to go to some church retreat with my dad that wknd

CHealeyPepper324: that sucks

FCBarcafan18: y?

CHealeyPepper324: just wanted to know what u guys were doing

FCBarcafan18: like who I'm going with? why? looking for a date?

CHealeyPepper324: NO!!!! but who are u going with? i kno michael's going with that molly girl

FCBarcafan18: not sure but there's no way tyler's hanging around sydney if that's why ur asking

CHealeyPepper324: what?

FCBarcafan18: u don't know?

CHealeyPepper324: know what?

There was no response for a minute. An eternity in IM.

CHealeyPepper324: Will?

FCBarcafan18: tyler asked sydney. but she shot him down. Assumed u knew

# CHAPTER THIRTEEN

**I PUSHED MYSELF AWAY FROM MY DESK AND COLLAPSED** into my beanbag. I felt like I'd been punched in the stomach. Of course Tyler liked Sydney. How could I have been so blind and stupid? She was so much prettier, skinnier, funnier, cooler . . . everythinger than I was. I don't know how I could have let myself believe that he liked me. I closed my eyes tight, feeling waves of embarrassment wash over me. Now I realized that everything he had done and I had obsessed over as proof that he liked me, he had done to Sydney as well. He had sat between us. He had put his arms around both of us. Yes, he put his hand on my knee during dinner and it looked like he liked me. But maybe it's just because I happened to be sitting next to him. I was an idiot. Boys would always like her over me.

A hard heavy rock of jealousy hit my stomach and lodged itself uncomfortably inside. Up to that point, I really hadn't felt envious of Sydney. Sure, she got a lot of attention from boys, but she never took it seriously. All through middle school, I had sort of accepted that Lauren and Ally got more attention than me because they tried so much harder—they were always shamelessly flirting, telling guys they were hot, and showing off their tiny cheerleader bodies. (I pictured Ally's signature "putting hair in a ponytail so you could see her stomach" move, and shuddered.) But Sydney was such a spaz and never seemed to be trying to get noticed in that way. It was easy to forget how beautiful she was. *God,* I thought to myself. *Am I ever going to be pretty enough? Would a guy I like ever like me back?*

I opened my eyes and stared at the ceiling. All of a sudden, it occurred to me that it was not just me that created my self-delusion. "He's so obsessed with you." "He's totally going to ask you to homecoming." Who had said that? Not me. That was Sydney. How could she have done that if she'd known Tyler liked her?

My phone vibrated on the floor in front of me. I had been so lost in thought that its sound startled me. As I grabbed for the phone, I caught the name flashing on the caller ID. It was Sydney. Before I could really process what I was doing, I answered.

"Hello?" I managed to utter.

"Hey, Charlie! I talked to my mom and she's totally cool with us hanging out at my house first before homecoming! You and Nidhi and I can get ready over here and then she will drive us," Sydney said excitedly.

"Cool . . . ," I barely said. The rock rolled in my stomach. I hated her. How was it that all of my girl friends ended up being so shady? Was I doomed to attract these people for the rest of my life?

She rushed on, oblivious. "She said you guys could sleep over after. So all we need now is to get Nidhi's parents to agree."

"Sure, whatever," I said.

"Charlie, what's wrong? What do you mean, whatever?" She was finally clueing in.

"Nothing, Sydney. It's fine." It felt good to be mean to her. Seriously, the girl deserved it.

"No it's not. You're barely answering me."

I sat up in my beanbag and crossed my legs. "If you really want to know, I just talked to Will."

"And?" she said, confused.

"He told me about you and Tyler," I snapped.

"Charlie, what are you talking about?" Sydney asked.

I didn't say anything for a moment. Becoming friends had been so easy. This was the first time I'd even had a moment of being mad at her. Now here I was.

"Will told me that Tyler asked you to homecoming. Is that true?"

That shut her up.

"Were you ever going to tell me, or were you just going to continue letting me make a complete fool out of myself?" I asked angrily.

"Charlie, I'm so sorry," she said slowly, her voice cracking. "I didn't want to tell you because I thought you'd be hurt. Please don't be mad at me."

"I'm not mad at you that Tyler asked you. You can't help if

Tyler likes you. I mean of course he likes you. You're way prettier than me."

"What? Are you insane? No, I'm not!" she argued.

Girls always say stuff like this when they get caught. All I could think was, *how could she do this to me?*

"That's not the point. I'm mad because you convinced me that he liked me and I've been walking around thinking that, when he really likes you."

"Charlie, I seriously had no idea he was going to do that. I really did think he liked you! Remember the sweatshirt? The movies? He was all over you. He didn't sit next to me at dinner. He sat next to you! He just asked me a couple of days ago. I was totally shocked and told him no right away—I guarantee he thinks I am a total bitch. But I didn't know what to do. I just thought I could pretend it didn't happen. I'm so sorry. I'll do anything to make it up to you. Just tell me what to do to fix it."

"Did you say no because you felt sorry for me or because you really didn't want to go with him?" I said, realizing this was going to be way worse if she did like him but only turned him down out of pity.

"Of course not. I said no because I don't like him like that, but even if I did, I still would have turned him down."

"Because you felt sorry for me?"

"No! Because you're my best friend. And it should always be chicks before dicks."

I laughed. I couldn't help myself. "What did you just say?"

"You know, chicks before dicks. Never choose a guy over a friend. It's one of the most important rules of feminism. If there is anything my mom has taught me, it's that no man is ever worth losing your friends for."

"Right," I said hesitantly. I'd never thought of it like that before but it sounded good.

"Please don't be mad about it. I've been feeling terrible the last couple of days. I wanted to tell you, but I didn't know what to say. I had no idea what to do."

I couldn't stay mad at her. I realized then that if it was a year ago and this had happened with Lauren or Ally, they would totally have gone to the dance with the guy and also done everything possible to dangle it in front of my face. "Fine. Just make me one promise."

"Whatever you want."

"Don't ever tell me a guy likes me until you have written proof, okay?" I insisted.

"I promise. Next time, written proof, I got it," she agreed. "So please say you're still going with me and Nidhi?"

I hesitated because a little part of me wanted her to work for my forgiveness. But just at that moment, I realized that it's better to have a friend who truly has your back than go to a dance with the guy you like. May seem obvious, but it hadn't been for me until right then.

"Okay . . . I mean I have to. You're the only person who's asked me," I said, laughing.

"Charlie, don't say it like that!" she protested.

"Sydney, it's fine. Really. We'll go and have an amazing time."

"So things are cool between us? I don't know what I'd do without you," she said.

"Things are good," I promised. "Thanks for being honest. . . . and you know what this means right?"

"What?"

"I'm going to have to throw away the sweatshirt."

"Wait, I have the best idea. . . . we can pour Axe all over it and set it on fire!"

"No thanks. Sounds good, but I can't deal with that smell anymore."

# CHAPTER FOURTEEN

**THE MORNING OF THE HOMECOMING PARADE WAS ONE OF** those perfect fall Saturdays. The sky was blue, the air was crisp, and as we drove over the bridge into Harmony Falls, colorful leaves fell gracefully from the trees. Only I couldn't really see them because I was once again crouched down in the Falcon hoping that no one would notice me.

"Charlotte Anne, is there a reason why you're playing dead back there?" my mom asked as we pulled into the school parking lot.

"Mom, don't know if you've noticed, but I'm dressed like an Arctic bird."

She laughed. "Honey, don't be silly. You look adorable!"

As my dad parked, I peeked my head over the edge of the Falcon to see where the rest of my float builders had congregated. At the opposite end of the massive parking lot, ten big floats were attached to pickup trucks and lined up ready to go.

The homecoming queen (Sarah Radner, senior volleyball captain) was adjusting her sash and smoothing her perfect blond hair while her king (Marcus Jordan, student body president) tried to look like he didn't feel stupid for wearing a big plastic crown. It all looked just like one of those homecoming scenes you see in the movies.

I snapped out of my momentary daze when I saw Nidhi running up to our car, camera in hand, with her mom following closely behind. Nidhi was dressed in normal clothes, while her mom wore a beautiful yellow sari.

"Charlie, get out of that car and let me see you!" Nidhi said gleefully.

"Could you be enjoying this more?" I said, climbing over the side of the car. As I hopped onto the pavement, she began laughing uncontrollably as she surveyed me. I was wearing black leggings and a black turtleneck—not so embarrassing. But attached to the front of the turtleneck was a big white oval piece of construction paper meant to represent my penguin belly. On my feet I wore bright orange Keds that Sydney had found for us at a discount shoe store.

"She's so cute!" Mrs. Patel said to my parents.

"Where's your beak?" Nidhi giggled.

"The elastic broke when I tried it on this morning," I said, holding up the plastic penguin beak Sydney had given me. "I guess I'll have to go beakless."

"And how did you get out of dressing up?" my dad asked Nidhi. "Didn't you help these guys build it too?"

She smiled widely, not trying to hide her triumph. "We flipped a coin, and unfortunately, I'm going to do the grunt work, like taking pictures and interviewing people."

"Yeah, I feel so bad for you, Nidhi! Well, hate to leave you all, but I need to go find the rest of my flock," I said. My parents and Mrs. Patel told us they'd be watching the parade along High Street, just outside the school, and to wave to them as we went by.

It didn't take Nidhi and me long to track down the rest of our freshman crew, seeing as our iceberg could probably be seen from space. As we walked closer, Michael and two other guys were gluing a few penguins back into place on the flatbed.

"Where have you guys been?" Sydney said frantically. "I have been calling you for, like, twenty minutes!"

I started laughing so hard I accidentally snorted. Sydney was saying this with her penguin beak strapped over her nose in full costume.

"Really? Sorry, I didn't bring my phone. There aren't any pockets on this penguin suit you forced me to wear."

"Well, we're leaving in ten minutes. I thought you and I could walk in the front and carry the sign. Wait a minute, where's your beak?" she demanded.

"Oh, the string detached, but don't you think people will get the idea when I am walking with fifteen other people in the same outfit?"

"Not a problem. I can take care of that," she said, running back toward the float and looking through some plastic bags. "Jen, where's that bag you brought with all the costume stuff in it?" Jen stopped tying one of her orange Keds and pointed a few feet away.

"Perfect!" Sydney exclaimed as she dug through the bag. She ran back over to me brandishing orange and black face paint crayons.

"Oh, no you don't!" I said, starting to back away from her.

"Come on, Charlie, just get it over with! You have to match!" She laughed.

I tried to pull away, but it was too late. Before I knew it, Sydney was furiously scribbling on my nose.

"I hate you, you know that, right?" I said, laughing, realizing it didn't matter if I looked ridiculous. This was my first homecoming and I was going to have a good time.

Nidhi yelled to all of the freshman penguins to stand together so she could get a picture for the *Prowler*. Me, Sydney, Michael, and thirteen other penguins all knelt and put our arms around one another in front of our icebergs and igloos. I ran to check out the picture on her camera, and laughed at the sixteen beaked faces that smiled back at me. If I ever got to put things on the *Prowler* wall, this would definitely be front and center.

Nidhi grabbed me. "Let's go see the other floats before the parade starts. We can get initial impressions for the column."

"Okay, but I promised Sydney I'd be back in time to hold the sign with her," I said, walking toward the other floats with Nidhi.

"They must have been working on that thing since school started," I said, taking in the senior class's perfectly constructed snow village and gingerbread houses. You have to give them credit, it's a classic. Boring but a classic."

"You see the little candies on the walls and roofs? The parents apparently paid for a float consultant to help out," Nidhi said.

"What are you talking about?" I asked.

"I'm not joking. Gwo told me all about it. He said some of

the parents here are always paying for stuff like that and being insanely competitive."

"Yeah, I'm not seeing either one of our parents doing something like that ever. But someone's going to have to break it to Sydney," I sighed.

Nidhi laughed. "She'll get over it. I think as long as she gets to be a penguin she's good."

Two senior girls dressed up as snow queens with sparkling silver capes walked by us. They didn't acknowledge us as we stood in awe.

"Well, don't just stand there. Write it all down so we have something to put in the column!" I said to Nidhi.

She began scribbling notes while I looked around, taking it all in, and froze, smelling Axe and knowing what usually followed it.

"Oh, no," I heard Nidhi say. She knew all about the Tyler–Sydney drama, but we had forgotten to discuss what I should do when I ran into him again.

"Hey, ladies, what's up?" Tyler said.

"Hey, Charlie. Hi, Nidhi," Will said.

"What are you guys doing here?" Nidhi asked. "Trying to walk with the freshman float last minute?"

"No, just got back from a scrimmage against Greenspring. What losers," Tyler said.

"Nice beak, Charlie," said Will, grinning.

Oh . . . my . . . God. I had completely forgotten how I was dressed.

"Thanks." I laughed nervously. "I'm a contestant on *Antarctica's Next Top Penguin*, so I always try to look my best." No one laughed. What was I saying? I should definitely not try to be funny anymore. Will cocked his eyebrows at my sad attempt at penguin humor. Shoot me now.

"Have you seen the senior float? It's amazing. It's like a professional float that you'd see in the Rose Bowl parade," Nidhi said, thankfully taking attention away from my costume and bad jokes.

"That's nothing compared to what the juniors did," Will said.

"Why? What do you mean?" Nidhi asked excitedly, flipping to the next page in her notebook.

"They're being all political. My dad's freaking out," Tyler said, pulling on the ends of the shirt that was wrapped around his neck.

"Controversy? I love it," Nidhi said, scribbling furiously. "Take me to the float!"

Tyler led us to where the juniors were assembled. When we got there, I could see Owen from the *Prowler* in the middle of a group of students. He was dressed in a green T-shirt and his signature black jeans. Today he'd accented them with green Converse.

"Owen, what is this?" I asked.

"You like it?" he said excitedly, putting his hair behind his ears.

My mouth dropped open. "Oh, my God, you did Chillin' in the Artic, global warming style."

On one end of a flatbed was a huge cutout of a silver Lexus SUV, which most of the Harmony Falls mothers drove, running over four stuffed penguins. Papier-mâché polar bears wearing sunglasses stood on small white icebergs surrounded by a fake ocean. On the front of the float, one of the junior guys was holding a huge papier-mâché sun. He was dressed in a tweed sport coat and a collared shirt over freshly ironed Dockers.

"Dude, Tyler," Will said, pointing at the junior holding the sun, "I think that's supposed to be your dad." Sure enough, a nametag on his blazer read, HELLO MY NAME IS BILL WICKAM.

Owen pushed a piece of paper into each of our hands. "Take a leaflet. We're throwing these out to the crowd instead of candy."

Nidhi read out loud, "Do you want to know how the HFHS administration is lying to you?"

Owen leaned over and said, "Wickam always claims he's doing things like being environmentally responsible, but he just talks a good game. There's a student committee at school that has tried to meet with Wickam about changing the school's business practices. Like, we've been trying to get them to stop buying paper from lumber companies that cut down old-growth forest, use different lightbulbs, and get different cleaning products so the custodians don't get poisoned. But he just blows us off. So today we're exercising our freedom of speech."

I looked over at Tyler to see how he was reacting to his father's effigy on the float. His arms were folded across his chest, and his lips were tightly pressed against each other.

I think that was the first moment Owen realized Tyler was there. For a second, a cloud of guilt passed over his face. "Sorry, dude. Nothing personal," Owen insisted.

"Hey, I'm not the one making an ass of myself. Do what you got to do, it's not like anyone cares," Tyler said, dismissively.

"Yeah, exactly. I will," Owen said harshly, his empathy gone.

For a moment, the air between the two boys crackled with tension. And then someone from the other side of the float called Owen's name. He shrugged and smiled. "Right . . . whatever. See you around," he said and disappeared under the Lexus.

As soon as Owen was gone, Tyler turned back to us. "No one cares about his hippy bullshit."

Will laughed nervously. "Isn't it kind of hypocritical for them to throw paper into the audience? It's not as if they'll be going back later to collect litter."

I saw Nidhi press her lips together as if she was trying to keep herself from saying something out loud. Instead she seemed to think better of it and said to me, "Come on, Charlie, we have to get you back to the other penguins before the parade starts."

"Right," I said, looking down at my watch. "Are you guys sticking around to watch the parade?"

"Maybe. First we have to go to some lacrosse preseason meeting," Will said.

"But lacrosse doesn't start until spring. Why are you meeting now?" asked Nidhi.

"Lacrosse is hard core here. Tyler and I are trying out for varsity, too. There's a meeting for underclassmen who are thinking of trying out."

"Do you have a chance?" I asked.

"Of course. But I'd love to watch these granolas make asses of themselves. That would be a lot more fun," Tyler said, smirking.

Tyler's comments were really starting to bug me, but something he said made my brain click.

"We interviewed someone who plays lacrosse about homecoming. His name is Matt Gercheck," I said.

"Yeah, everyone knows him. He's one of the top players," Will said.

"I went to lacrosse camp with him. If we make varsity, Matt will look out for us," Tyler said. "So maybe we won't get towel snapped every time we change. Right, Will?"

"Yeah, sure," Will said, but he sounded unconvinced.

"We've got to get back," I said, hearing someone on a megaphone instructing us to get in place for the start of the parade.

Nidhi and I quickly walked back to our float while I heard the marching band music and the engines of all the float-pulling trucks rumble to life.

"There you are! You keep disappearing! Take the other end of the banner," Sydney said, lifting the metal pole that held it into position. "Are you ready?"

I grabbed the other end of our banner. "Ready!" I said, following the procession of floats ahead of us.

"Take lots of pictures," I yelled to Nidhi as we left the parking lot. She waved as we waddled onto the street.

## CHAPTER FIFTEEN

**"LET ME SEE YOUR DRESS!" SYDNEY SQUEALED.**

I lifted the beige plastic over the top of the hanger. "You like it?" I said, holding the midnight blue dress against my body.

"I *love* it!"

"What did you end up getting?" I asked.

Sydney walked over to a chair and lifted up a shiny purple dress with tiny spaghetti straps.

"What do you think? I'm not going to look like an eggplant, right?"

"Are you kidding?" I said. "You can totally pull that off!"

"Thanks. . . . Look, there's something I want to tell you. It's not a big deal, but yesterday I heard this girl in my geometry class say that Tyler's bringing some girl from another school."

"Sydney, don't worry about it. I'm fine, I promise," I said, surprised that I actually meant it. "It was a stupid crush, and he was totally bugging me at the parade this morning anyway."

At that moment, the bedroom door swung open and Nidhi walked in.

"Hey . . ." I started to say, but my voice trailed off as I registered what she was wearing. Nidhi had on a navy blue floor-length dress with a high neck and short sleeves. On her feet were plain brown flip-flops and she had a huge backpack slung over her left shoulder. The only thing that looked good was her long, jet-black hair which, as usual, was perfectly straight and shiny.

"Girl, why in world are you dressed like a forty-year-old Sunday school teacher?" Sydney asked.

"Sydney, shut up!" I said.

Nidhi sighed as she closed the door. "I had to wear this to get out of the house. My mom is downstairs talking to your mom to make sure we're coming straight back here after the dance. As soon as she leaves, I'm changing."

"Do you need to borrow something?" Sydney asked.

"Don't worry about it. My cousin Leena took me to the mall last week and I got a dress and shoes," she said, unzipping the overstuffed backpack and removing a plastic bag. She pulled out a short, bright blue dress that tied at the neck. "This was pretty much all my babysitting money from the last three months, but it's so worth it."

An hour later, after singing and dancing along to our predance playlist, putting on our makeup and dresses, and getting Sydney's curlers out of her tangled hair, we were ready to leave.

"We all look so good!" Sydney said, throwing some lip gloss into her silver clutch purse.

"Your legs are so long in that dress!" Nidhi said.

"Thanks and your boobs are huge! Where have you been hiding those?" Sydney laughed.

"I just take them out for special occasions. Like when there's no chance my parents will see me. And no offense, Sydney, but, Charlie, as soon as Tyler sees you, he's going to kick himself."

"You're totally right! Charlie's smokin'. Even Will would notice tonight!" Sydney said, giggling.

"Oh, my God, Sydney, shut up!" I said.

"Whatever! Who cares? You look hot! Let's go!" Sydney said.

The senior class had transformed the gym into a winter wonderland. Blue, silver, and white balloons hung from every inch of the ceiling—there must have been a thousand of them. Fake snow was scattered all over the floor, and dry-ice machines were all over the basketball court, so you couldn't really see that we were surrounded on all sides by bleachers. I was glad the school hadn't gotten one of those terrible local bands that plays weddings and instead had gone with a DJ (some skinny guy who called himself Blaze).

"Look over there, there's ice sculptures on the food tables!" Sydney half yelled over the thumping of the bass.

"I am so glad we came together," I said as we were taking it all in. "This is so much better with you guys."

"Me too!" said Nidhi. "Hey, there's Michael and Molly!" She pointed to one corner of the gym where couples were lined up to get their pictures taken in front of a cheesy back-drop of a snowy landscape.

"Girls, I definitely need one of those souvenir photographs with my dates," Sydney said, throwing her arms around our shoulders.

As we joined the line that now extended a third of the way down the dance floor, nobody could miss Ashleigh, my not best friend from the *Prowler*, and Matt.

"If it isn't the most generic, boring couple ever," Nidhi said, whispering into my ear.

"But you have to admit the pink bubble dress is amazing!"

"You're joking right?"

"I'm not going to even answer that question."

"What?" Sydney asked too loudly. "Tell me what you said—no secrets!"

I glared *Shut up* to her with my eyes, but it was too late. Ashleigh had already noticed us.

"Charlie!" trilled Ashleigh as she turned around. "It's so good to see you!" She leaned forward and gave me a hug like we were best friends.

"Hey," I said as I awkwardly crooked one arm around her back.

"Who are you here with?"

"Oh, um, you mean like a date? I just came with friends," I said, gesturing to Nidhi and Sydney.

"Oh," she said, jutting out her lower lip in a fake pout. "I'm sorry. That sucks so bad! Don't be embarrassed! I'm sure someone will ask you next year."

I was about to tell her that I didn't feel embarrassed at all—that I'd rather have horns and a tail than have to go to a dance with Matt, when he jumped into the conversation. "Hey, Ashleigh, I may have to dump you so I can hang out with these girls! Charlie, I'd be happy to get in the picture with you and your girls. You all look totally hot!"

"Um . . . thanks but that's really not necessary, Matt. You really don't have to worry about us," I said, noticing Ashleigh's cold stare.

"Hey, this line is really long," Nidhi said, pulling on my elbow. "Let's go get something to drink and come back later."

"Great idea!" We all quickly moved over to the side of the gym. I didn't know what about them bothered me the most—how fake Ashleigh was, Matt's arrogance, or Ashleigh letting Matt get away with treating her like that. Maybe it was all three.

"Does that girl's boyfriend always hit on other girls like that? Like, right in front of her?" Sydney asked. "So uncomfortable."

"Matt? Yeah, he's a total creep—" But I didn't have a chance to finish my thought because Nidhi suddenly gasped.

"What?" I said, turning around to follow her gaze.

"Oh, my God, he couldn't have," I whispered. I shook my head, trying to convince my brain that I really wasn't seeing what I saw. My heart was racing a million miles an hour. All I wanted to do was run.

Will and Tyler had just walked into the gym arm in arm with Lauren and Ally.

## CHAPTER SIXTEEN

**"CHARLIE, WHAT'S WRONG?" SYDNEY ASKED. "I THOUGHT YOU** said you were over Tyler."

Nidhi grabbed my arm with one hand and Sydney's with the other hand and started leading us across the gym.

"Where are we going?" Sydney protested. Just then, Michael walked up with his date, a beautiful Asian girl. "Hey, ladies, I want to introduce you to Molly," he said. But we definitely did not have time for this—I was in full-blown panic-mode.

"Sorry, Michael, emergency," Nidhi said as we rushed past him.

"Nice meeting you!" Sydney called back over her shoulder.

Nidhi took us straight to a corner of the gym and sat us down on the bleachers, safely behind a cloud billowing from one of the dry-ice machines.

"Okay, seriously, what's going on?" Sydney demanded.

I couldn't talk.

"Charlie and I know those girls from Greenspring."

"Shut up! Those are the girls you hate from your old school?" Sydney asked.

I nodded. It was too insane to comprehend. Why on earth would Will have invited Lauren and Ally? Why had he lied to me about it? And—more importantly—how could he do this to me?

"I don't believe it! Why would Will be such an asshole? Doesn't he know what happened last year?" Sydney said.

"I didn't go into all the details, but I thought he knew enough," I said miserably.

We all looked back over. Lauren and Will had clearly come together. Her right hand was holding his while she smoothed the front of her short black dress. Ally looked like she'd been sleeping in a tanning bed for weeks.

Kill me now.

Sydney cocked her head to the side and said, "So that's the infamous Lauren. She's not as pretty as I thought she'd be."

"Thanks. . . . That's why you're my friend," I said, trying to laugh. "But what are we going to do? We can't sit over here all night, and your mom isn't coming to get us until eleven. Should I call Luke?"

"Charlie, are you six years old?" Sydney said, clearly not impressed by my gut reaction to run and hide. "You're going to stay here and stand your ground and pretend like it doesn't bother you."

I groaned. "I'd really rather go home."

"Not a possibility, I won't let you. This is your territory, not theirs." I just stared back at her, paralyzed. Nidhi was still looking over in Lauren and Ally's direction. It suddenly made me feel guilty all over again for how I'd helped them be so mean. And now Nidhi had to deal with this, too.

"Look, Charlie," Sydney continued, trying to motivate me, "you can't let these people control you like this. So, come on. We're going over there and getting it over with."

"Nidhi, what do you want to do?" I asked. I didn't want to leave her here on the bleachers, but I doubted she'd want to face them either.

"Why would Nidhi care?" asked Sydney.

I looked away. I wasn't really planning on telling Sydney that part of the story. It's one thing to confide in a new friend about a difficult situation you went through where you come out looking good at the end. It's totally different when you look like the evil one.

"Let's not get into it now. And Sydney's right. We can't avoid them for the rest of the night. Let's just say hi and then we'll keep doing our own thing," Nidhi said.

I looked at Nidhi gratefully. "Yeah, I guess you're right."

Sydney crossed her arms. "Look, I'm not sure what's going on, but you're both telling me the whole story when we get home." Sydney got up and pulled both of us up from the bleachers.

Sydney was right. This was our school, and even if Will was completely insensitive, I couldn't let my past take control of my present. Everything was different now. Nidhi and I had managed to forgive and forget. Maybe Lauren and Ally had matured since I'd seen them five months ago.

"Oh, my God, Charlie, it's been sooooo long!" Lauren squealed as she threw her tiny arms around my neck, and I could feel her sizing up Sydney and Nidhi behind me.

"Hey, Charlie! Look who I brought!" said Will.

My eyes bored into him, but I didn't say anything.

"Hey, Lauren, Ally. You both look great," I said. It was amazing how just being around them generated compliments I didn't mean.

"I know, thanks! My parents and I went to Mexico last week and I got so dark!" Ally giggled, holding out her arms so I could examine her tan. "But, oh, my God, Charlie, I can't believe you're at Harmony Falls with Will!"

"Yeah, it's kind of crazy," I said, glaring at Will.

"So you all came together?" Tyler asked.

Sydney, all five-feet-ten of her, stepped up next to me. "Actually, yes. Charlie and Nidhi got asked by like a hundred guys, but I made them come with me," Sydney said. She turned to Lauren. "Hi, I'm Sydney! It's so good to finally meet you. Charlie's told me all about you."

"Really?" Lauren laughed and put her arm on Will's shoulder and leaned against him. If I could have ripped her arm out of its socket, I totally would have.

Nidhi stepped forward. "Hi, Lauren. Hi, Ally."

They looked at her blankly. They had no idea who she was. It was like they had tortured so many people that they couldn't keep track anymore. Then the next second, Lauren's smile widened. She got it.

"Nidhi? You look so nice I didn't even recognize you,"

Lauren said, once again crowning herself the queen of the noncompliment.

Ally looked confused. "Wait, why are you here? Don't you go to Greenspring?"

"Actually, no . . . ," Nidhi said slowly, trying her hardest not to seem condescending. "I go here too. With Charlie."

"Are you sure you're not in my Spanish class? With Señor Fisher," Ally pressed.

"No. I'm not in your Spanish class. I go to Harmony Falls," Nidhi said.

Lauren looked back and forth between us. "So you're all friends?" she asked mockingly.

My eyes darted to Will for just a second to see if he was picking up on how awkward this was, but his smile only communicated complete stupidity.

"Hey, Nidhi, looking good tonight," Tyler said, totally staring at her boobs. That was his contribution to this conversation? The guy was a genius.

"Hey, I am going to get a Coke," Will said to us. "Anybody want one?"

"Get me a diet!" Lauren asked.

"I'll go with you," Nidhi said, seizing her moment to escape. At least Sydney was still here.

"So how's Greenspring?" I asked, as DJ Blaze announced the mandatory participation in some group dance.

"Ahhhhh! I love this song!" Ally shrieked, nearly splitting my eardrum, and dragged Tyler onto the dance floor. Lauren and I were now alone, unless you count Sydney, my bodyguard in the purple dress, loitering about three feet behind me—far enough away to not be eavesdropping but close enough to let me know she had my back.

"What were you saying?" Lauren said, not missing a beat.

"Um, I can't remember," I said. I just had nothing to say to her anymore. All I wanted to do was find Will, figure out why he'd brought them in the first place, and then kill him.

"So, when did you start hanging out with Will again?" I asked. "It must have been, like, three years since you guys have seen each other."

"I know, isn't it crazy? I mean, we kinda emailed back and forth all through middle school, but I didn't ever see him. I mean, I pretty much knew he still really liked me, but there was no way I was going to be in a long-distance relationship, you know?"

Long-distance relationship? She had to be joking. She didn't actually think I believed that she and Will had been talking all through middle school and she wouldn't have rubbed it in my face? I knew her better than that.

"But he called me right when he got back in June and we hung out a bunch over the summer, and I don't know, Charlie, but I definitely think something is still there."

"What did you say?" I asked. Will had been back since JUNE? My stomach dropped and I fought to catch my breath while Lauren stood there gloating.

"What?" she said innocently.

I almost asked her again, but I knew what she'd said, and I couldn't give Lauren the satisfaction of making me feel worse.

Lauren sighed and looked away. "Anyhow, that's weird that you're friends with that girl now."

"Why is that weird?" I asked defensively.

"What, did you forget you totally trashed her and then tried to get me in trouble for it?"

I narrowed my eyes at the target. She was going down.

"Lauren, you do realize you are completely delusional, right? You walk in here thinking that everyone is going to bow down and let you get away with your shit when that is so not happening. And by the way, Nidhi is one of my best friends now, so I'd appreciate it if you don't start trashing her in front of me. Or else I'm going to have no choice but to accidentally put my fist in your teeth."

I must have said this loudly because suddenly I was aware that Sydney was right next to me.

"Relax! I didn't say anything about her. But you're always blaming me for stuff I didn't do, so I'm not surprised," Lauren said smugly.

"Lauren, I really don't care what you believe anymore because I've never been happier than the day we stopped being friends. But I hope you remember you're at my school tonight, and I'd think really hard about it before you start saying things you can't back up."

I didn't wait for her to respond. I turned around and almost ran straight into Will, who was trying to carry four drinks without dropping them. As Sydney and I walked away, he called to us, "Hey, I got you drinks!"

I kept walking. I had never been so mad at someone.

"Great to meet you, Lauren," Sydney called out cheerfully as we walked to the other side of the dance floor.

As soon as we were out of sight of Lauren and Will, she started jumping up and down. "Oh, my God, Charlie, that was amazing! I can't believe you told her off like that! Doesn't it feel so good?" Sydney said, practically skipping in her heels as we wove through the couples who were now slow dancing to some bad nineties love song.

"I guess so," I said, my voice nearly shaking. Lauren made me so angry I could feel it in my bones. And Will . . . I didn't even know what to think. I was suddenly so tired, but the clock on the wall above the bleachers said it was only nine thirty.

Sydney and I saw Nidhi and Michael on the bleachers laughing.

"Nidhi just filled me in. Damn, Will is so stupid," Michael said. I wished I could find this as funny as he did.

"Michael, where's Molly?" I asked, trying to distract myself from what had just happened.

"Good question," he said, clearly not that concerned. "Last time I saw her, she was all over this guy on the basketball team."

"That's so mean! How could she do that do you?"

"Don't worry about it. Girls come and go. Didn't really like her anyway."

"It still sucks," Nidhi said.

Sydney rolled her eyes. "Michael, we know you really wanted to go with all of us," she teased. "Ladies, I think we have no choice but to let Michael join our group for the rest of the dance. Is he in?"

"He's in," we both said.

"Thanks, but I'm not sure . . . I have my reputation to protect. I can't let people think you all felt sorry for me."

144

"Would it help if we told everyone we stole you away from Molly because we were so in love with you?" I asked.

"Not bad, Charlie! I like the way you think!" laughed Michael.

"Good. Now that that's settled, I've had enough of this sitting around," Sydney said, stretching out her hand to me. "Charlie, Nidhi, Michael, come shake what yo' mama gave you."

Michael, Nidhi, and I burst out laughing.

"What?"

"Girl, don't say that again," Michael said, putting his arm around her and leading us onto the dance floor.

For the next hour or two, I danced my butt off and almost managed to obliterate Will, Tyler, Lauren, and Ally from my mind. Will tried to talk to me a couple of times, but I refused to answer him in anything but one-word responses. Tyler spent the whole night all over Ally. Or she was all over him. It was hard to tell. And of course I'd get daggers of hatred from Lauren, but every time I felt them, I got weirdly stronger. By the time we got home that night and rehashed every moment of the dance, I was actually grateful that I'd had the opportunity to tell Lauren what I really thought of her. Not that I had forgiven Will for bringing her.

# CHAPTER SEVENTEEN

**"CHARLIE, CAN I TALK TO YOU FOR A SECOND?" WILL ASKED,** standing next to our table in the cafeteria.

"Maybe I should come, too, Will," suggested Sydney. "You may need protection."

"Thanks, but I think I can take care of myself," he said, shoving his hands into his Harmony Falls soccer jacket.

"Why are you here? Shouldn't you be in class?" I asked. This was the most I'd spoken to him since the dance a week before. If he was such a loser that he wanted to hang out with Lauren, then I was done with him wasting my time. Completely, forever done.

"I have a free period," Will said impatiently.

"Whatever you need to say, you can say it right here," I said.

"You sure about that?"

"Excuse me?" I said.

He backed away from the table and crossed his arms. "Charlie, give it a rest and just come with me for five minutes, okay?"

"Fine," I said, following him to an empty table.

"Are you going to tell me what your problem is?"

"If you can't figure it out, then I don't see why I should tell you," I said, glaring at him.

"Are you serious? You're mad at me and won't tell me why?"

"I'm not even going to answer that. You know what you did."

He clasped both his hands behind his neck, closed his eyes, and leaned back in his chair. "Why don't you do me a favor and tell me what I did that was so wrong. Assume I'm completely stupid."

"I don't have to assume anything. You are totally stupid. I don't even know where to begin. Oh, wait, yes I do. How about you didn't tell me you were back but you called Lauren as soon as you got here and you're almost back together? You lied about it to my face. And then you bring her to the dance, knowing that I hate her? How about we start there?" I crossed my arms triumphantly.

"Wh-what?" he stuttered.

"You heard me," I said, glaring.

"I didn't lie to you about it. I was going to tell you that I was bringing her, but Lauren told me not to. She said she wanted it to be a surprise."

"You expect me to believe that? You couldn't possibly be that dumb."

He didn't say anything.

"Oh, my God, you are that dumb, and she's that psychotic. The girl is unbelievable," I said, putting my head on the table.

"I thought you were friends! Or at least I didn't think you hated each other's guts!"

"Why would you think we were friends? I told you that I hated her."

"You never said that! All you said was that you weren't close anymore."

"Maybe I didn't explain it word for word, but you still should have known," I said, lowering my voice because I'd just realized Nidhi and Sydney and everyone else in the cafeteria were looking over at our table.

"Charlie, you're insane. Am I supposed to read your mind?"

"You should have known," I said stubbornly.

"Well, I didn't. But it would help me out a lot if you tell me now what's going on."

"What difference would that make?" I argued.

"Because I need to decide who to believe. After the dance, Lauren said some crazy shit about you."

My eyes narrowed. Of course Lauren talked trash about me. That was just like her. "Fine, I'll tell you." And for the next five minutes, I told him what happened. Not every detail, but the important ones, including the part with Nidhi.

"Charlie, why didn't you tell me before?" he said, leaning his elbows on the table.

"Well, it's not exactly something I love talking about. And I thought with us going to Harmony Falls that I wouldn't have to deal with Lauren anymore."

"Do you think I'd have invited her if I'd known any of this?"

"I don't know—"

"I wouldn't have done that."

I looked up at him. A wave of relief flooded my body, plus a tiny feeling of victory that I'd just beat Lauren. But then I remembered a crucial detail.

"Okay, so, why did you call her and not me when you got back?"

"I can't really explain it, but calling you was more intense somehow. I knew I should have, and I wanted to, but every time I sat down to do it, I don't know, I just didn't. And I invited her to the dance because she asked me to go to hers."

"You went to Greenspring's homecoming dance?" My stomach dropped. I hadn't seen this coming.

He nodded. "Tyler and I went about two weekends ago. He's been hanging out with Ally ever since." He saw my grimace. "Charlie, trust me. He's better off with Ally. They're perfect for each other."

"So . . . then . . . are you back together with Lauren?"

"What? Are you kidding? The girl's a nightmare. It just took me a little while to realize how superficial and stupid she is. And whatever you said to her at the dance got her so mad I thought her head was going to spin around."

"Really?" I said, a little too happily. But I couldn't help it.

"Definitely. I had no idea she could talk such crap about someone. It was pretty freaky. Anyway, I actually haven't seen her since, even though she's been texting me, like, twenty-four-seven."

I'm sorry, but that just made me so happy. In fact, nothing Will could have said would have been better.

"So have you two made up yet?" Sydney asked, sitting down next to Will.

"Not sure. Are we good? Or do you still hate me?" asked Will.

"I definitely hate you less than I did thirty minutes ago," I said.

"I'll accept that."

"Good! I'm feeling much better now!" Sydney said.

"Well, it is all about you," I said, laughing.

# WELCOME TO THE FRESH VIEW!

*Hello, Freshmen!*

*Welcome to the Fresh View! Don't know how we pulled this off, but the* Prowler *is letting us, Nidhi Patel and Charlie Healey write a column for freshmen by freshmen. For our first edition, we're covering Spirit Week. Why? Because basically from the day school started, Spirit Week would come up at least once a day and we were clueless. Seriously, if you were an outsider and saw how intense this school is about Spirit Week, it would be a little weird, right? So what did we learn last week about the school where we will be spending the next four years?*

*1. Harmony Falls is ridiculously competitive. Our best examples are the lunchtime contests. So first, congratulations go to sophomore Mark Abrams for overthrowing Junior Franklin Sanders in a stunning upset of root-beer chugging. Mark gave freshmen this advice for any future chuggers: "Whatever you do, stand next to the garbage cans because the second you're done, you're going to hurl. Trust me." Thank you, Mark. This is the kind of invaluable information freshmen depend on. Then there was the chubby bunny contest, when students stuff as many marshmallows in their mouth as they can, while singing the school anthem. This year's winner, Junior Amanda Moore, said, "I'll never eat another marshmallow again, but it was totally worth it." We'd like to point out that Amanda beat about twenty guys in her quest for marshmallow domination. Way to go, Amanda!*

*2. Harmony Falls loves fire—and we're even competitive*

about that. Every year, the juniors are responsible for building a bonfire the night before homecoming. And every year, the juniors try to make it bigger than the year before. We have to say, they did an amazing job, although we weren't reassured when junior Max Neely said, "Good thing we got over sixty pallets so we didn't have to sacrifice any freshmen to the bonfire gods." We assumed Max was joking, right?

3. Harmony Falls has a lot of talent: Anybody who walks by the Good Karma Café knows we have some serious musicians at this school. So it was no surprise to us that the talent show was amazing. Brian Garcia and Amanda Clark's acoustic performance of Maroon 5's "She Will Be Loved" was incredible, and when the sophomore boys started juggling fire, we were nervous but impressed. The only thing we'd like some clarity on is why the football team dressed up like girls in lingerie and lip-synched a song about how hot they were. We're not criticizing. We're just curious. Is there something you want to tell us?

4. Harmony Falls loves tradition. There are a ton of things we could write about here, but we chose the one we had the most experience with. We're talking about the floats. We were drafted to help, even though neither of us had a clue what we were doing. So we would like to take this opportunity to officially apologize to our fellow float makers for our poor contributions. But it was all worth it because one of us (Charlie) had the honor and privilege of walking in the parade as a penguin. If that's not the way to start high school, we don't know what is. And as far as the competition went, we weren't surprised that the seniors

won. Let's face it—it looked like the kind of float you see on TV. But we also want to recognize the junior class's efforts. We know a lot of people thought the parade wasn't the right way to "raise an issue." But even if you hated it, you have to admit they brought up some important issues, and people are still talking about it.

We know people have different opinions about Spirit Week, but all in all we had a great time. We did feel more a part of the school after the week was over. And whatever experience you had, let us know and we'll post it on the website. Remember, let us know if there are any topics we should cover for future columns!

*Nidhi and Charlie*

# CHAPTER EIGHTEEN

**"CHARLIE, WAIT UP!" JOSH WAS WALKING TOWARD ME WITH** a stack of *Prowler*s in his arms. I'd been waiting all day to get one.

"God, I haven't been in this hall in three years! But I wanted you to have the chance to congratulate me in person."

"For what, and are you going to give me one?" I asked, desperately reaching for a copy.

"Because I'm such a genius for letting you do the Fresh View! Wait, where's Nidhi? Isn't her locker around here too?"

"I'm not sure where she is. Why?"

"Well, whose idea was it to put that thing in about the football players?"

"Mine . . . is someone mad about it?" It had been my idea. I couldn't help it. The song they "sang" was ridiculous, and they still got more applause than anyone else.

"Well, I am now officially in love with you. I know you're a freshman girl, but I don't care."

"I'm glad you're happy with it. I was a little worried people would get angry at me."

"You have no idea! Those assholes have been doing that every year I've been here, and everyone always thinks it's so funny. You're the first person to call them out. I loved it, and so did a lot of the other people. Owen may even like you now."

"Thanks, but it wasn't like I was trying to make some kind of political statement. I just wrote what I saw."

"That's what makes it even better! I'd never have been able to get away with that without getting major flack for it."

"But are people mad at me?" I didn't want to give Matt a reason to get in my face about anything ever.

"Who, like the football players? Don't worry about it. They're too embarrassed. And Gwo will back you up anyway. Why he stays on that team is a mystery to me, but it's not my life."

"Wait, why would Gwo need to back me up?"

"Charlie, you really need to relax. Everyone I've talked to loved it—the whole column. That was just the best part. But I have to run and make sure all the printed editions get out. Here's two. One for you and one for Nidhi. And, Charlie, good job. You're not turning out to be the pathetic freshman I thought you'd be."

"Wow, Josh, I don't really know how to thank you for that," I said.

"Don't worry about it! Got to run!"

## CHAPTER NINETEEN

**IF I NEEDED ANY MORE MOTIVATION TO BE A WRITER WHEN**
I grew up, having people like something you write was it. Wait,
actually it was even more than people liking it. It was that
people were talking about it. I even had students come up to
me in the hallway and congratulate me. And it was critical for
my sanity to think about something else besides the homecoming dance drama and Lauren's thinking she could play me.
Then it didn't matter what I thought about writing or Lauren
or anything else because all of a sudden I was buried in an ava-
lanche of work and then midterms. Seriously, how is anyone
expected to be smart in five simultaneous subjects? I mean,
why do we have to be well-rounded? What exactly is so good
about that? But of course I have no say on that, so I complied
like everyone else.

I couldn't get up early or go to bed late enough to fit it all in. And it was the same for all of us. Nidhi was splitting her time between the *Prowler* and the debate team, Sydney was busy with basketball practice, Will was in pretraining for lacrosse (apparently you could be in training for "lax" all year), and Michael was trapped in the science lab working on some insane project he was submitting to the Westinghouse science award.

The only problem was Tyler. His fat ego still couldn't accept that Sydney had rejected him. Whenever he saw her in the halls, he'd stick his tongue out in this way that was totally disgusting. In Mr. Jaquette's class, he'd talk over her whenever she tried to speak until Mr. Jaquette stopped him. Sydney always laughed it off, but anyone with half a brain could see she hated it. We all told her to ignore him, but I knew about putting up with people who attacked you in little ways. Sooner or later, those things build up, and one day you can't take it anymore. You have to do something to make it stop.

"Can you believe LT pulled a groin muscle in the first five minutes of the game? It killed me," Sydney said, opening her milk at our lunch table.

I told you, you should have picked Eddie Royal off the waivers last week!" Michael said.

"Do you think we could talk about something else besides fantasy football?" I begged.

Out of nowhere, the Axe was upon us.

For a second I assumed Tyler was only walking by, but just as I thought we were safe, he swooped down from the side and grabbed a slice of pizza off Sydney's tray.

"Tyler, give that back!" Sydney screamed.

"You know you want me," he teased, his mouth filled with pizza.

"You are so delusional! But whatever, it's so not worth it," Sydney said, turning away from him.

"Tyler, why are you bothering this beautiful girl?"

I looked behind Tyler and saw an all-American good-looking guy, coming over from the junior tables. He had brown hair and wore a black Harmony Falls varsity lacrosse jacket. I'd never seen him before, but from the way Tyler jumped, clearly he had.

"Hey, Dylan, don't worry about it. I'm just playing with her," Tyler said anxiously. This was interesting. I'd never seen Tyler like this before. All his cockiness was gone.

"Why don't you get my lunch, Wickam? And make sure to get the tots. Then meet me back at my table," Dylan ordered.

"Sure, man, no problem." Tyler scurried away.

Dylan leaned over and rested his hands on the back of a chair. "Hey, Michael. How's your brother? Still playing at Duke?"

Michael nodded. "Yeah, going well."

"Tell him I said hello." Dylan was talking to Michael but looking right at Sydney.

"Absolutely," said Michael.

"So what's your name?" he asked Sydney.

"Sydney."

"Sorry about Tyler. If he ever bothers you again, just let me know," he said, smiling. Then he walked back across the invisible divide to the other side of the cafeteria where the upperclassmen ate.

"Who was that?" I asked.

"Dylan Vorhees. Lacrosse player. I guess my brother knew him," Michael said.

"Well, whoever he is, it was nice of him to get Tyler off my case. I swear I'm going to kill that guy one day."

"Well, I think Dylan may have had other reasons," Michael said, smirking.

"Shut up! Can't someone do something just to be a good guy? Is that possible?" Sydney said, throwing her napkin at him.

Michael looked around, pretending to be deep in thought. "In this situation? I would say . . . no. The boy's definitely creeping on you."

"He is not! And anyway, I don't care. He got Tyler to leave me alone!"

Michael leaned back in his chair and shook his head. "Yeah, but what you saw right there is why I'll never try out for lacrosse."

"What do you mean?" I asked.

"You see Dylan ordering Tyler around? There's no way I'd be a slave for anyone. Just for a team? And lacrosse is always the worst. So not worth it," Michael said.

"How are they the worst?"

"My brother always told me to stay away from them. Like he told me last year that if I was even thinking of trying out for the team, he'd kick my ass."

"That's so sweet? But what do the lax guys do?"

"I don't really know exactly what goes on now. But when my brother was a sophomore, they made the freshmen run naked in front of the varsity cheerleaders."

"You must be joking!" I said.

"Totally true story. At least they made the freshmen do it at night. Much less embarrassing. Wickam loves them, so they basically get to do whatever they want."

"But the sports editor on the *Prowler* told me they had a new coach this year," I said.

"Oh, right. I forgot about that. Who knows? Maybe it'll be different this year. But some of those guys are pretty into that stuff. I mean you just never know."

"But Will's on the lacrosse team! Shouldn't we tell him?"

"Charlie, he'd have to know."

There was no way I wasn't grilling Will about this at the first opportunity. Homework could wait.

CHealeyPepper324: u know what happened at lunch with T and S?

FCBarcafan18: what now?

CHealeyPepper324: t being usual tool. took pizza off her plate. i swear he's 5 but that guy dylan from your lax team told him to lay off. ordered t around like a servant. what's up with that?

FCBarcafan18: its nothing lax tradition the new guys do stuff for the older players

CHealeyPepper324: that's not what Michael said. he said it was way more intense

FCBarcafan18: its not we get them drinks hold doors for them carry their stuff

CHealeyPepper324: r u sure? they aren't gonna duct tape u and throw u in some pool? i saw that on Dateline last year it was out of control

FCBarcafan18: Charlie, its nothing. u really don't need to be worrying about this

CHealeyPepper324: if u say so but promise me u won't let those guys do anything really bad to u

FCBarcafan18: fine promise

CHealeyPepper324: 1 more thing keep t away from s

FCBarcafan18: she can take care of herself really think we should stay out of this

CHealeyPepper324: u always want to stay out of it if we don't do something it'll get worse

FCBarcafan18: ok can we just give it a rest right now?

CHealeyPepper324: fine i'm just worried not sure what to do. have a bad feeling about this

FCBarcafan18: ur freaking over nothing. t cant help being a tool. and he worships Dylan so if he said to lay off he will. u don't need to get involved

CHealeyPepper324: whatever but I still think ur wrong

# CHAPTER TWENTY

**"SO FAR WE HAVE BEEN READING ABOUT AMERICAN HISTORY** through the eyes of only one kind of person. Does anyone know what I am talking about?" Mr. Jaquette asked.

I didn't have a clue. I'd heard that every year he came up with some weird new final project before winter break. I guessed this was it.

"Anyone?" he said, scanning the room hopefully.

We all shook our heads.

He sighed. Clearly we weren't being gifted and talented or whatever Harmony Falls students were supposed to be.

"All the people we're reading about were in positions of power or did the right thing." Mr. Jaquette walked to the side of the room. His eyes twinkled, his inner geek coming out full force. "For your final project before break, you are going to find someone outside the usual history books. You'll research their lives and present a ten-minute report in front of the class."

I raised my hand. "But Mr. Jaquette, how are we supposed to find these people?"

Mr. Jaquette arched his eyebrows and smiled. "Charlie, don't underestimate yourself." He scanned the room. "And a word of warning for those of you who usually like to wait until the last minute. I'd strongly advise against that with this project. It'll be twenty-five percent of your grade, and invisible people are hard to find at midnight the night before your presentation is due."

Two weeks later, I'd chosen Isaac "King" Sears, one of the founders of the Sons of Liberty. From their name, I thought they'd be heroic revolutionary fighters. Wrong. They were like Mafia guys, beating up and bullying anyone who got in their way. The night they threw the tea into Boston Harbor, they dressed up as Indians so people wouldn't think a bunch of white guys were responsible. Nice.

Sydney didn't have a hard time finding someone to talk about, but she was terrified of public speaking. She practiced in front of Nidhi and me a hundred times, but she was still sure she'd get up there and choke.

"Hey, you all! Bad news! Mr. Jaquette just went home with the stomach flu, so I'm afraid you guys are going to have to put up with me!" Ms. Fieldston said, walking into our classroom the day of Sydney's speech.

"Don't worry, Ms. Fieldston, we'll take care of you," Tyler called out from the back of the room.

"Thanks, Tyler, I know I can count on you," she said brightly.

The room buzzed with the noise of people talking.

Ms. Fieldston raised one hand. "Okay, everyone, let's be quiet, okay? Mr. Jaquette instructed me to go ahead with the class presentations as planned."

"Ms. Fieldston, how are we going to be graded if Mr. Jaquette isn't here?" Brian Reitman whined.

"I know it isn't perfect, but I'm going to give a grade and video the presentation for Mr. Jaquette to review later," Ms. Fieldston said, patting a small video bag hanging at her side.

"So, then, let's get started! If you have a PowerPoint, I'd be happy to advance the slides for you. Brian, why don't you begin?" she asked cheerfully.

Brian's was so boring that honestly I have no idea what he talked about. Then this guy Trevor did one about a doctor, and then it was Sydney's turn.

"You'll do great. Remember to pick out your friendly face in the audience," I said, pointing at myself.

Sydney gave me a small, tight smile, dropping the piece of hair she'd been twisting, and walked to the front of the class. She took a deep breath and began.

"In this class we have learned a lot about Thomas Jefferson. He wrote in the Declaration of Independence that all men are created equal. But when he wrote that, Thomas Jefferson owned over two hundred slaves. I thought finding out about their lives, people owned by a man who talked about freedom, was important," Sydney said, her voice cracking a little.

"One of Jefferson's slaves was a woman named Sally Hemings. Advance slide."

Sydney cleared her throat. I sent her all my telepathic powers of confidence.

"Sally Hemings was born in 1773, the daughter of Elizabeth Hemings, a slave, and John Wayles, Thomas Jefferson's father-in-law. In 1774, Jefferson inherited Sally from the Wayleses when she was a year old. She and her mother came to live with Jefferson in his Virginia home, Monticello, in 1776. Advance slide, please."

Sydney looked up hesitantly, making eye contact with everyone in the room like she'd practiced.

"There aren't many descriptions of Sally, but all of them say she was very beautiful. Before researching this topic, I had never thought about slaves having children with their owners but in 2004, scientists proved that Jefferson was the father of several of Sally Hemings's children."

Tyler called out, "Nice one!"

Sydney stared at Tyler, her hands clenched at her sides. She breathed deeply and began again. "In 2004, scientists proved that"—she paused. She was repeating herself. She looked at the index card outline she had in her hand but didn't continue.

Come on, Sydney, you can do this, I said to myself.

She started again. "Even though his political rivals tried to use it against him, the rumors never completely died. Throughout his life, Jefferson and his family denied his relationship with Sally. But until 1998, it seemed impossible to prove that Jefferson was the father of Sally Hemings's children."

Sydney's voice was broken by the sound of clapping. I turned around and saw that it was Tyler and a couple of other boys. Sydney stopped talking, totally confused. I was, too.

Sydney waited for them to stop clapping before she spoke again.

"However, in 1998, Dr. Eugene Foster, a retired pathologist, compared genetic material from the Y chromosome of a descendent of Jefferson's uncle with genetic material from the Y chromosome of the descendents of Sally Hemings's sons—"

Again, the boys applauded, but it was combined with laughter. Sydney looked at the boys and then Ms. Fieldston. Ms. Fieldston stood up. "Come on, boys. Settle down please," she begged, her singsong tone at full force.

Sydney tried again, but she couldn't get two words out before the clapping returned. The boys doubled over laughing.

Ms. Fieldston said, "Okay, guys, you've had your fun. Let Sydney get on with her presentation."

"Now . . . history shows that Jefferson was the father of Sally Hemings's children," Sydney whispered and raced back to her chair.

"Don't pay attention to them. You were amazing," I whispered.

Sydney blinked back tears. She shook her head and didn't say anything else for the rest of class.

The bell rang a few minutes later, and I watched Tyler leave with his friends.

"Let's get out of here," Sydney said, swinging her backpack over her shoulder.

I followed her, desperately thinking of what I could say to make her feel better.

We made it as far as five feet outside the classroom before Sydney stopped and leaned against the wall. "That's it. I'm going to go so Girl Scout on his ass. He has no idea."

"What? Sydney, speak English. What's Girl Scouting?"

"Oh, I made that up when I was ten. I was in a troop and

got into a fight with a girl about who sold the most cookies. She and her crazy mom freaked out on me. So that's what I call it when you get so angry at someone you want them to die."

Just then we both became aware of Ms. Fieldston standing in the doorway. "Sydney, I'm glad you're still out here. Can you come in and talk to me for a second?" Ms. Fieldston said.

"Will you wait for me while I talk to her?" Sydney asked me.

"Of course. I'll be right here."

I leaned against the wall near the door so I could hear their conversation.

"Now, before you say anything, I know you're not happy about what those boys did to you. But don't be too upset about it. Boys always do things like that when they like a girl," Ms. Fieldston said.

"You're saying they did that to me because they like me?" Sydney asked.

"Of course, honey. Boys can't help themselves when they're around pretty girls. They get intimidated so they act out. But they didn't mean anything by it. I'd be complimented if I were you."

"But, Ms. Fieldston, I couldn't concentrate while I was doing my presentation. I didn't even get to finish, and I worked really hard on it. It's not fair."

"Sydney, don't worry about it. You obviously worked on the project. I'll tell Mr. Jaquette you did a good job and you can just put it behind you. Okay?"

"I guess."

"Sydney, think of it this way. You're lucky. They could have done that to any girl in the class but they chose you."

"But will Mr. Jaquette see the video?" Sydney said quietly.

"Actually I just checked and the tape seems not to be working properly. If you want, I could talk to Mr. Jaquette and you could do it again for him? But either way, I'll make sure your grade is covered so there's really nothing to worry about."

"Okay. Thanks, Ms. Fieldston," Sydney said hesitantly.

"No problem. It's what I'm here for."

The door opened wider, and Sydney came out.

"Did you hear that?" Sydney said as she closed it behind her.

"Yeah, what do you think?" I asked, walking away from our classroom.

"I don't know. She's going to talk to Jaquette, so that's good."

"I mean it wasn't her fault that those guys did that, and you did the work. So I guess it seems fair. But what are you going to do about Tyler?"

Her eyes narrowed. "I don't know, but I'll think of something."

# CHAPTER
# TWENTY-ONE

**IT DIDN'T TAKE SYDNEY LONG. SHE TEXTED ME SIXTH PERIOD:**

Meet at our lockers after school.

When I got there, Sydney's eyes were blazing.

"Okay, I know where he is. You coming?"

"Sure. You tell Nidhi or Michael?" I said, hurrying after her

"Didn't see Nidhi. I think she's doing some debate thing. Michael told me to drop it. That it wasn't worth it."

I thought Michael had a point.

"I've been ignoring him for weeks. Now it's time to destroy him," Sydney said, stubbornly.

For a brief moment, I wished I'd been busy this afternoon, but I couldn't walk away now. Sydney needed my support.

But as I followed Sydney through the academic buildings

and the gym, and down into a narrow hallway of gray cinder blocks, I got a very bad feeling.

"You're not going to kill Tyler, right? Because I have a Spanish test tomorrow that I need to study for, so I don't have time to spend the night in jail," I joked to break my own tension.

She stopped and turned around. The smell of stale sweat and dirty socks permeated the air. "Charlie, I can't just let him get away with it. And he's not going to stop until I make him."

"I know, you're right."

The girl was on a mission. I was just along for the ride.

She stopped at a red door that said WEIGHT ROOM and looked through the glass. Even through the door, I could hear the sound of some kind of hard-core rap I didn't recognize and the clanging of weights. Sydney took one deep breath and marched in like she was entering the cage in *Ultimate Fighting Championship*.

I fought my instinct to run away. Beyond the inescapable and absolutely horrible smell of boys' feet and old sweat, I got the feeling girls weren't supposed to be here. At all. It was us and about fifteen guys in long shorts and T-shirts, grunting and lifting.

Sydney walked right over to where Tyler stood above Will, who was on his back, bench pressing.

"So you think what you did in class was funny?" Sydney said loudly over the music.

The clanking of the weights stopped. So did the music.

Tyler looked around the room and laughed nervously. "What are you talking about?" he asked, picking at his shirt.

"Don't pretend to be more stupid than you are. You know exactly what I'm talking about," Sydney said, arms crossed, hips out.

I heard someone in the background cough and mutter, "Wickam, regulate, dude."

Tyler's ears turned bright red.

"Syd, rest. It was a joke. Are you PMSing or something?"

A laugh bounced off the wall. I looked up and saw Matt grinning, taking in the whole scene.

"First of all, don't call me Syd. Second, what are you, in seventh grade with that PMS crap? Third, the stupid shit you pulled in class today was the last straw. Do you actually think you're funny? Because you're not. You think people like it when you're such a dick? Let me help you out on this one, Tyler, they don't."

Will sat up on the bench and brushed his hair out of his face. "Sydney, seriously, take it easy."

"Will, you weren't there so you don't know," I said, taking a step forward.

"I'm just saying maybe they can talk about this somewhere else?"

"Tyler doesn't care where he embarrasses me. Why should I care when I do it him?" Sydney sniped at Will.

"Sorry—whatever you say," Will said, putting his hands up in the air.

Sydney turned to Tyler. "Here's the deal. Just because I rejected you doesn't give you the right to be a total tool. Got it? You stay out of my way, and I'll stay out of yours. And if you mess with me again, we'll take this outside and find out what kind of man you really are."

Laughter ricocheted around the room along with several mutterings of "Damn, Wickam! She's calling you out!"

For one second, Tyler was absolutely paralyzed. "You don't want to take it there," he choked out.

"Good! I'm so glad we got this cleared up. And one last thing. Axe sucks!" she said, spinning on her heels as she walked out.

Outside the red door, Sydney let out a big breath and shook her hands in front of her. "Well, I feel better!"

It took me a second to speak because I was still regaining my breath from the combined effects of how horribly tense that situation had been and the stench in there. "I definitely think you've traumatized that boy for life," I said.

"Good! Mission accomplished. He so had that coming to him."

"You saw Matt Gercheck there, right?"

"Matt? Which Neanderthal was that?"

"He's the idiot who hit on us at the dance. Looks like a pig with a bad attitude?"

"Oh, yeah! I guess he was there. Even better!" Sydney gloated.

"He was watching the whole thing."

She shrugged. "I really don't care. Now Tyler knows what it feels like to be humiliated."

Later that night, of course Will IM'd me. It had become the only place we could really talk.

FCBarcafan18: guess S is proud of herslf

CHealeyPepper324: u have to admit he deserved it

FCBarcafan18: all he did was clap how bad could that b?

CHealeyPepper324: trust me

FCBarcafan18: but S was over the top so bad after you lft

CHealeyPepper324: how??????

FCBarcafan18: bad. M was the worst S shouldn't have done that—not there

CHealeyPepper324: fine. but no I cannot stop her when she's like that. . . . cant believe I ever liked T such a tool

FCBarcafan18: it was pretty pathetic

CHealeyPepper324: whatever. i was temporarily insane we can let it go now

FCBarcafan18: no problem. T's life is going to be miserable now M will tell the whole school

CHealeyPepper324: i forgot about that

FCBarcafan18: T won't. M won't let him

## CHAPTER TWENTY-TWO

**OUR CONVERSATION BOTHERED ME. THERE WAS NO DOUBT** in my mind that Tyler had it coming to him, but I wondered if Sydney was wrong, too. She had humiliated Tyler in front of the people he was the most desperate to impress. I thought about it a lot over the two-week winter break, but I didn't say anything to Sydney. It's not because I was scared to—well, I was a little bit—but she was visiting her grandmother and I didn't feel like this was something I wanted to text her about. I wanted to wait until it felt like the right time.

A week after school started back up, I got my chance.

"I swear, I live for snow days. I had like five tests today," Sydney said, handing me a bag of Kettle Corn and settling down on my couch.

"I know, I prayed to the snow-day gods last night before I went to bed," I said, stuffing my face with popcorn.

Suddenly Sydney stopped eating and sat up. "Oh, my God, I forgot to tell you about Tyler yesterday. It was absolutely amazing!"

"What happened?" I asked, thinking that my Tyler moment had arrived.

"It was when I was walking out of lunch and you were talking to someone on the newspaper. That big Asian guy. And by the way, I love Matt."

"Sydney, you can't say that even if you're joking. Yesterday Ms. McBride and I walked in on him and Ashleigh totally making out in the staff room. I never need to see that again."

"Okay, fine, but you have to listen," Sydney insisted, sitting up and grabbing another handful of popcorn. "You know how the lax team makes the underclassmen get their lunch? So Tyler was holding Matt's lunch tray and he tripped or fell. Not really sure how but food, plates, everything fell all over the place. The best part was the whole cafeteria just stopped and stared at him. And then everyone started laughing and clapping. Totally made my day!"

Will's words came back to me. "Don't you feel the slightest bit sorry for him?" I asked.

"No! Why should I? He totally deserved it!" she said looking at me like I was crazy.

"Yeah, but come on. Do you have to be so happy about it?"

"I have a right to be happy. Anyone who crosses me will forever be on my bad side."

"Look, I'm not saying he wasn't a total ass, but ever since that weight room thing, I don't know, I've sort of been feeling sorry for him. The whole school knows about it."

"Are you kidding me? You hate the boy as much as I do!"

"I know but . . ."

"Wait, you still like him. I can't believe it!"

"No I don't!" I said in disbelief.

"Why else would you be taking his side?" Sydney said, her voice rising in anger.

"Sydney, I'm not taking his side. But I still think we shouldn't be gloating when he screws up in front of the whole school."

"Well, I guess that makes you a better person than I am," Sydney said sarcastically.

"No I'm not. I've just been thinking about what happened in the weight room, and I think it may have been a little too much. I know he was being horrible to you and you had every right to be incredibly angry. But what you did in the weight room was sort of like what he did to you."

"Exactly. That was the point," Sydney said, refusing to look at me.

"But then you're sort of acting just like him, don't you think?" I said anxiously.

"You have got to be kidding me with this! This must be because you still like him. If Tyler still liking you is more important than our friendship, then obviously we aren't as close as I thought we were."

"Sydney, that's ridiculous. Why are you getting so mad at me?"

"I'm not mad! I just happen to think being loyal is really important in a friendship. Look, forget about it. I don't want to talk about it anymore. I'm going to call my mom to pick me up."

"Sydney, don't go! Anyway, you can't go. It'll take your

mom forever to get here," I said, at the same time desperately trying to figure out how to calm her down.

"Whatever, I can walk," Sydney said, putting on her coat.

"Sydney, don't go."

"I just really need to be by myself right now," Sydney said, flipping her cell phone open.

Two seconds later, the door closed on me.

## CHAPTER TWENTY-THREE

**"HEY, SYDNEY,"** I SAID CASUALLY WHEN I SAW HER AT OUR lockers the next morning. The night before, I'd mulled over what I should do when I saw her next and had decided on the "I'm going to pretend our fight didn't happen" strategy.

"Oh, hey," Sydney said like a speck of dirt on the floor had just spoken to her.

"Did you do the reading for Jaquette's class? It was like a hundred fifty pages. I don't know why he assumes we can all speed-read."

"Yeah, I did it, but I have to go," she said, again refusing to look at me.

"Okay, fine," I answered, but my words were ignored. She had already run up to Candace Patterson, a girl on her basketball team. I watched as Sydney laughed at something Candace said and then disappeared around the corner.

For the next six days, I'd get up in the morning, look out the window at the gray cold, and wish that somehow I could get mono and not have to deal.

"This war must end," Michael said, catching up to me in the hallway by our advisory class.

"Which war?" I asked, because there were a lot to choose from.

"The cold war between you and Sydney."

"Talk to Sydney because it's not my fault," I said.

"You do realize you all are acting like you're in seventh grade?" Michael teased.

"I'm not the one giving her the silent treatment!" I said.

"At least tell me why she's so mad. Because I've already asked her and she won't say anything. Nidhi won't say anything either."

I stopped, because we were getting close to our advisory room and I didn't want to risk the chance of Sydney hearing me.

"She's mad at me for absolutely no reason! All I did was tell her to stop being so damn happy every time Tyler makes an ass out of himself," I said.

"Oh," Michael said nodding, leaning against a locker.

"That's all you have to say, genius?"

"Hey, I'm not the one you're mad at, remember?"

"Sorry. It's just this whole thing puts me in a really bad mood. Nidhi's caught in the middle, and every time I see Sydney she's hanging out with the girls on her team. I mean, I don't care. She can be friends with whoever she wants, but it's like she wants me to feel bad."

"Charlie, you know Sydney. Of course she flipped out. Don't get me wrong, Sydney's my girl, but she's stubborn, especially when she thinks she's right . . . which is all the time."

"I should never have said anything," I grumbled.

"No—she needed to hear it. Just give her some time. She'll eventually come around."

"Yeah, like, in about a hundred years," I grumbled.

"I don't know. Maybe twenty," Michael said, grinning.

"Very funny."

"Come on, we got to go to Advisory." Michael said, putting his arm around me.

"Yeah, maybe I should write something for Ms. Fieldston's question box. You know, 'I have a friend who's being a total bitch for no reason. Any advice?'"

"Well, it would make the class more interesting. But seriously, Charlie, she'll come around."

I don't know if it was my conversation with Michael or how Sydney made a point during class of completely ignoring me and kissing up to everyone else, but by the time the bell rang at the end of Advisory I was furious. Honestly, Sydney was being so stupid that I wanted to shake her. Did I talk behind her back? No. Was I mean when I told her? Again—no. Did I bring it up around other people? No. No. No. It was so irritating and unfair that she thought the only reason I said anything about Tyler was because I liked him. She should have been way cooler about the whole thing. Instead, she was acting like I had totally betrayed her. So if she was going to pretend I didn't exist, then I could play that game too. I hadn't put in three hard years with Ally and Lauren for nothing.

"Sydney and Charlie, can I talk to you for a minute?" Ms. Fieldston asked as everyone was gathering their stuff to leave.

"Oh, great, this should be fun," I muttered under my breath.

"Girls, I have a very serious problem that only the two of you can fix," Ms. Fieldston said gravely.

"Okay . . . ," I said, bewildered.

"Two of my most favorite, coolest girls I know aren't talking to each other and I don't know what to do about it. Do you have any solutions?"

"Not really," Sydney said flatly.

"Charlie, Sydney, I'm not blind. You all are usually inseparable and now . . . you won't even look at each other. Girls, I don't know what's going on, but if you want to talk about it right now, I'll give you a pass."

I glanced over at Sydney, who was staring out the window with her jaw clenched, tapping her foot.

"Thanks, Ms. Fieldston, but it's okay," I said. There was no way I was going to wait around for Sydney the drama queen to get over herself. At this point, I'd be there forever. On top of that, since the Tyler thing, I doubted Ms. Fieldston was the best person to help me out in this situation.

"Girls, you should know by now that I would do anything for my students, especially the two of you. And there's nothing more important than girls sticking together. So we aren't leaving until this gets worked out."

"There's nothing to work out, Ms. Fieldston," Sydney said bitterly. "You know that Tyler has been completely obnoxious to me, and I finally told him that he had to back off. Charlie is mad at me because I'm not nicer to him now."

If she wanted to do this in front of Ms. Fieldston, fine by me. "That is not what I said, and you know it, Sydney. I'm not asking you to be nice to him. I just don't think you should be gloating about every bad thing that happens to him. You're completely overreacting."

"Okay, I can see that there are a lot of hurt feelings on both sides. And each of you is probably a little bit right. Sydney, do you think Charlie said those things to make you feel bad?" Ms. Fieldston asked gently.

"How should I know? But friends back each other up, and she is so clearly taking Tyler's side over mine," Sydney said.

This was incredible. "Sydney, you're being totally unfair! When have I not backed you up? Name one time."

"It only takes one time for it to count," Sydney said.

"What do think about that, Charlie?" Ms. Fieldston asked.

"What do I think? I think she's wrong. Sydney, if I tell you I disagree with you about something, I am sort of backing you up. Think about it. Do you think I wanted to talk to you about the Tyler thing? Did I wake up in the morning that day and say to myself, 'Great, today I get to talk to Sydney about this whole Tyler thing'? I mean seriously. I knew you weren't going to be happy about it, but I did it because . . ."

"Why?" Sydney asked.

"Because I guess that's what friends do sometimes. You tell each other when you think the other person is wrong. I'd want you to do that for me."

"So, girls, we need to find a common ground here. Sydney, it really seems like Charlie thought she was doing the right thing. Can you see that?" Ms. Fieldston said.

"I guess." Sydney shook her hair back and looked at me for

the first time in a week. "It's not like I don't know I'm a freak sometimes."

"And I'm not saying you aren't right about Tyler. He's the worst."

"So, wait a minute. Are you saying I can tell you when you're doing something that annoys me?" Sydney asked.

"Sure," I said, positive I'd just totally set myself up.

A small smile broke out on Sydney's face. "Okay. . . . No more rolling your eyes when I talk about fantasy football."

"Fantasy football? You're serious?"

"When am I not serious about fantasy football?"

"Okay, does this mean you see what I'm trying to say?"

"Yes," Sydney said.

"I'm so glad you all have worked it out," Ms. Fieldston said, her voice shocking me a little. I'd sort of forgotten that she was standing there.

"Thanks, Ms. Fieldston. I guess we needed a little help."

"No problem. I'm just glad you all feel better. But I better get you those passes and get you to class, or else I'll get in trouble," she said.

## CHAPTER TWENTY-FOUR

**"WHO ARE THE FLOWERS FROM?" NIDHI ASKED.**

"I don't know," Sydney said, holding two pink carnations in her hand. "Wait, that's not technically true. One is from that weird guy in science class who stares at me but I can't remember his name. Oh, yeah, and Will," she said, turning back to her locker.

"Will?" I guessed.

Nidhi bent over laughing. "Okay, that was so mean. Relax, Charlie, Sydney's joking. But you should see your face," Nidhi teased.

"I'm so glad you're amused," I stumbled. "Anyway, I knew you were joking."

"You are so lying! And just so you know, Nidhi and I have decided that you are totally in love with Will," Sydney insisted.

"I'm not in love with him!"

"Really? Nidhi, do you think the girl is in denial, or is she just refusing to admit it?"

Nidhi's eyes danced mischievously. "Charlie, admit it. Today is Valentine's Day. If you got a flower from him, would you one, be indifferent, two, think it was nice, three, be totally excited?"

"None of the above, because there's no way he would ever give me a flower," I insisted.

"Don't avoid the question. What if he did?" Nidhi said.

"I don't know."

"Maybe we should go ask Will how he would feel if you bought him one?" Sydney said.

"Don't even think about it. If you do, I'm never speaking to either one of you again!"

Just then we all saw Will walking down the hallway toward us. Nidhi and Sydney burst out laughing again, and I turned bright red.

"Hi, guys. What's so funny?" Will asked, blond hair in his eyes. He was wearing a dark red T-shirt. This would have been way easier to deal with if he had been uglier.

"Oh, nothing. We're talking about how much we love you and think you're the hottest boy in school," Nidhi said.

"Cool!" Will said, grinning.

Boys believe anything as long as it feeds their ego.

"Will, don't be an idiot. Just keep walking to class," I said, pushing him away from us.

"No way! I want to know what you all were talking about! It had to be good because Charlie's all red. What's up?"

"Go to class, Will! We're not talking about you. I'm getting my period, and I was asking them if they had a tampon," I said, pulling the girl trump card to get a boy to leave her alone.

Will winced. "Oh, man! No problem. I'm leaving right now!"

We watched Will scurry away. "Good one, Charlie. I'm impressed," Nidhi said.

"Thank you. Always use the period in case of emergencies. Never fails. So anyway . . . next topic. . . . So who's the other one from?" I asked, pointing to the flowers.

"Actually, I really don't know. All it says is *Hey, beautiful. . . . D*. Any ideas? Do I know anyone named D?"

I shrugged. "No one comes to mind."

"Me neither," said Nidhi.

"It's probably some other really weird freako guy," said Sydney.


"Gotten any flowers today?" Josh said as I entered the newspaper room.

I slammed my bag on the table, way harder than I intended. "Why does everyone care so much about flowers? And carnations have to be the ugliest flowers anyway!" I said.

"Charlie, am I detecting a bit of Valentine bitterness in your voice?" Josh said cheerfully.

"No, it's just that I don't see why the student council thinks it's a good idea to make money off a popularity contest," I said.

"So even if someone gave you a flower, you would reject it in protest?"

"Since I'm pretty sure that everyone sends them to themselves anyway, I guess I'm not really interested in bankrolling my own social status."

"Okay, Ms. Bitter," Josh said, with a huge smirk on his face. "Well, not to ruin your day or your politics, but this came for you," he said, reaching behind him and taking a red carnation off his desk.

He held it out for me.

I sheepishly took it out of his hands.

"You want me to take it back?" Josh said, enjoying this way too much.

"No, that's okay."

"I'm assuming you're throwing it in the trash, right? Wouldn't want you to sacrifice your principles just because someone likes you."

"Uh-huh," I mumbled, needing to get away from Josh as soon as possible.

I sat down on the couch and opened the little white note attached to the stem. "I hope you have a good Valentine's Day." There was a little heart at the bottom but no name.

*Who could have sent me this flower?* I wondered.

"Do you know how much the student council makes on those every year? Last year it was over twenty-five hundred dollars!" Gwo said, walking by me.

"It's total capitalist oppression. Everything is a commodity. It's disgusting," Owen said, without taking his eyes off his laptop.

"Yeah," I said, barely hearing them.

A few minutes later, I was on the couch, completely obsessing on the possible identity of my flower giver, when Nidhi interrupted my thoughts.

"Did you get a flower, Charlie?" Nidhi whispered.

"Looks like it."

"So . . . who gave it to you?"

"I have absolutely no idea," I said, handing her the note, my heart pounding. "What do you think?"

"Well, it's definitely from a boy. You can tell from the handwriting. But it doesn't matter—you know what I think," she said, giggling.

"Nidhi, it can't be from Will. That would just be too weird," I said, but my stomach was fluttering.

"Well, I'm not going to argue with you about it. But it seems pretty obvious to me. Anyway, do you still want to do the column like we planned, or have you changed your mind?" Nidhi asked.

"Of course I haven't changed my mind. It would take a lot more than one flower."

# WHY WE HATE VALENTINE'S DAY

*Dear Fellow Freshmen—*

*We hate Valentine's Day. It's true. Hate it. Why would anyone think it's a good idea to have a day where people are reminded that no one likes them? Now, maybe you're reading this and thinking, "What's wrong with these girls? I love Valentine's Day!" If you are, then you must be one of those annoying people who ever since third grade have had a steady stream of "Be Mine," "You're the best!" and "I love you!"*

*At the cost of sounding bitter and loserish, we would like to formally register our dissatisfaction with this holiday and, more specifically, the Harmony Falls tradition of buying flowers for people on Valentine's Day. Isn't there a way the student government can make money that doesn't stomp on people's hearts?*

*Don't get us wrong, it's great for those people who get a lot of flowers. What's better than starting off your day with a flower sent by someone who thinks you are flower-worthy? Or you're sitting in a science lab dissecting a frog and in comes someone with that unmistakable sign that you are better than all the other flowerless people sitting around you? On the other side, it's a convenient, low-risk way to say that something special to your latest obsession. Why? Because if they don't like you, they can pretend they never got it, you can pretend that you never sent it—and all is well.*

*That said, come on, people. Are we the only ones who are freaking annoyed at these popularity contests masquerading as fund-raisers? Tell us you aren't irritated when you see* someone walking around with a whole bouquet in their arms.

Now, we know it's not cool to whine and it's important to be "solution-oriented." So we are asking our fellow class members what they think. And if you agree, send us your ideas for replacement fund-raising activities. In the meantime, we're going to Iris's flower store on Commercial Street and buying ourselves a big bunch of roses.

*Nidhi and Charlie*

# CHAPTER TWENTY-FIVE

**IT WAS THE END OF THE THIRD PERIOD. THE SCOREBOARD READ** 54 to 50. Sydney and the four other players jogged off the court and sat on the bench, exhausted. We were up, but it had been going back and forth the whole game.

"This is killing me," Michael said. He cupped his hands around his mouth. "Nidhi! How many fouls does fifteen have?"

"Four!" Nidhi yelled back, from the front bleacher, behind the ref's table.

"Fifteen needs to go. She's been in Sydney's face the whole time."

"Yeah, and look at Sydney. She's fading. I don't know how she's going to make it through the last quarter," I said.

"Yeah, she needs inspiration." He looked around at the mostly empty bleachers. "As soon as they go out again, we have to make some noise."

"I forgot you guys were up here," Nidhi said, walking up the bleachers and sitting down next to us. "I'm sorry, but it's so annoying that this team is doing really well but no one comes to the games. This place will be packed in a little while when the guys play, and the girls' basketball is twelve and two, the boys' team is six and nine."

"I'm here!" Michael protested.

"And I love you for it. But there're forty-three people here. I know. I counted."

"Hey, Michael, you always sit with the most beautiful girls in the room?" said a voice from above us.

"Hey, Dylan," Michael said, grinning at the compliment.

Dylan Vorhees, Sydney's knight in shining armor from the cafeteria, sat down next to me. And I will admit he was super cute—like, in that I-am-so-much-older-than-you-I-live-in-a-completely-different-world way some guys had.

Unfortunately, Matt was right behind him.

"Hey, my favorite freshmeat!"

"Hi, Matt," I said, trying to show absolutely no enthusiasm. It suddenly dawned on me that I'd never seen Matt without Dylan or Ashleigh. Did Matt have some separation anxiety thing like little kids have with their security blankets?

Matt looked down at Nidhi's writing pad. "What, are you keeping score or something?"

"I've been helping cover games for the *Prowler*."

"Damn! I'll come to the girls' games more often. Can I be your assistant?"

"Thanks, I can manage," Nidhi said, not taking her eyes off the court.

The sound of the buzzer momentarily deafened us.

We all watched Sydney go back out. Within thirty seconds, the other team had scored a three-pointer: 54 to 53. My stomach clenched.

"Go Panthers!" Matt yelled, jumping up so I got a glimpse of his pasty white freckly belly. I shuddered. That was absolutely the most of Matt's body that I ever wanted to see.

"So . . . you're a friend of Sydney's, right?" Dylan said quietly to me.

"Yeah, since the beginning of the year. She was pretty much my first friend here."

Dylan nodded like I had just given him some top-secret information.

"That's cool," he said, watching Sydney run down the court.

"Yeah," I said again. I wanted to say something like, "So, Dylan, you're way into my friend—how does that feel?" But I just concentrated on the game.

For the rest of the quarter, it was pretty funny to see how people would walk into the gym and do a double take when they saw these random freshmen (that would be me, Michael, and Nidhi) sitting with Dylan and Matt. But it made me jumpy. And I wasn't the only one. Michael and Nidhi couldn't act normal either. It was like we couldn't risk being ourselves. So to be safe, we all concentrated on the game.

The other team called a time-out, and that's when Sydney noticed the seating arrangement. Her eyes widened and even though she was sweating, I could see her blush and look away too quickly.

"Does she have any boyfriends I should know about?" Dylan asked.

"Oh . . . countless. There's a waiting list on the weekends,"
I said.

"Really? Like who?" Dylan said. Apparently Dylan was a
very literal thinker.

"Why? Did you want to sign up?" I asked.

Dylan didn't laugh. And I'm sorry, but that was funny.

"No thanks—just curious, but you can tell her I asked."

"Sure," I responded.

"See, what did I tell you. Look at all these people showing
up now for the guys' game!" Nidhi said. She was right. All of
a sudden, the bleachers were filled.

"No offense, but girls' basketball is boring. It's just so
slow," Dylan said matter-of-factly.

Nidhi stared at him, a moment away from debating him.

"Relax," Dylan said, seeing Nidhi's face. "It's not my fault
that girls are never going to be as fast as guys."

Sydney scored and the whole place erupted in cheers. The
score was now 56 to 53 with one minute left in the game. I bit
my nails until the buzzer sounded and we won.

"Looks like Syd got her inspiration," Michael whispered
to me.

For a second, I didn't know what Michael was talking about
and then I realized how obvious it was. He was sitting right
next to me.

"Edwards! Wickam!" Dylan called out, raising his arm.

"Hey," Will said, his eyes skipping over all of us like he was
approaching a potentially dangerous animal. Tyler was right
behind him.

"Just getting to know your friends a little better," Dylan
said, grinning. "Guys, I just got an idea. Come with me for a

second." Dylan got up and put his arm around each of them and walked up the bleachers.

I looked at Michael, hoping he knew what was going on. But all he did was shrug.

The players shook hands and then I assumed Sydney would come hang out with us like she always did, but she didn't. She wouldn't even glance over in our direction.

I watched Dylan laugh and Tyler and Will walk alongside the court and then walk up the bleachers to our right.

"You have no idea what they are doing?" I whispered to Michael.

He shook his head.

Tyler and Will approached a group of students and then sat down next to a girl. Wait, let me clarify, two extremely pretty girls. Will was talking to one who had gorgeous long brown hair. And not just talking. He had changed into a younger version of Dylan. He kept brushing his hair out of his eyes and staring at the girl. OMG . . . Will was flirting. I'd never seen him like this.

Five minutes later, Will returned with a hugely annoying grin on his face. I hated that grin.

"Are they coming?" Dylan asked.

"Yeah," Will said.

"Well done, Edwards. You can thank me now," Dylan said.

# CHAPTER
# TWENTY-SIX

**"HAVE A GOOD TIME AT THE GAME?" I ASKED, NOT BOTHERING**
to say hi when he answered his phone.

"What are you talking about?" Will said, knowing EX-
ACTLY what I was talking about.

"Going over to those girls? What was going on?"

"It's nothing. The lacrosse team has a party in a couple of
weeks. Tyler and I invited those girls."

"But do you even know them?"

"Now I do. The girl I'm taking is Barbara. She has Spanish
with Tyler."

"Seriously? Her name is Barbara? What is she, fifty?"

"What's wrong with Barbara?" Will said defensively.

"Nothing, it just sounds like an old woman who crochets,"
I said.

"Well, she's not, and the party's just this thing the team
does every year."

"That's really weird."

"Why? She's totally hot! And it's way better than what they made us do last time."

"What did they do to you? Pour ketchup on your head?"

"No, ketchup and hot sauce was the first week. Actually, maybe I shouldn't be talking about this," Will said, suddenly hesitating.

"Will, why not? This is me, remember?"

"I know but—"

"Come on, you know I won't tell anyone," I insisted.

"We went on a scavenger hunt."

"Excuse me?" That was probably the last thing I thought he'd say. Lighting something on fire? Sure. Memorizing some secret handshake? Okay.

"So what did you have to get?"

"Lots of things. A napkin from a bar signed by the hostess, a condom out of a men's room, a six-pack of beer. Things like that. Then we had to get into these really dirty old clothes and beg for money on the street."

"You can't be serious! You had to beg for money?"

"Pretty much."

"Where? Because I'm not really seeing you doing this in Harmony Falls."

"Yeah, right. They took us to some super sketchy part of the city and left us there—after they took pictures of us. Actually, first we had to go to a park where a lot of homeless people hang out and yell, 'Get a job!'"

"There's no way that's true," I said. And I meant it. I really couldn't believe what Will was telling me.

"Totally true. It was sort of funny. They were screaming all sorts of stupid things back at us."

"Will, there's nothing remotely funny about that," I said, disgusted.

"I knew I shouldn't have told you!"

"I'm not going to tell anyone, but you promised me that if it got too crazy you would stop."

"Charlie, it's not like they're beating me up or making me drink poison or anything."

"But does it have to get that intense for you to think that?" What was wrong with boys? Why do they think this way?

"Well . . . yeah. I don't need you to freak out about this. It's not that big a deal. I got through it, didn't I? The only thing left is this party where I have to hang out with this hot girl. Why would I quit now, when it's almost over?"

"Whatever, but I don't understand how any of this will make you a better lacrosse player."

"I just have to pay my dues. Can we stop talking about this now?" Will whined.

"Fine." I grumbled, wanting to say about a million things more about "Barbara" and how stupid the whole thing was. But whatever. Will could do what he wanted.

I hung up. Okay, clearly these guys were complete jackasses, but I had to admit Will was right—in a way. They weren't beating him and they hadn't made him drink until he had to get his stomach pumped. But at the same time, I couldn't believe Will was buying into all of this. I had a sinking feeling that he wasn't finished paying his dues. And I had learned by now to pay attention to those feelings.

# CHAPTER TWENTY-SEVEN

**TWO WEEKS LATER, IT WAS ONE OF THOSE RARE SATURDAY** afternoons when I had the house to myself; my parents were running errands, and Luke was at an all-day welding class. All I wanted to do was hang out in my room and read *A Complicated Kindness*, which wasn't even for school.

I was fully engrossed in chapter two when Sydney's ringtone brought me back to reality. "What's up?" I said, rolling over on to my back.

"Whatareyoudoingtonight?" Sydney blurted into the phone.

"I don't even get a hello?"

"Sorry. . . . Let me start again. Hi, Charlie! By any chance are you available tonight?" she chirped.

"I think so. Why?"

"Dylan Vorhees invited me to a party," she said.

"Dylan . . . ?" I asked, pretending I didn't know who she was talking about.

"Charlie, shut up! You know exactly who he is. He invited me to a lacrosse party."

"A lacrosse party?" I said, my stomach sinking, realizing I knew which lacrosse party this was.

"Come on, not every guy on the team is that bad. Will's on the team, right? Anyway, you have to come with me because I need a wingman."

"But you're going to go off into a corner somewhere and make out while I have to stand there all night and awkwardly pretend to text people so I don't look like a loser."

"That's not true! You can hang out with Will!"

"Yeah, not sure if I really want to do that."

"Oh, right, he's going to be with that girl."

"I don't care. He can hang out with whoever he wants," I said, gritting my teeth. But that wasn't exactly true. The thought of having to see him be so stupid the whole night made me furious.

"Let me call Nidhi. If she'll go, I'll go," I said.

"Nidhi's in Chicago for her cousin's wedding, remember? She won't be home until tomorrow morning."

"Damn, that's right. So when did Dylan ask you?"

"Yesterday. We've been sort of hanging out recently," Sydney said shyly.

"Really? When? How? Have you been hiding this from me?"

"I haven't been exactly hiding it. We just talk sometimes at night."

"Wait a minute, is Dylan the guy who gave you that Valentine's flower?"

"Maybe."

"You really like him, don't you?" I said.

"I do *not* like him. I'm just sick of always doing the same thing on weekends," she said flippantly. "I mean, how many times can a person be expected to eat at Five Guys and see bad Adam Sandler movies?"

She was lying.

I knew it, and she knew I knew it. But she was my friend and unconditional friendship included throwing yourself into potentially mind-blowingly stupid situations.

"Okay, I'll go under two conditions," I said, sitting up and looking at myself in the mirror. If my hair was any indication, going to this party meant doing some major damage control.

"Anything you say. Just name it!" she squealed.

"First off, stop squealing. You're freaking me out. Second, maximum time you're allowed to disappear with this guy is thirty minutes."

"Got it."

"Third, anybody, meaning Tyler, gets in your face, you can't flip out on them. No Girl Scouting."

"Absolutely. I'll control myself, no problem. But that's three things."

"Asking you to stop squealing didn't count."

"Okay, fine. . . . So you're coming?" she said breathlessly.

"When should I come over?"

"YES!" she yelled over the phone. "Actually, I was kind of hoping he could pick us up at your house and maybe I could spend the night?"

"Why don't you want him picking you up at your house?"

"You know my mom. As soon as she sees Dylan, she won't let me go."

I had to admit she was right. If Heidi took one look at a guy

201

like Dylan, she'd close the door in his face and sit us down for the don't-expect-older-boys-to-respect-you primer, followed by the scare-you-out-of-your-mind pregnancy lecture. Not that that was anything I even remotely needed, but Heidi was inclusive that way.

"Okay, come on over," I said.

"Great! I'll be over at five so we can get ready!" she gushed.

Sydney had never been this freaked out about a guy. Maybe Heidi was right.

Four hours later we ran down the stairs, summoned by a text from "Dylan V."

"Hey, Mom, our ride's here," I called out.

"So where are you going again?" she asked, coming out of the kitchen. I immediately employed Will's name to defuse her suspicion. "Mom . . . remember . . . I told you? It's a party for Will's lacrosse team? I told you Will made varsity, right?"

My strategy worked. Her face relaxed, doubts cleared. "Oh, that's right, I forgot. Your dad and I need to make it to one of his games sometime," she said. "Tell Will we said hi. And you'll be back by eleven, right?"

"Definitely," I said, suddenly wondering if I could convince Dylan to get us home before curfew.

We heard Dylan beep his horn twice. "Bye, Mom," I said, giving her a quick hug.

"Bye, Mrs. Healey!" Sydney called out.

"Be safe!" my mom yelled back.

Outside, a shiny black Jeep Cherokee idled at the side of the curb.

"Hey, beautiful," Dylan said to Sydney as I got into the back-seat, fully embracing my third-wheel status for the evening.

"Hey, Dylan, you remember Charlie, right?" Sydney said.

Dylan stretched his arm over the back of Sydney's seat. "Yeah sure, Sydney told me you write for the *Prowler*?"

"Oh, um, yeah," I stammered, as Dylan put the car into gear and drove down the street.

"So you must know Owen Parker."

"Sure. He writes the op-ed section."

"What a waste. The guy just walked away from the team."

"Well, I'm sure he had his reasons . . ."

But our conversation was over. Dylan blasted the radio, apparently no longer interested in what I had to say.

"This band is the shit! I love this song!" he yelled to Sydney as we sped down a main road heading to Harmony Falls.

The ride was only four ear-shattering songs long, but every time we had to stop Dylan didn't hesitate to try and kiss Sydney. By the time we pulled into the driveway of a big brick house in Harmony Estates, I had already devised a plan to lock myself in a bathroom if this party was even half as awkward as the car ride.

"So whose house is this?" I asked as we walked up a stone pathway leading to the front door.

"Matt Gercheck's," Dylan said.

My head whipped over in Sydney's direction. She pretended not to notice my "are you friggin' kidding me?" face. Any shred of hope I had that this night wouldn't be so bad disintegrated.

"Are Matt's parents here?" I asked.

Dylan nodded as we got to the front door. "Yeah, but the

Gerchecks are really cool. They usually just say hi to everyone and then hang out upstairs all night," he answered, opening the door without even knocking.

"Hey, Mrs. G!" Dylan said to a tiny woman with short blond hair wearing a yellow polo and long khaki shorts. She stood in the enormous kitchen thumbing through a magazine.

She beamed at Dylan when she saw him. "Hi, sweetie! You guys were great today!" Her eyes landed on Sydney and me, and she frowned just slightly before she smiled again.

"Thanks! Mrs. Gercheck, this is Sydney and Kelly."

Fabulous. He had no idea what my name was.

"Everyone's downstairs," she said, completely ignoring Sydney and me. "Paul and I are just going to be up here watching a movie, but let us know if you want any snacks or anything."

"Thanks, Mrs. G."

Dylan led us downstairs into a large rec room that put my basement to shame. As Dylan announced his entry by high-fiving every guy in the room, Sydney and I stood back and looked around. There were about twenty people there, and everyone was drinking. I was confused. Did the Gerchecks really not know what was going on down here? I guess as long as you don't look like an alcoholic drug addict, Matt's parents were completely fine looking the other way, or in this case, not looking down the hall and a flight of stairs.

"You so owe me," I said to Sydney as I absorbed Ashleigh and another girl pretending they had nothing better to do than watch three guys play basketball on a flat screen.

Barbara or no Barbara, I needed to find Will fast. I took out my phone and texted him.

No response, and he was nowhere to be seen. Instead, I saw Tyler playing pool with two idiot giggling girls. Or at least I thought he was playing pool. Mostly he was leaning on the pool stick and telling them how to play.

"You realize my price is going up by the second, right?" I whispered to Sydney.

"Come on, ladies, don't be shy," Dylan said, coming up from behind us. He led us into the center of the room.

"Vorhees!" Matt came sauntering over to Dylan, can of Bud Light in hand. I could see Ashleigh's head snap toward us.

"Hey, Gercheck, can you get these ladies some beverages?"

"Absoluuutely," Matt said, grinning. "Vorhees, what are you having?"

"I'm sticking with water for now. But why don't you get them taken care of? I have to check in with some of the guys for the team-building exercise we're doing later."

"Oh, right! Sure, no problem," Matt said, laughing.

Matt led us down the hall and into his room. The walls were covered in posters of *Sports Illustrated* swimsuit models except one corner, where there was a dartboard and a "beer pong" scorecard. And of course there was a barbell set. Classic.

Matt opened up his closet door and lifted a towel off of a lump in the far right corner. Underneath were three cases of Bud Light on ice and some bottles of Smirnoff Watermelon Ice. He turned toward us and smiled proudly.

"So do you girls drink beer, or am I going to have to convince Ashleigh to let you have some of her girly drinks?"

"Beer's fine," said Sydney, taking one as if all this was totally normal.

"No, thanks. I'll just start off with a Coke," I said.

As I was reaching for my drink, Tyler fell into the room and slammed into the wall, making Sydney almost drop her beer.

"Aw, shit, Gercheck!" Tyler laughed. His face was red and sweaty. "I didn't mean to interrupt your threesome!"

"Dude, Wickam, relax," Matt said.

"I just crusssssshed in pool." Tyler smiled, eyes closed. He stretched both of his arms in the air triumphantly, spilling the remaining contents of whatever was in his red plastic cup onto my hair.

"Tyler!" I shrieked, in a much higher pitch than I meant to.

"Tyler, seriously, check yourself," Matt said, throwing me a towel.

Tyler lumbered over to a bottle of Dr. Pepper and cinnamon schnapps and refilled his cup.

"Why don't you stay and hang out with me while you're drying off?" Matt said. "I want to give you an exclusive interview for your next column."

I had no idea what to say. Was he really doing this in front of my friend while his girlfriend was in the next room? Tyler started laughing and pushed past Sydney and me to go back to the rest of the party. And then, of course, Ashleigh walked through the door.

"Hi, girls," she said flatly. "I'm surprised to see you here." She sat down with Matt on the bed and rubbed his leg to make sure we knew whose property he was. "Baby, can you hand me another Ice?"

Did she seriously think it was necessary to prove that Matt was her territory?

"Hi, Ashleigh," I said. "Sydney and I were just leaving."

"Well, this is off to a good start," I said to Sydney as we walked down the hall.

"I'm so sorry! I can't believe Tyler just spilled his drink all over your hair!" she said, feeling the back of my head. "It's really not that bad, though—you can't even tell unless you're touching it."

"It's okay, I'll live," I said, giving her a weak smile.

Then Sydney leaned in closer and whispered, "So, what do you think of Dylan?"

My eyes quickly scanned the room to where he was sitting on the couch talking animatedly to a group of guys.

"He seems nice enough," I said, knowing that's what Sydney wanted to hear. And I could see why Sydney liked him. In some ways, who wouldn't? He was totally hot and seemed to be in control of everything around him. He didn't seem beyond redemption like Matt, but still there was something about how sure he was of himself that made me distrust him.

"Hey, there you are, beautiful. Are you going to ignore me all night, or what?" Dylan called out to Sydney.

"You go. I'm fine," I said. "I'll try to find Will."

"Are you sure?" she said, smiling.

"Just go!" I said, leaning against the door frame and pulling out my phone to text Will again.

As Sydney walked toward the couch, I noticed four girls off to the side staring at her with full-on hatred in their eyes. As beautiful as Sydney was, watching her in that situation made me wonder if it was worth the attention she got for being so pretty. But I pushed that thought aside and texted Will. Again there was no response. I had no choice but to accept my fate and bore myself to tears by watching some guys play video games at the far end of the den.

As soon as I walked over there, though, I could see why Will wasn't answering any of my texts. He was too busy hanging all over Barbara. Technically, I realized she was hanging all over him, as she was sitting on his lap in a reclining chair.

*OMG!* I thought, shifting my eyes away from them. *I can't be here!* But what exactly was I supposed to do? Was I going to lock myself in a bathroom, or wait outside on the front step until Sydney was ready to go? No, I wasn't. I was going to go play pool with Tyler and his idiot girls—and pretend that recliner didn't exist.

"Charlie!" Tyler smiled happily as he threw his sweaty arms around me in a bear hug.

"Can I play?" I asked, pushing him back so we both wouldn't fall over.

"Sure. You know how?" asked another red-haired guy I hadn't noticed.

"Yeah," I said, taking a pool stick.

"Okay. I'm Alex. You can play with me against Tyler and— what's your name?" he said to one of the drunk girls.

"Kim," the girl said, dissolving into giggles.

Thirty minutes later, Alex and I had beaten Tyler and Kim three times. And it wasn't exactly fun, but I didn't look over at that recliner once. When I finally did, it was empty. Somehow that was worse than seeing them going at it. I needed air.

"I'm going to take a break," I said, handing my stick to Alex.

"Okay, but you're good. If you want to play later, let me know," Alex said.

"Thanks," I said, and opened the French doors that led outside.

There were no lights on the porch when I got outside, so it took my eyes a minute to adjust to the dark. I strained to see, but all I could make out were the silhouettes of four or five people standing in the middle of the yard talking. Then off to the side, I heard a grunt coming from a lawn chair.

"Will?" I said, praying I wouldn't see Will and Barbara totally going at it. I walked closer and was so relieved to only see one body with an arm crooked over his face.

"Hhhhuhhh?" the lump said, as I sat down on the chair next to it and shook him by the shoulder.

"What?" he said, rubbing his eyes. "Oh, heyyyyyy, Charlie!" He grinned. Will leaned over and pulled me into an awkward hug.

"Hey, Will. Where's Barbara?"

"Barbara? Who? Oh, yeah, she's in the bathroom or something," Will said, grinning at me. "I didn't 'spect to see you here—you hate these people," he slurred.

"I don't *hate* anyone," I said, and then reconsidered. "Well, maybe Matt, but that's still a very short list. But you're right. I'm only here because Dylan invited Sydney and she didn't want to go alone."

"Vorhees?" Will looked at me like I had said something in German. "Vorhees has a girlfriend." Will hiccupped loudly. "She's smokin'."

"GIRLFRIEND!" I almost shouted. "Who's his girlfriend? Oh, my God, I have to tell Sydney!"

Will looked alarmed. "No! Sit down!" he said emphatically, leaning forward and holding my shoulders down. "Maybe they broke up. I can't remember. Everything is a bit fuzzy right now, you know? Just stay with me."

I looked him directly in the eye. He hiccupped again. "You better get your information straight, Will Edwards, because I'm not letting my best friend get used."

"I think I got him mixed up with Matt. Mmmatt's the one with the girlfriend." He nodded, assuring himself.

"Yeah, Ashleigh. And she wasn't exactly excited that I'm here," I said.

"Whatever, she sucks," Will said. "She was probably just jealous because you're way hotter. Matt's always bitching about her to everyone because she acts like his wife or something. Don't worry, you're not like that. You would make"—another hiccup—"the best girlfriend ever."

Did he just say what I thought he did? I laughed uneasily. "Whatever. You're just saying that because you're drunk." Will's green eyes were staring at me so hard that I laughed again. "Why are you being so weird?"

"Charlie," he said, taking his free hand and putting it over the top of mine, "you're amazing. You know that, don't you?"

I didn't say anything and kept my body completely still. I didn't know what was happening, but I suddenly didn't want to miss a word Will was saying.

"It's so hard because you've been like, my besssst girl friend since forever. Like, girl that's a friend. Not girlfriend. . . . You know what I mean."

He put his hand on my knee.

"You just don't get it," he said. "You've always been soooo much different."

My heart was pounding a hundred miles an hour. Will looked up at me again and leaned into my chair, kissing my cheek.

"Am I interrupting something?" Sydney said loudly, bringing us back to reality.

"What? No! We were just talking!" I blurted out.

She paused but then shook off whatever thought was in her head. "Whatever you say, but we can talk about that later. Right now we have to go home."

"I have to pee," Will announced, getting up and stretching. He shuffled past Sydney into the house.

"Um, okay," I said, so confused about what had just happened. "Why do you want to go? Is Dylan going to drive us?"

She laughed angrily. "Ha. Not on his life. He's such a loser. Is there any way you could convince Luke to come get us?"

"Luke? He's not going to like it, but I can ask."

"Tell him it's an emergency," Sydney snapped, looking back into the house. Over her shoulder I could see a stunning dark-haired girl all over Dylan.

"What the hell is Dylan doing?" I asked.

"That's Naomi Brewer," Sydney said angrily. "Apparently, she and Dylan were on a 'break,' but I seem to have brought them back together."

"Sydney, I'm so sorry," I said, getting up to hug her.

"Oh, please, whatever—he sucks. I already deleted him from my phone. Just please call Luke."

After about ten minutes of repeatedly dialing Luke's number, he finally picked up.

"Charles, what the hell is with all the phone calls? You better be kidnapped or bleeding."

"Worse. Sydney and I are stuck at a really lame party, and I need you to come get us."

"No way. I'm at Dave's house. Call Mom. I'm not your slave." I could hear the blare of a TV in the background.

"I can't. People are drinking here and I don't want her to freak out."

"Please tell me you're not drunk," he said.

"No, we're not. We just want to leave. It's just one of those typical Harmony Falls parties. The people are terrible." I knew if I played the "Harmony Falls sucks" card he might give in.

He sighed heavily.

"Please," I begged. "I promise to take out the garbage for you for the rest of the month. Just come get us."

"Fine," he said. "Where are you?"

"343 Steeplechase. In the Estates."

"Typical," he snorted.

"Thank you, seriously."

"Meet me out front so I don't have to pull into any driveways," he said and hung up. Before I closed my phone, I noticed I had a text message flashing across my screen. It was Will.

C. hav 2 go, will call u tomorwx.

I smiled to myself and noticed I had goose bumps all over.

"Ready?" I asked Sydney and closed the phone.

Sydney didn't even want to wait inside, so for the next fifteen minutes we waited on the curb outside of Matt's house.

"So what happened in there?"

"I wish I'd never come! Right after you left, Dylan and I were hanging out and everything was fine. That is, until one of Naomi's friends came up to us and asked to speak to Dylan— alone. Fifteen minutes later, he still hadn't come back so I went looking for him. Finally, I asked Matt if he knew where Dylan was. He said he had no idea but to let him know if there was going to be a catfight."

"What?"

"I know. So stupid. Like she had a chance."

We both giggled.

"Anyway, I left Matt talking to some other guy about his favorite 'Girls Gone Wild' scene and decided I needed to go to the bathroom. The next thing I know, I'm surrounded by these senior girls who think they can intimidate me."

"What did they say?"

"I think their exact words were, 'You need something explained to you. You're a freshman. There's only one reason freshman girls ever get invited to parties like this, and it's to be used. You do know that, don't you?'"

"Oh, my God, I don't even want to think about what you said back."

"Charlie, I promised you I wouldn't get into any fights, didn't I?"

"So what did you say?"

"All I said was thanks so much for the advice, but I was using him."

"I'm sure they took that well."

"Yeah, not so much. They pretty much told me it was time to go home, and I told them nothing would make me happier."

"God, why do they care so much?"

She shrugged. "Whatever . . . but you know what the worst part was? Dylan totally saw them go after me and he did nothing about it. He just stood there. I mean, what the hell is his problem?"

Finally the Falcon turned onto the street and stopped in front of us.

"If you're gonna puke, you better not do it in here. I just detailed the car," Luke said, holding a plastic bag.

I threw the bag back at him. "We're not drunk. The party just sucked."

"If you're not drunk, why do you smell like you are?" Luke asked.

"Oh, because some huge loser spilled a drink on my head."

"Nice, Charles!"

"Oh, my God, would you give it a rest please?" I begged.

Sydney climbed into the backseat. "Thanks, Luke. It's totally my fault. The guy I came with turned out to be such an asshole I had to leave before I punched him in the face."

He laughed. "Wow, it was that good, huh?"

"And his ex-girlfriend was being a nightmare. Not that I knew he had a girlfriend, but whatever, it's all good now."

"So, Sydney, am I taking you home, too, or are you coming with Charlie?"

"She's sleeping over, so you only have one place to go," I said.

"Fine, but first I have to get gas."

"Even better, because I have to get to a bathroom immediately," Sydney said.

As Luke put the car in reverse, I looked back at Matt's house. I could see a blue TV light from a room on the other side of the house where I guessed Matt's parents were watching a movie while their son and all his friends got drunk right under their noses.

"You have no idea how much better I feel!" Sydney said, climbing back into the car. "I mean I didn't want to scare you, but it was a close call."

"Sydney, look!" I yelled out, lurching forward.

"What?" Sydney said just in time to see Dylan's black Cherokee drive by. "I wonder if that douche even noticed I was gone," she muttered.

"I think I saw Matt too!"

"That's the guy who invited you?" Luke asked.

"Yes."

"Where do you think they're going?" I whispered.

"Why are you whispering, Charlie? It's not like they can hear you. Why don't we find out? It's not like we have anything better to do, right?"

## CHAPTER TWENTY-EIGHT

**THE JEEP WAS LEAVING HARMONY FALLS. WHEN WE CAME** down the hill before the bridge, I remember thinking how pretty the town looked. The gazebo's lights sparkled on the water, and I could see a big banner announcing the Spring Jazz Festival. But then I felt the Falcon slow down. Ahead, someone was driving a moped with a pizza delivery box attached to the back.

The Jeep rode alongside the moped, and we could see that it wasn't just Matt in the car with Dylan. First I saw a fire extinguisher and then I saw Tyler lean out of the window with it. He sprayed the guy on the moped in the chest. This white foamy powder was all over the guy. I'll never forget seeing Tyler's face as he laughed and yelled, "Go! Go! Go!" In the next instant, everything went into slow motion as the pizza guy grabbed the open window of the now accelerating Jeep to steady himself. Tyler's face changed to shock and then horror as the driver was pulled further off balance and then thrown off his moped, disappearing down the embankment. The Jeep slammed on its brakes as Tyler and Matt stuck their heads out of the car, looking back where the driver fell. I kept waiting for them to get out of the car but they didn't. They just sat there for a few more seconds and then the Jeep gunned the engine and sped away.

"Those assholes! Luke, stop the car! Stop the car!" I screamed.

"I am! I am!" Luke yelled.

"Oh, my God, what if he's dead? What if he's in the water and he can't swim?" Sydney cried.

Even in the semidarkness I could see that Luke's hands were white from clenching the steering wheel. He stopped at the side of the road and grabbed a flashlight out of the glove compartment.

"Charlie, call an ambulance!" Luke said, opening the door.

"I'll call," said Sydney. I could see her hands shake as she pulled out the cell phone.

"Charlie and I will go down and try to find him," Luke said.

"I'm right behind you," Sydney said, as she put the phone to her ear.

Our feet crunched on the gravel as we raced down the embankment. I could feel my heart pounding in my chest as I tried to focus my eyes on any spots where the guy could have landed. The drop wasn't that steep, maybe six feet, but it was covered in rocks until the water's edge. I listened to the lapping of the water. Usually that sound calmed me. Now I looked at the dark water and was terrified.

Luke aimed a flashlight beam on the water. "Can you see anything?"

I shook my head. "No, it's too dark."

We slowly scrambled along the rocks.

"Hello! Hello!" I yelled. "Are you here?"

Silence.

I yelled again.

Ahead of us something moved. "Luke! Shine the flashlight over there," I said, pointing near the water.

"I see him!" yelled Luke.

The guy was lying on the ground and his head was bleeding.

"Ayúdame . . . mi pierna . . . mi cabeza," he groaned.

Luke pushed me forward. "Is he speaking Spanish? Charlie, speak Spanish to him."

"Right." I reminded myself, "I speak Spanish." I bent down so I was kneeling at his side.

"Hola . . . cómo me llamas?"

"Qué?" He looked at me like I was crazy.

"Cómo me llama?" I said, desperately trying to remember the most basic thing ever in Spanish.

Sydney leaned over. "I think you just asked him what your name was."

I nodded, right. I took a deep breath and mentally went through the conjugation chart in my head.

"Cómo te llamas?" I tried, hoping I had gotten it right.

"Carlos, Carlos Salinas."

"Yo soy Charlie. Are you okay? I mean, estás bien?" I asked.

"Ayúdame, mi pierna, no puedo movar mi peirna," he pleaded.

I forced my brain to try and understand him. "I got it! His leg, he can't move his leg!"

"Y mi pierna. Me quema . . ." He grimaced as he clutched his leg.

"I think he's saying it burns."

"Ask him if he can get up," said Luke.

"Puedes caminar?" I asked hesitantly, hoping I got the right word for "walk."

"No. No." He grimaced.

"We're not going to be able to get him up to the road by ourselves. Sydney, how long do you think it'll take for the ambulance to come?" I asked.

"They said they were on their way," Sydney said, looked up the embankment.

"Okay . . . Sydney, Charlie, we need to talk . . . over here," Luke said, gesturing away from Mr. Salinas.

"Look, he's going to be fine. When the ambulance gets here they're going to ask us what we saw," Luke said.

"What do you mean?" I asked, bewildered.

"Look, I hate those guys as much as you do, but I think we should just get this guy help and leave it," Luke said.

"Luke, I don't get it. Why wouldn't you want to tell who did this?" I said, unbelievably confused.

"Because it won't matter. They won't get in trouble. Somehow they'll get out of it."

"That makes no sense. They just ran someone off the road," Sydney cried.

"Trust me. The less involved we are the better. We'll tell them we saw the pizza box and the moped in the street and got out to look."

"That's just wrong," I said.

"Charlie, I know these guys and I know the police. Matt and Dylan have been getting away with this crap forever. Nothing we're going to do is going to make a difference."

"I don't understand. You're talking like you know them."

"I do. And I know their parents will do whatever it takes to cover their asses. Look, just trust me. After the guy gets to the hospital, he'll be fine. We already did the right thing."

My thoughts swirled around me. Luke hated guys like Matt and Dylan. He should be jumping at the chance to get them in trouble, so why did he want to cover for them? The whole thing made no sense.

A few minutes later, we heard sirens. I looked down at the guy and smiled. "Ambulancia?" The ambulance lights reflected off the water.

"Here they are," said Luke, pointing at us.

A man with a big box kneeled down and put his hand on my shoulder. "We got it from here."

"He only speaks Spanish. I only understand a little, but he said his leg was hurting him and something burns."

Immediately the other paramedic bent down near the guy and said, "Señor, soy Officer Garcia. Entiendes? Somos los paramédicos. . . ."

We stepped out of the way while they took out their medical supplies and got to work. Feeling like we were no longer needed, we slowly climbed up the rocks to the road.

• • •

It seemed like it took forever, but they finally brought him up in a yellow stretcher and put him into the ambulance.

The Spanish-speaking paramedic put his gear back and walked over to us. "You guys did a good thing tonight. He's going to be fine, but if you hadn't seen him, it could have been way worse." He looked at each of us one at a time. "So did you see what happened?"

Luke shook his head. "I picked up my sister and her friend from a movie and on the way back home we saw the pizza box. When we got out, I saw the moped."

Officer Garcia handed each of us a card and said, "Well, usually the police come out to something like this, but there was a big accident on the highway an hour ago and every-body's tied up. It's pretty late. You all heading home?"

We nodded.

"Drive home safe," he said, climbing into the back of the ambulance.

"Don't worry. We've seen enough for one night," I said.


What made them think it would be funny to hurt some-one? Did they really not care that they could have killed that guy?

I shook my head thinking about Tyler. Sydney was so right. He was desperate to please those guys. Everything he did was about getting those boys to respect him. How could he not see that they'd never respect him? They had him wrapped around their finger.

Tyler was like me last year with Lauren and Ally. I mean,

really, what was the difference? That we were girls and Tyler and those idiots were guys? That I was in eighth grade and Tyler was in high school? It was all the same.

My rage choked my words. "I . . . I . . . how could they think . . . they could get away with that?"

"They just do," said Luke, staring hard ahead at the road.

"Do you think Will was in the car? Oh, my God, Sydney, remember Dylan said something about not drinking because they were doing some team-building thing? Do you think that was it?"

"Could be. I wouldn't put it past them," Sydney said.

"But, Charlie, why would Will be in the car?" Luke asked.

"Because he made varsity a little while ago. They've been making him do tons of stupid stuff. But nothing like trying to run someone over," I said, my stomach clenching. "Will promised me he wasn't going to let this get out of hand. I hope he meant it."

We weren't ready to go home just yet, so we stopped at Wendy's, the only place that was open that time of night. If we had been thinking clearly, we would have realized that everyone who was out that night would be going there too.

We pulled into the parking lot, and I saw the black Cherokee Jeep. The back door was opened and Matt and Dylan were both sitting on its edge with takeout trays between them stuffing their faces. I couldn't believe it. They had practically just killed somebody for fun, and now they were just sitting there having a late night snack like it was no big deal?

I walked right over to them.

"Hi Dylan. Just getting something to eat after your little team-building exercise?" I said.

Dylan's face contorted in shock. For a brief moment, the cockiness was gone.

"What are you doing here, Charlie?" Matt asked, staring at his fries as he spoke.

I heard footsteps behind me.

"Hey, Matt, Dylan," Luke said in deadly calm.

"Luke Healey? Haven't seen you in a while. Is that your car?"

Luke ignored the question.

"So how do you know these two?" Dylan asked.

"Charlie's my sister. I just picked them up at Matt's house because they were bored out of their minds. Had to take a little detour though to help someone who had been run off the road," Luke said, steadily. ·

Matt quickly reached for his drink, knocking it over.

"Damn it! Gercheck! Now you spilled Coke all over the interior!" Dylan yelled, grabbing napkins and throwing them at Matt.

"Sorry! Sorry!" Matt said, hurriedly putting the ice cubes back in the cup.

Luke crossed his arms and shook his head. "Charlie, you see why I don't let you drink or eat in the car? Sorry, man," Luke said to Dylan. "I just got mine detailed, I feel your pain."

Dylan hesitated, trying to figure out if Luke was making fun of him. "So . . . that motorcycle thing sounds bad, anybody get hurt?" he asked, smoothly. His arrogance recovered.

"Why would you care?" I asked.

Dylan ignored me.

"Strange you didn't see it. It was right on the way. The guy's going to the hospital right now. He's hurt but he'll live," Luke said.

"That's good," Dylan said.

"Yeah, especially for the person who ran him over. Hard to imagine who could be such a dick that they would run someone off the road and run away. . . ." Luke said.

"Hey, what are you guys doing here?" Will asked as he crossed the parking lot. His words were coming out thick and slow. Clearly, he was still drunk—but not nearly as bad as Tyler, who stumbled out from behind the bushes.

Dylan leaned over and said, "Wickam, stop being such a tool. I'm not covering for you if a cop drives by."

Tyler groaned, turned back to the bushes, and threw up.

I was not going to stand there and be ignored. "Yeah, I bet you don't want any police coming around right now," I hissed.

Matt laughed nervously. "Healey, seriously, you need to get your sister under control."

Will picked his head up, looked over at Luke and then back to me and Sydney, who I just realized had been standing there the whole time.

"How do you know what happened? It was an accident. I swear, an accident," Will mumbled.

"Shut up, Edwards. We'll handle this," Dylan said, slowly taking a sip from his drink. "Apparently she thinks we had something to do with that guy being hit. Charlie, I think you're getting us confused with someone else. There are tons of people who drive Jeeps."

"You think you're going to get away with this?" I said, trying desperately to keep my voice from shaking.

"What I'm saying is that it's dangerous to throw around accusations when you can't back them up," Dylan said.

"Are you threatening me?" I asked, my heart pounding against my chest.

Luke quietly stepped forward, stopping short about two feet in front of him. "No. Dylan's not threatening you, Charlie. Because if he is, he knows I will destroy him. Isn't that right, Dylan?"

I turned and looked at Luke in shock.

Dylan put his arms up and then slid them into his pockets. "Hey, no one is threatening anyone. I'm just sitting here eating my burger, minding my own business," Dylan said.

I couldn't stand any of this one more second. "Will, come home with us," I pleaded.

Dylan stood up and closed the back of the car. "Hey, Will, if you want to go home with them, don't let us stop you."

"Come on, Will," I pleaded again.

"Charlie, don't worry about me. I'm fine," Will said.

"Why do you want to go back with them?" I asked, incredulous.

"I'm fine. Seriously. I can't go home. Parents will see. Can't go home now."

Luke put his hand on my shoulder. "Charlie, leave it. But Will, if you need anything, call okay?"

"Sure, sure. Don't worry, I'll be fine," Will said.

"Will . . ." But even as I said it I knew it was hopeless.

"You should listen to your brother, Charlie," Dylan said. *Well,* I thought, *at least the jerk finally got my name right.*

Sydney, Luke, and I walked back to the Falcon, and all I could think was, *I can't let them get away with this. I just can't.*

I opened the door. My cell phone was on the seat. The Jeep was parked in front of me. I wasn't sure exactly what I wanted to do with it, but as Luke pulled away, I took a picture of Dylan's license plate. "Let's go home," I said.

# CHAPTER
# TWENTY-NINE

**"SO, YOU GOING TO TELL ME HOW YOU KNOW MATT AND** Dylan?" I asked as I sat down on Luke's bed.

"I think I first had the pleasure of their company at hockey camp. Seventh grade," he said, never looking up from the book he was reading.

"What did they do?" I prodded.

Luke shrugged. "The usual 'You're gay and retarded' comments. They were relentless. We were constantly getting into fights. Then one day Matt went after another kid on the team and just wouldn't stop."

"What happened?"

"We got into it pretty bad. I pretty much rearranged his face. I got blamed for it, so I was kicked off the team."

"Oh yeah! I remember that! What did Mom and Dad do?"

"I don't know. I got punished."

"Didn't you tell Mom and Dad that it wasn't your fault?" I asked.

"Sort of, but I was getting into so much trouble back then that they really didn't want to hear it. Plus, Matt's parents threw a fit. The coaches took his side."

"God, that's so unfair!" I said.

Luke finally closed the book and put it on his bedside table. "Who do you think was one of the coaches?"

I looked at him blankly.

"It was Matt's dad. And he didn't care what the other kids said Matt was doing. He said that since he didn't see Matt do anything, you couldn't prove who was to blame."

"What, like the only way a kid like that can get in trouble is if he's stupid enough to do it front of the adults? That's crazy."

"That's the thing, Charlie. Some adults only see what they want to see. The sooner you realize that, the better. And I wouldn't tell you to keep quiet just because I had some fight with him when I was a kid. Matt and Dylan do messed-up stuff all the time and they still get away with it. Last year, Matt drove down a street with a baseball bat and smashed a bunch of car windows. When school started this year, Dylan's parents let them have a party at their house. Dylan left, totally drunk, to pick someone up and bring them back to the party and ended up crashing his car into a tree in the front lawn of the house. When the police came his parents denied they knew anything about the party and all Dylan ended up getting was community service at his church. A couple of months later, both of them went to a party and started shit with me and some guys I know. All they got was more bullshit community service. So the thing you should be taking away from this is they do whatever they want and their parents bail them out."

"And that's why you didn't want us to report it?"

"Exactly. And look, we got the guy help. That was the most important thing, don't you think?"

"But it just seems so wrong to let them get away with it!"

"Can we talk about how unfair the world is tomorrow? Because right now I'm beat."

I got up and threw him the pillow I was leaning on. "Sure. But one more thing."

"What?" he said impatiently.

"Thanks for coming to get us. And that whole big-brother-I'm-going-to-kick-your-ass-if-you-mess-with-my-sister thing was pretty amazing."

"No problem. I live for bailing you out of trouble although you could have taken them if you really wanted to," Luke said, reaching over to his lamp. "Now, please leave so I can go to bed." He turned out the light.

## CHAPTER THIRTY

**"CHARLIE! DO YOU WANT BREAKFAST?" MY MOM YELLED UP** to me. I opened my eyes to face the bright sunlight. A groan came through the heap of blankets next to me. A long arm emerged, followed by the most intense bed head I'd ever seen in my life.

"We're sleeeeeeping!" I whine-yelled as loudly as I could and turned onto my back and put the pillow over my eyes.

"What time is it?" Sydney croaked, sitting up.

"Way too early, but of course my mom thinks she needs to wake us up."

"Oh, my God, Charlie, last night was completely out of control."

"I know."

"We have to tell Nidhi."

I looked over at my desk clock. "It's ten, do you think she's up right now?"

"Who cares? We have to tell her."

She grabbed my cell off my bedside table and hit speed dial.

"This better be important because I got home from my cousin's wedding at three A.M.," Nidhi grumbled over speaker phone.

We told her everything.

"I seriously cannot believe this! And all I did was watch my uncles drink Scotch."

"I know. Crazy, huh?" I said.

"So are you really not going to tell anyone?" Nidhi asked.

Sydney and I looked at each other.

"I don't know. Luke says we got the guy help and we should leave it at that. He told me all these stories about those guys never getting into trouble for anything. It was so intense. He really thinks we should keep quiet. And if we tell, it won't make a difference," I said.

"But we didn't exactly keep quiet. Or at least Charlie didn't," Sydney said, grinning. "It was beautiful. As soon as Charlie saw those guys, she jumped out of the car and totally Girl Scouted them."

"No I didn't," I insisted.

"Charlie, yes you did. Trust me, Nidhi, it was amazing!"

"I just told Dylan he wasn't going to be able to get away with it. Honestly, I don't think I ever wanted to beat anyone up more in my life. But there's sort of one more thing I need to tell you. I mean, it's not nearly as important as this stuff, but it definitely adds to the weirdness factor."

"God, what else could have happened last night?" Nidhi asked.

"Well, after Sydney went off with Dylan—"

"For like two minutes!" Sydney interrupted.

"Whatever, it was more like fifteen, but that's not the point. So I was walking around the party trying to find Will, and I couldn't find him anywhere. I finally went outside and saw him almost completely passed out on a chair. . . ."

I stopped talking. I was now at the part where I had to tell them about Will, and I really didn't want to because then I would have to admit they were right about the whole Will thing, and I wasn't sure how I was feeling about Will anyway at that moment. I just wanted to keep it private—sort of.

"And . . . ," Nidhi said.

"Okay, don't freak out, but I mean this is really weird—"

"What!" yelled Sydney.

"Remember, he was really drunk so maybe he was temporarily insane, but when I sat down next to him, he started babbling about how much I meant to him and it's weird because we grew up together, but he can't help how he feels—"

"I knew it!" Sydney screamed, jumping up and down on the bed.

"Sydney, can you yell that a little louder so my parents can hear you?" I said, grabbing a pillow and throwing it at her.

"Sydney, don't get her off track! Then what happened?" Nidhi asked.

"I was completely in shock. So I'm just staring at him and he leans over and says something about how I'd be an amazing girlfriend and then Sydney burst in."

"I knew something was going on!" Sydney said, raising her arms up in the air again.

"So, Charlie, are you telling me that you're surprised by this?" Nidhi asked.

"Of course I am! In case you've forgotten, this is Will we're talking about!"

"Okay, Charlie, I mean this in the best way, but you're being totally stupid!" Nidhi said.

"Why?"

"Because it's always been obvious that Will likes you! He's just so shy that he had to be drunk to tell you."

"Ughhh! This is so weird!" I said, diving under one of my pillows.

"Charlie, I can barely hear you. You sound like you're under water," Nidhi said impatiently.

"Sorry," I said, removing the pillow. "But you have to admit this is super awkward."

"It's so cute!" Sydney shrieked again.

"For the last time, Sydney, you have to calm down about this."

"So . . . ?" Nidhi said.

"So what?" I asked.

"So do you like him like that?" Sydney asked.

"What am I supposed to think? How could I like him after what happened last night?"

"He was only doing that to be tough in front of all those guys," Sydney said.

"But how pathetic is that? He doesn't even like them. For the last four months, he's been complaining to me about the things he has to put up with to be on the team. And he promised me that nothing would get out of hand. If spraying someone with fire extinguishers and running someone off the road isn't out of hand, I don't know what is," I said.

"I don't think it's really fair to blame him for what happened. Dylan and Matt made him drink all night, and they made him get into that car," Sydney said.

"I seriously doubt they physically forced him into that car. A part of him likes them," I said.

"It's complicated," Nidhi said. "Will's a nice guy, but I agree, it's still pretty bad. Charlie, I think you need to talk to him. See what he says. Maybe from there, you can figure out what to do."

# CHAPTER THIRTY-ONE

**"ANYONE WANT TO HEAR SOMETHING SCREWED UP?" GWO**
asked, entering the newspaper room. The Monday *Prowler*
staff meeting had just started, but we all stopped talking with
that intro.

He grabbed a stool and sat down at the table next to Ms.
McBride. "You know my mom's a nurse, right? Well, some
pizza delivery guy came into the emergency room on Saturday
night because he was run over near the bridge going into town.
And it looks like it was a Harmony Falls student that did it."

I grabbed either side of my chair as hard as I could. I forced
myself to relax and not scream *Oh, my God* to Nidhi, who was
sitting across from me, mouthing *no way*.

"Why do they think it was someone from here?" Josh asked.

Gwo shook his head and took out a huge bottle of
Gatorade from his backpack. "He didn't get the license plate,
but the guy saw a Panther Paw on the back of the car."

"Oh, my God, that's terrible! Is he okay?" Ashleigh asked.

"My mom said he has a really bad broken leg and he's all bruised up. But the weirdest thing was that he was sprayed with a fire extinguisher."

"A fire extinguisher? Seriously?" Josh asked.

Gwo took a big swig from the bottle. "It was totally messed up. My mom said someone sprayed him on purpose. His wife was at the hospital with his three little kids. He kept talking about having to get back to his construction job the next morning because he didn't have insurance and couldn't pay for it. I think my mom had to sedate him or something."

Ashleigh rolled her eyes. "Gwo, people don't run people over and then spray them with a fire extinguisher. It must have been an accident."

Owen rolled his eyes. "Come on, Ashleigh. Are you telling me you don't know anyone at this school capable of doing that?"

Josh looked over at Gwo. "What do you think? Anyone on the football team capable of that level of stupidity?"

Gwo shook his head. "Hell, no, not that I'd tell you, anyway." We all stared at him. "Guys, seriously, no. I could see that happening a couple of years ago, but not anymore. Now, it'd have to be hockey or lacrosse."

"Whoever it was, if they got caught, that's like no joke. That's definitely juvy because it's hit and run. You'd at least get massive community service and probation," Raj said.

Gwo leaned over and asked, "Do you know this because of last year's firecracker incident?"

"That was an accident! We didn't know the field would catch on fire!" Raj said.

"Right, of course, because Roman candles and dry grass are always a great combination!" Gwo laughed.

"Shut up! Anyway, this is different because whoever did this did it on purpose. All I'm saying is that if whoever did it gets caught, they're totally busted," Raj said.

Ms. McBride got up and went to her desk. "Okay, you all. Let's not speculate about anything we really don't know about. We're journalists. If we get more information about the story, then that's different, but for right now, let's just be grateful the guy's alive. So let's get started with our meeting."

Josh got up from his stool and looked at the story schedule posted on the wall. "Raj, you wanted to go first, right?"

Raj opened his computer. "I have to leave early to cover a tennis match, but I want everyone to know that, thanks to Nidhi, we've been able to cover most of the games this season. And our new feature on the coach profiles is also going well." He glanced at the clock and gathered his things into his backpack. "But I've got to go. Girls' softball game," Raj said, rushing out the door.

Ms. McBride started talking about the production schedule, but I couldn't take being in that room one more minute. I quietly excused myself and went to the bathroom.

My steps echoed down the hall as I walked. I wondered if it was possible for a person to pace in their head? Walk back and forth, wearing out the floor in your mind? Because that's what I was doing. It was so frustrating. This last year I had promised myself that I wouldn't stand by when people did bad things. But, another part of my brain couldn't stop arguing that this wasn't my problem. This was Will's mess to fix. But I knew he wasn't going to do it. What was I going to do?

I came back a few minutes later and everyone had spread out to work on their own projects. When Nidhi saw me, she waved me over to the couch.

"Charlie, I totally forgot about this, but do you know who I'm interviewing next week?"

"Who?"

"The lacrosse coach, Coach Mason."

I sat up. "Nidhi, what are you thinking?"

"Well, Ms. McBride told us not to speculate, right? So let's go dig up some facts. Maybe he doesn't know anything about his players' team-building exercises, but maybe he does. You want to find out?"

## CHAPTER THIRTY-TWO

**"I HATE BOYS. I MEAN IT. THEY COMPLETELY SUCK," I SAID,** closing my locker.

"Just so I'm clear, we are talking about Will, right?" asked Sydney.

"Have you noticed he's giving me the silent treatment? It's so completely ridiculous. Every time I see him in the hallway, he looks the other way."

It was Friday, almost a week after the party, and I had been waiting for him to call, email, or text me. And every second that went by without talking to him made me more angry and tense. Not that I would ever admit this out loud, but it was all I thought about.

"Charlie, you can't let him get away with this. You need to step up and take control. So the next time you see him, go up to him and say you need to talk and then force him to do it."

"But I can't force him to talk to me, can I?"

"Of course you can!" Sydney insisted.

I wasn't at all sure that Sydney was right about the forcing part, but I did know that if I didn't talk to him soon, I was going to explode.

Two hours later, I got my chance. There he was, just sitting on the stairs at the end of the freshman hall, laughing his head off with Tyler and some other guys from lacrosse like nothing in the world was bothering him.

"Hey, Will," I said coldly, walking up to him.

"Hey, Will! Look who it is! It's Mrs. Edwards!" one of his lacrosse buddies called out.

My heart leapt in spite of my anger. Maybe they were calling me that because they knew Will liked me?

"Hi, Will, can I talk to you for a minute?"

Will didn't seem to hear me. He pushed his hair out of his face and leaned back further.

"Will, can I talk to you for a minute?" I said more loudly.

"Sure. Go ahead," he said, shrugging.

"I'd like to talk to you alone."

"Maybe later," Will said. "Now is not a good time"

The boys around him snickered and looked away.

Thoughts of liking Will disappeared. I stared at him in disbelief. I had seen that combination of arrogance, rudeness, and indifference before. He had become a mini-Matt right before my eyes. My chest tightened as I fought back tears. I couldn't believe he would treat me like this. Not Will.

"Okay, whatever, I'll catch up with you later," I said, hearing my voice begin to catch. I had to get away from these boys as soon as possible.

I walked down the hall a few feet, but from behind me I still heard one of the boys call out, "Hey!" I turned around without thinking, something no one should ever do when walking away from a group of guys. "Go make me a sandwich!" he yelled and then all the boys laughed again, including Will.

I stared at the boy, completely confused. Make him a sandwich? What did that mean? All I could do was stand there feeling unbelievably stupid.

The rest of the afternoon went by in a blur. I longed to go home, be miserable by myself, and think about what to do. By five, I had been fantasizing for two hours about all the things I wanted to say to Will to make him truly feel like the little insignificant speck that he was.

At five thirty, I was at Will's door.

"Hi, Mrs. Edwards, is Will home?" I asked sweetly, hiding my anger behind my smile.

"Hi, Charlie! He just got back from practice. I think he's in his room."

"Can I go upstairs?"

"Of course!"

My heart was pounding as I walked up the stairs to his room. His door was open.

"Hey," I said casually.

He looked up from a comic book he was reading. "I thought I heard you come in," he said flatly.

"You owe me an explanation."

"About what?" Will said, picking up his phone and playing a game.

"What do you mean about what? Obviously, you're mad at me, which is pretty stupid because if anyone should be mad at anyone, I should be mad at you."

"Right . . . you should be mad at me. Yeah, Charlie, you're completely right. I'm the one who's completely in the wrong here," he said.

"I'm sorry, is 'make me a sandwich' a new way to say 'I'm so sorry for being such a tool'?"

"I knew you would totally blow that out of proportion. But if that's what you came over here to say, you've said it. . . ." He went back to reading his comic book.

That was it. I wasn't leaving until I forced him to deal. I didn't care how long it took or how pathetic he thought I was, I wasn't going to budge.

"Will, you and I are going to talk, whether you like it or not."

He closed the book. "Fine. But not here."

Will got up, grabbed a baseball hat, and put it firmly on his head. "Mom! I'm going out for a little while," he yelled as he walked by me and down the stairs.

"Okay, but be back in an hour for dinner. Charlie, you want to eat with us tonight?"

Somehow I didn't think I was invited. "Thanks, but I promised my mom I'd be home for dinner," I said, following Will out of the house.

For three blocks, we didn't say a word to each other, then we got to a playground near his house.

"So why am I here?" Will said, sitting down on the bottom of a slide.

"You can't be serious," I said, flabbergasted. He was treating me like we barely knew each other. Like I was this crazy girl who was making some kind of unreasonable demand to even be talking to him.

"What? I don't even know why I'm here," Will continued.

"Excuse me?" Even after the silent treatment and how horrible he had been to me the last few days, I was still shocked. I still thought I was going to get something like "Charlie, I'm so sorry for being such a pathetic loser. I was totally wrong." But these things never work out the way you play them out in your head. Not even close.

"You heard me."

"Well, for starters, I want to know why you're avoiding me."

"I'm not avoiding you. You're being dramatic."

"I'm being dramatic? You're giving me the silent treatment and being an unbelievable jerk every time I see you, and I'm the one who's being dramatic? Are you on some kind of weird hallucinogenic drug that's making you see everything backward?"

Will crossed his arms and said nothing.

"Just admit that since Saturday night, you have been a complete jerk."

"What did you expect? That I would come crying to you for help?"

"I'm not that stupid, Will." Although as soon as he said that, I realized that's exactly what I wanted to happen.

"What the hell were you thinking? Following us? Begging me to go home with you on Saturday night? Were you trying to make my life more difficult?"

I walked a few feet away from him so I could squash my overwhelming desire to strangle him.

"I didn't realize offering you a ride when you're completely drunk surrounded by arrogant, useless assholes was so unforgivable. Believe me, next time I see you with your douche-bag friends, I'll completely ignore you."

"Excellent."

"You have got to be joking with this."

"Charlie, you were like my mom out there. It was totally embarrassing. Now whenever my friends see you, they call you Mrs. Edwards."

I paused to fully absorb my embarrassment, realizing how completely I had misinterpreted that.

"You know what's worse? Watching you turn into a mini-Matt."

"You have no idea what you're talking about," he said, turning his face away from me.

"Really? It certainly looks like that to me. But maybe you've forgotten that you've been screaming at homeless people to get a job and you almost killed someone Saturday night?"

That shut him up. Finally.

He leaned back on the slide, his arm resting across his eyes.

I heard a giggle and looked up to see two kids at the top of the slide, bouncing up and down waiting for Will to get up.

"Will, you have to move or you're going to be run over by some five-year-olds. Not that you don't deserve it."

He turned around and looked up. "Very funny," he said and shuffled over to the nearest bench.

He sat there, legs crossed straight out and arms folded. "I thought Luke said the guy was fine. . . ."

I was tempted to tell him Mr. Salinas had died, but I told him the truth. "He'll live, but he broke his leg badly. The worst is that he has no insurance, so he can't pay for the hospital and he'll probably lose his construction job. He has three little kids, by the way. . . ."

Will closed his eyes again. For a few minutes he was gone, lost in his own thoughts. Then he drew his legs in, rested his elbows on his knees, and dropped his head so I couldn't see his face.

"Things have just gotten so out of control. Charlie, you don't understand. I didn't have a choice. It's not like I wanted to be in that car," he mumbled.

"Will, what are you saying? Don't you remember what you said after the basketball game? You said that I shouldn't worry because all this stuff with the lacrosse team wouldn't ever get out of hand. Don't you think this qualifies?"

"They kept telling us all this stuff was almost over, but it just kept coming."

I looked back over at the kids playing on the slides and thought about how much easier things had been when we were little. Now in comparison, all that drama with Lauren and Ally seemed like nothing.

"Okay, maybe I don't get it. But why should Mr. Salinas have to pay the price for your decisions? It's not fair. He's hurt, and you're not. He's the one who will lose his job because he can't work. He's the one who has to pay. You get to wake up in the morning and go school like nothing ever happened."

Will ran his hands through his hair, and I thought I saw his green eyes well with tears. But the next second, he had brushed them away and it was as if they had never been there.

"Will, those guys are completely controlling you. And you're turning into them. I hate it."

"You think I like this?"

"I don't know. Do you?"

"Shit, Charlie. You know me better than anyone. . . . You know I hate all of this, don't you?"

"Will, sometimes you're completely tolerable. Other times—"

"I'm the biggest dick you know, right?" he asked miserably.

"Well, not the biggest, but close. I don't think you've totally gone over to the dark side yet," I said.

He looked away and then dropped his head again. "Look, I'm sorry about the last couple of days."

I exhaled with relief. "And I'm sorry about the mom thing. I didn't have a clue that's the way it looked. I just wanted you to get away from those guys."

We sat there side by side in silence for a minute.

"So what are you going to do?" I asked gently.

"What do you mean?"

"Don't you think you should tell someone?"

"Who? Like my coach?"

"Sure."

"I don't know. He's new, but he has to know. It's been going on forever. Since Saturday night I've thought about talking to him a hundred times, but I don't know. I guess it's because I'd really like to live, you know, past this year. I just need to get through the season and then it'll be some other freshman's problem."

"They run over people with fire extinguishers every year?" For some reason, this thought had never occurred to me, even though this is exactly what Michael had told me.

"No, don't be stupid. They don't do the exact same thing every year, but more or less, yeah. They treat you like shit and you put up with it until you break."

"How bad would it be if you told? What could Matt and Dylan do to you?"

"Charlie, I don't even want to think about it. If I snitch, I may as well leave the school."

"Okay, but what about Wickam? I know he's totally fake, but won't he care at least a little bit because Tyler's involved?"

Will laughed bitterly. "You don't think Wickam knows what Matt and those guys do? As long as they win, he looks the other way. Who do you think encourages Tyler to be on the team?"

"But it's his kid."

"Trust me, all Wickam cares about is doing whatever it takes to make him look good. Tyler told me he wants to run for superintendent or something."

"Damn, this is complicated."

He nodded. "It's not like I don't know what to do. I know the right thing is to tell, but I just can't. If somehow it could just stop. . . . I don't know, but, Charlie, please don't think I'm turning into Matt."

"I don't. I just wish there was some way I could help you."

"Thanks, but it'll be fine. Anyway, I should be getting back. You want to stay for dinner?"

"Sure, but only on one condition."

"What?" Will asked.

"Are you going to make me a sandwich?" I said, giggling.

"Ha-ha! Very funny but I guess I deserved that," Will said pushing into me.

"Totally."

Now that Will and I had worked things out, I should have

slept easier that night. And I did, sort of. But it still really bothered me that Will was going to let Dylan and Matt get away with everything they had done—to him, to the delivery guy, to next year's freshmen. I just couldn't get it out of my head.

## CHAPTER THIRTY-THREE

**"YOU WANT SOME?" SYDNEY ASKED.**

It was 7:20 A.M. on Monday, and spring had finally committed. Girls already were wearing really short shorts and flip-flops, like it was one hundred degrees, but it couldn't have been more than sixty-five. Even though I had a lot on my mind, it all seemed easier and better outside in the sun with Sydney before the first-period bell rang.

I took the iced double caramel macchiato out of Sydney's hand and had a sip. "You are so addicted to these," I said, immediately feeling the caffeine and sugar buzz.

"I know. My mom says that if I saved all the money I spend on these, I could buy a car. Not that she'd ever let me have a car anyway. . . ."

"What's up? Why the urgent must-talk-before-school text?" Nidhi said, walking up from behind us.

I scanned the front entrance to make sure no one was

listening. "I've been thinking a lot about what happened, and we can't just let Matt and Dylan get away with this."

"Me too! Every time I think about them, I get so angry I want to explode," Sydney said, wiping the whipped cream from her mouth.

"Well, whatever we do, we have to be smart about it. Charlie and I can find out what the lacrosse coach knows when we interview him," Nidhi said.

"How is that not going to be incredibly obvious?" Sydney asked.

"I have to write a short profile on him," Nidhi said. "We just thought that maybe we could use the opportunity to ask a few more questions—"

"Maybe this is crazy, but what do you think about telling Ms. Fieldston? She's always telling us to go to her for help if we have a problem," Sydney asked tentatively.

"I don't know. After what she allowed to happen to you in history class, do you think she can be trusted?" Nidhi said.

"Since then she's been pretty cool," Sydney said.

"Well she shouldn't have to tell who told her. Unless you're in imminent danger, you can be anonymous."

"What the hell does 'imminent danger' mean, and how do you know this stuff?" Sydney asked.

"Because I read it in the student manual. And imminent danger means you're about to have something really bad happen to you, like if you just swallowed a bottle of Valium or your parents are abusive. Then she has to say it's you. Other than that, she can report the information but not say who she heard about it from," Nidhi said.

"Nidhi, you realize you're a bit of a freak, don't you?" I said.

She nodded. "But it comes in handy, doesn't it? So, Charlie, you really think Will isn't going to talk?"

"No way. He's terrified of what Dylan and Matt would do to him," I said.

"Yeah," said Nidhi. "They'd have to put him into a hazing protection program."

"Very funny. But he is acting like they have some kind of superpower control over him. Honestly, this may seem weird, but I think it's like the kind of power Lauren and Ally had over me. Every time I thought about standing up to them, I just couldn't imagine it. All I could think about was all the ways they would make my life miserable," I said.

"Well, then, obviously, the boy needs our help. Plus, Charlie's right. Those boys have to learn their lesson, and they aren't going to if people continue to let them do whatever they want and say nothing about it," Sydney said.

Nidhi tossed her bag over her shoulder. "I agree. So the plan is we go to Ms. Fieldston as soon as we can. In the meantime, Charlie and I will see what we can learn from Coach Mason."

## CHAPTER THIRTY-FOUR

"HI, COACH MASON, I'M NIDHI PATEL, REMEMBER? READY FOR your interview?" Nidhi said as we hovered outside his office.

Coach Mason stood up and smiled widely. "Of course, come on in!" he said, getting up.

At first glance I was surprised. He wasn't wearing a Harmony Falls lacrosse jacket or anything else Harmony Falls, for that matter. Instead, he was wearing perfectly ironed khaki pants, Merrill shoes, and a white button-down shirt.

"This is my friend Charlie. We're both assisting on the coach profiles."

"Hi, Charlie! Well, girls, have a seat. What can I do for you?"

Nidhi beamed a huge smile Coach Mason's way. "Like I said in my email, I just want to ask you a few questions for the profiles we're doing for all the coaches."

"Well, I'm sure mine will be one of the most boring, but I'll try to come up with something interesting."

"Oh, I doubt that," I said, surveying the walls of his office. There were none of the inspirational posters I hated. The only thing I saw were diplomas, a picture of Coach Mason with another guy holding a huge fish, and a poster of a lacrosse team.

Coach Mason's eyes caught mine. "That's the first team I ever coached. Poor guys. We lost almost every game—the parents wanted to kill me."

Nidhi pulled out her notebook. "Well, how about we start with where you grew up and where you went to school?"

"Not much to tell. I grew up in Richmond, Virginia, and went to high school there. After high school I joined the marines and then I went back to college to get my degree."

The marines? That seemed like a bad sign. I imagined the marines were into all different kinds of hazing, and on top of that, he was probably a war freak. Of course he knew. He might even have given Matt and Dylan pointers on what to do. My blood started to boil.

"That's interesting. Why the marines?" I asked.

"I needed the structure in my life. They gave it to me, that's for sure," he said chuckling.

"Did you like it?" asked Nidhi.

"It was good for me, wouldn't trade my experience in the corps for anything. That's not to say I liked everything, but overall it was what I needed at the time."

"So this is your first year at Harmony Falls?" I asked.

"Yep, I coached back East for a few years, but my wife grew up here. Once we had our daughter, she wanted to be closer to her family. She's good friends with Mr. Jaquette, and he's the one who told me about the job opening. So I'm here teaching lacrosse and three health classes."

"I have history with Mr. Jaquette," I said.

"He's the godfather of my daughter, Lucy. Want to see a picture?"

"Sure," we both said. He turned around and took a picture off his bookshelf and passed it to us. There was a sweaty Coach Mason holding a smiling, drooling infant in his arms.

"She'll be a year in two weeks," he said proudly. "That was at the Marine Corps Marathon. I came in right behind a seventy-eight-year-old grandmother."

I had to give it to him. He was charming, but I'd been at Harmony Falls long enough to know better than to trust that.

"Okay, as I said, we don't want to take up too much of your time, so we only have a few more questions. Harmony Falls has a tradition of athletic excellence, and the lacrosse team is no exception. Do you feel any pressure because of that?" Nidhi asked.

He laughed. "Well, I'd be lying to you if I said winning didn't matter to me. I like to win, and so does the rest of the team. But I want my players to be model athletes on and off the field. I know that in the past this team has struggled with its reputation a little bit, and I'd like to improve that."

"Care to elaborate?" I asked casually.

He shrugged. "Unfortunately, lacrosse has gotten a bad rep recently. Some deserved, but most of it not. I want my players to be a positive influence."

"Really? Do you think that's happening?" I said a little too pointedly. No journalistic objectivity there at all.

"I think we're doing better. We have great guys on the team."

"You really think that?" I asked.

"Is there a reason I shouldn't?" Coach Mason had stopped smiling.

"Maybe," Nidhi answered.

I shifted in my seat and tried to keep my eyes from leaving his.

"Is there something you want to tell me?"

"I don't know. There's been some talk of the younger players having to do things. . . ." Nidhi said casually.

Coach Mason leaned forward and put his elbows on the desk. "Like what, exactly?"

I shrugged. "I don't know. Aren't the marines really hard on the recruits?"

"Sometimes, but that's not always a bad thing. Depends on the leader."

"Yeah, I guess it would."

"Well, I would hope if anybody knew anything about my players, that they would tell me about it."

"And then what would you do?" Nidhi asked.

"Is this still part of the interview? This doesn't seem like something you'd put in a little profile."

"No, this is off the record," I said smiling. "We're just curious."

"Well, I would take any potential hazing matter very seriously. My job would be to find out all the facts before anyone is found guilty. Gossip about things like this can destroy someone's future. But why are you asking me these questions?"

We were past the line of what we could get away with. It was time to back off.

"It's just that hazing is such a big issue right now in the

media, so we thought we would ask you what you thought about it," Nidhi said quickly.

"Well, there have been some very unfortunate stories in the news recently. It's sad for everybody when that happens," Coach Mason said.

"Well, we just have one last question," Nidhi said. "Any predictions for how the team will finish the year?"

He leaned back in his chair, and I got the distinctly unpleasant feeling that he was examining us. "I don't like to make predictions, but if we play right, we should have a good chance to win the division."

Nidhi closed her notepad. "Thanks, Coach Mason. I think we've got what we need."


"So what do you think?" Nidhi asked, once the front door of the athletic building closed behind us.

"He knows. I mean, he was a marine. They love that hazing stuff."

"Nice stereotyping, Charlie!"

"Come on! Didn't you think he was trying too hard to be all politicianlike? He always had the right answers."

"I don't know what to think. Part of me thinks he's a good guy and he doesn't know," Nidhi said.

"Well, I think it's time to tell Ms. Fieldston. We just don't know enough about him to go in there and say, 'Hey, Coach, by the way, your players are huge hazers and they ran someone over.'"

## CHAPTER THIRTY-FIVE

**"GIRLS, THANK YOU SO MUCH FOR TELLING ME! IT'S HARD TO** believe those boys are capable of doing something like that," said Ms. Fieldston. After the meeting with Coach Mason, it had taken two more days to set up this appointment, so Sydney and I were beyond impatient.

"Well, if you had seen them, you wouldn't have a problem believing it at all," said Sydney.

"It's just that I've never heard of them doing something like that before . . . but if you say it happened, I'll look into it right way."

"Thanks, Ms. Fieldston," I said. "We really didn't know who else to talk to."

"Of course, it's what I'm here for. I'll talk to the coach and Mr. Wickam and get to the bottom of this."

"Ms. Fieldston, what will happen to the guys?"

She leaned in closer to us, her hair dropping forward so she had to quickly tuck it behind her ears. "The school has strict policies for these kind of things. I'll have to talk about it with Mr. Wickam. But, girls, now that you've told me, try to put it out of your minds. It'll get taken care of," she said reassuringly.

"How do you think that went?" I asked, as my steps echoed down the hallway.

"Not bad. I think she believed us, if that's what you mean. I guess now all we do is wait to see what happens," Sydney said.

"How long do you think that'll take?"

"I don't know, a few days at the most? You know as soon as it gets out, everyone's going to be talking about it."

"Do you think they'll all be kicked out of school?"

"It's possible. At the very least, they should get kicked off the team and get some kind of suspension."

"Are you as freaked out about this as I am right now? I mean, I can't help feeling like the least I should do is tell Will," I said.

"Don't do that! He'll just get mad. What he doesn't know can't hurt him."

"I don't know, just seems like I'm lying to him somehow. I mean, I told him I'd let him handle it."

Sydney looked at her watch. "Come on, we need to forget about this for a little while. Let's go see if Michael's still around. We can go get coffee. I'm buying."

Two days later, nothing had happened.

"Ms. Fieldston!" I called out when I caught a glimpse of her between the crush of students fourth and fifth periods.

"Hi, Charlie, love to catch up but I'm running late for a faculty meeting," Ms. Fieldston said, her black high-heeled shoes clacking against the floor.

"I just was wondering, since it's been a few days, if there was anything you could tell me about what we talked about the other day?" I asked, trying to keep up with her and dodging people simultaneously.

"I'd really like to, but I'm not really allowed to say anything about it," she said.

"But is there anything you can tell me?"

"Charlie, don't worry about it. It's being handled. And I'm really glad you told me, but I want you to keep in mind that there're always two sides to a story," Ms. Fieldston said with a tight smile.

"What do you mean? We know what we saw. Those boys did it on purpose," I insisted.

"I know you feel that way, Charlie, but from our investigation, it looks like an accident. You know boys will be boys sometimes. You can't punish them for that."

I watched her walk down the hall in her pencil skirt, and I knew without a doubt that I was being blown off. We had trusted her, and she betrayed us.

# CHAPTER THIRTY-SIX

**THAT AFTERNOON I DRAGGED MYSELF TO THE *PROWLER*. I** walked in, got a cup of tea, and tried to concentrate.

"Hey, Charlie! Can you help me look at this layout?" asked Ms. McBride.

"Sure," I said.

I gave a cursory glance at the monitor. "Looks fine, Ms. McBride, but I'm sure Josh will come in and want to change everything around." I tried to smile, but just the attempt to pretend everything was fine sent me into a tailspin. Before I could stop myself, tears were running down my face.

"Charlie, what's wrong?" Ms. McBride asked, putting her arm around me.

"It's nothing. I'm just having a really bad week," I said between my tears.

"Charlie, why don't you come into my office. Maybe there's something I can do to help."

"I really doubt that."

"Try me."

All I could think was how pointless it had been talking to Ms. Fieldston. Why would this be any different? But still I followed her to her office and sat down.

"By any chance, would this have anything to do with the interview you and Nidhi did with Coach Mason the other day?" she said, looking directly at me.

"What did he tell you?" I asked defensively.

"Well, he stopped by my office yesterday. He was concerned about some of the questions you asked him."

"Why? Was he mad about it?"

"No. Not at all. But he was worried. He thinks you may know something about hazing on the team."

"Why would I know anything about that?"

"Aren't you friends with some of the freshmen on the team?"

"Yeah."

"If there's a problem on Coach Mason's team, I think he'd want to know."

"Do you really believe that?" I asked skeptically.

"Did he give you any reason to believe otherwise?"

I didn't know what else to say because telling her meant trusting another adult, and so far they were failing me 100 percent. I stared at the wall behind Ms. McBride and said nothing.

"Charlie, something is clearly going on. If you don't want to tell me, I can't force you, but for whatever it's worth, I've watched you really come into your own this year—which isn't an easy thing to do. You've made a place for yourself at this school, and I'm really proud of you. Whatever it is that you're dealing with, I know you will do the right thing."

"Ms. McBride, no offense, but adults always say things like that. Doing the right thing is a lot more complicated than it seems. And even if you do the right thing, sometimes I don't think that changes things all that much. Believe me, I've tried."

"What do you mean?"

"I don't know. It's complicated. . . . Ms. McBride, you really trust Coach Mason?"

"I do. He's also a close friend of Mr. Jaquette's, and you like him, right?"

"I don't know why he needs to talk to me about what's going on with the team, because he's been told already."

"What are you talking about?"

"He already knows. A few days ago, I told Ms. Fieldston everything that happened, and she said she would tell Coach Mason."

"What did you tell Ms. Fieldston?" Ms. McBride asked, picking up a pencil and tapping it against her hand.

"I told her about something I saw after a party."

Now it was Ms. McBride's turn to sit and say nothing.

"Okay, Charlie, I don't know anything for certain, but I think there is a possibility that Coach Mason doesn't know. Or at least doesn't know your side of the story."

"You mean like Ms. Fieldston didn't tell him?"

"I'm not saying anything one way or another. Remember, you gather your facts first before you make a decision about something."

"One thing's for sure, Ms. Fieldston's been blowing me off ever since I told her."

"Well, I'm not going to blow you off, and neither will Coach Mason if you go talk to him. I know this means taking a big leap of faith, but I'm asking you to trust me."

I took a deep breath. For some reason I wanted to give it one more try. I wanted to believe there were adults who could make it better.

"Okay, I'll do it, but I want you to go with me."

"I'll be behind you every step of the way," she said and picked up the phone.

"Coach Mason? I have Charlie Healey with me, and I think we should come down to your office and talk."

## CHAPTER
## THIRTY-SEVEN

**IT'S FUNNY WHAT HAPPENS AFTER YOU CONVINCE YOURSELF** to do something courageous under the category of "doing the right thing." You assume you'll feel good. No confusion. No regret. If I had known that my initial feeling of confidence would be swiftly replaced by fear and paranoia, I'm not sure I would have done it. I was totally paranoid that Will would find out and never talk to me again. Or, Dylan and Matt would find out and I'd be known as a snitch for my entire high school life.

So it wasn't like I was thrilled to find myself in Principal Wickam's office the next day sitting between Ms. McBride and Coach Mason, spilling my guts.

"Well, Charlotte, these are very serious charges you are making. You're sure you want to make them?" Mr. Wickam asked, methodically rocking back and forth in his chair.

"Yes, sir, I am. I am absolutely positive," I said, looking him right in the eye. I didn't trust one perfectly styled hair on this man's head.

"You need to be certain about what you are saying, young lady. Those boys are leaders in this school. . . . An accusation like this could ruin their future. Are you sure you want to do this to them?"

I sat there speechless. How was this my fault?

"With all due respect, sir, I don't think Charlie is doing anything to them," Coach Mason said softly but his jaw was clenched.

"I just want Charlotte to be careful. People see things sometimes that look one way but in reality aren't that way at all."

"I know what I saw," I said, my anger rising.

Mr. Wickam smiled. "Of course you do, Charlotte. But we need to think about what's best for the school, and besides, there really may be a rational explanation that you don't know."

That was it. He could talk to me like I was five, but I couldn't let him defend those guys anymore.

"Principal Wickam, what explanation could there be for hit-and-run driving? I saw them. Everyone knows the lacrosse guys get away with whatever they want at this school."

"I don't think that's entirely accurate. And I know you can't understand this yet, but it's my job to think about all the different repercussions here," Wickam said, tightly.

"Right. I get it. It's just like you said. You have to think about what's best for the school. Which means you're going to do what's best for the school's image."

"Umm . . . perhaps we should thank Charlie for her time before we go any further," Ms. McBride said quickly.

Wickam smiled, "Yes, of course. Charlotte, you are free to leave."

"Yeah, thanks," I mumbled, getting up from my chair.

"Charlie, thanks for telling me. It was a brave thing to do," Coach Mason said.

I closed the door behind me, thinking about what Luke had said. You couldn't trust adults in these situations. They *could* say the right things, but that didn't mean they actually would. Wickam and Fieldston definitely fit into that category. But not everybody was like that. I'd been dead wrong to make all those assumptions about Coach Mason. Along with Ms. McBride, I had to believe Coach Mason would do the right thing. They had to.

## CHAPTER THIRTY-EIGHT

**UNDER THE CIRCUMSTANCES, THERE WAS NO POSSIBLE WAY** to concentrate on my schoolwork. Seriously, how can a person focus on conjugating the subjunctive when my faith in the moral order of the world was at stake? Exactly. It was impossible, but I did at least try to do my homework that night for about ten minutes, and then my phone vibrated. Will was texting me. Homework could wait.

charlie u there? coach mason just left my house!

what?

he knows just finished telling my parents about car thing. I'm dead.

ru in trouble?

mom wants to kill me wants to kill dylan and matt maybe them first not sure ru still on the team?

texting is too annoying im calling hold on

"Okay, that's much better," Will said breathlessly.

"I can't believe he came over!" I said.

"God, this whole thing is so bad. I'm not saying I didn't totally screw up. I did. I know I did. I thought my dad was going to kill me. He told the coach to do whatever he wanted to me. Then he told the coach to kick me off the team."

"What did the coach say?"

"He told my dad he didn't want to do it. Actually, he apologized to me for not seeing what was going on, which was weird."

"But that's good, right? You're happy you're still on the team?"

"Well, I am, but I'm sitting out the rest of the season. And my mom wants me to be the water boy for the team and pick up all the trash after games. And my parents said they're coming to every game to make sure I take it seriously. It's going to be great," he said sarcastically.

"That's a little harsh," I said, stifling my laughter. I mean I felt bad for him, but it was also the least he deserved.

"Oh, and there's more. My mom and dad are taking half of my savings and giving it to Mr. Salinas' family so we can help pay for the guy's hospital bills. And your best friends are gone."

"You mean Dylan and Matt?"

"Yep—kicked off."

"Yes!" I yelled, and jumped for joy. "But I can't believe Wickam would agree to that."

"Oh, yeah, that was crazy. Coach brought that up when he was leaving. They didn't think I could hear them because I was walking upstairs, but he said he'd need my parents to support him."

"For what?"

"That if Wickam wouldn't back him up kicking them off the team, Mason would go public with all the things they've done in the past. Tell people what's been going on and that Wickam knew about it."

"I can't believe how intense this is," I said.

"I just need this thing to end," Will said. He sounded exhausted.

# CHAPTER THIRTY-NINE

**"WAY TO GO, WILL!" SYDNEY YELLED AS SHE JUMPED UP AND** down on the bleachers. The scoreboard read GUEST 7 HOME 0. We were home. Highland was kicking our butt.

"Sydney, shut up! It's embarrassing enough for him!" Michael said, leaning over and covering her mouth.

Sydney pushed him away. "I'm just trying to show my support! What's wrong with that?"

"Because he's in a suit and tie carrying water back and forth to the guy who replaced him on the team," I said.

"I feel bad for him! But will someone tell me why people are wearing those black ribbons on their shirts? Did someone die or something?" Sydney asked.

I glanced around the crowd of parents and students in the Harmony Falls bleachers. About half of them wore little black ribbons like Sydney was talking about, and a group of kids were wearing black T-shirts that had either 12 or 34 or them.

"Those people are protesting Matt and Dylan being kicked off the team. How stupid can people be? And look, some parents are doing it too!" Nidhi said.

"All I can say is, Coach Mason is one very brave man. I wouldn't mess with those lacrosse parents for anything," Michael said under his breath.

"People have lost their minds," I said in disbelief.

Michael shrugged. "They just don't want to deal. They see what they want to see."

"Nidhi, I think we have our last Fresh View for the year," I said quietly, taking out my notebook.

"What's the angle?" Nidhi asked.

"Look around. There's all these people here protesting about how unfair it is for Dylan and Matt to be kicked off the team. But if I know anything about this school, there's probably plenty of people who think they deserve what they got but are too scared to say anything out loud."

"You're right and it would make a good column! We can't let these people think they speak for everyone else," Nidhi said, eyes shining.

"Exactly my point."


Forty-five minutes later, the game was over. Most of the crowd had left; only parents and friends stayed behind as the team dragged themselves off the field. That is, except for Will, who was collecting water bottles and picking up trash as his parents looked on from the bleachers.

"Hi, Mrs. Edwards! Mr. Edwards!" I said, walking over to them.

"Hi, Charlie! You waiting for Will too?" Will's dad said.

"Yeah, um, I know it's Will's punishment, but would you get really mad at me if I went down there and helped him pick that stuff up?" I asked.

Mr. Edwards put his hands in his windbreaker and looked at Will below us.

"I think Will would appreciate a little support right now."

"Great!" I went down a few stairs and then stopped. "I know what Will did was wrong, but I think he got in over his head. He just wanted to make varsity so bad. . . . I don't know. He just didn't know what to do."

"We know, Charlie. We've made some mistakes too. We put way too much pressure on Will to be on that team. We just had no idea what he was dealing with," Mrs. Edwards said.

"Me too," I said, turning back around and walking onto the field.

"Hey, trash boy," I said, putting a paper cup in his garbage bag.

"Can you believe how people just throw their stuff everywhere? Who do they think is going to clean it up?" Will said irritably.

"You?" I said, trying to make a joke, as I bent down to grab more cups.

"Yeah, you're so funny."

"Hey, Will, you have another bag for all this stuff?" called out a voice from the side.

We turned around to see Michael, Nidhi, and Sydney picking things up under a bench.

"Looks like the other team trashed the place," Nidhi said.

"Oh, my God, this is disgusting! There's chew in here!" yelled Sydney, holding up a cup.

"You guys don't have to do this. I'm okay," Will said.

"Don't worry about it. I know you'd do the same for me," Michael said.

"No, I wouldn't," Will joked.

"You're so full of it, Will. Just give me a bag," said Nidhi, smiling.

That's how Will's lacrosse season ended. With all of us picking up trash and water bottles off the field. Honestly, in that moment I knew without a shadow of a doubt that these people were my friends for life.

# THE FRESH VIEW: WHAT EXACTLY
# DO WE STAND FOR?

*We know we're only freshmen and neither of us are on an athletic team, but we felt we had to share our opinion about the controversy on the lacrosse team. It's really hard to see the school tearing itself apart over it. From what we hear in the halls, cafeteria, and classrooms, people fall into one of two camps. One believes the players weren't punished enough, and the other believes the players were punished too much.*

*What we want to ask is, Why are people so angry at one another about it? Why are people accusing Coach Mason of being politically correct, when what he's trying to do, at least from our perspective, is teach his players that he will hold them to certain standards even if that comes at the cost of a division championship? Why is that so bad?*

*What we know is that after a year at this school, we love it here. We are proud to be Harmony Falls students. We want this school to be unified.*

*So while we don't have any answers, at least we wanted to ask questions. Why do people think it builds team unity to haze the younger players? Why, if people know about it and hate it, don't they say anything? Lastly, we know that one of the reasons people like being at this school is because of its traditions. If there are traditions based on people being humiliated or forced to do unethical things, are those the traditions we really want at this school? As we talked to students in the older grades we heard stories that made us shudder. Why would a group of girls think it's funny to smush tuna into a girl's locker? A group of boys think it's team building to duct-tape a boy to a chair for hours and pour disgusting things on him because he had the honor of making it onto a varsity team as a freshman? Do people really not get why that kid decided to drop off the team?*

*We want to be proud of this school. We want to have PRIDE. How can we do that if we don't really challenge ourselves to look at the things we don't like and speak out? And like we said, we know we're only freshmen and not supposed to have opinions, but too bad. That's what we think.*

*Nidhi and Charlie*

# CHAPTER FORTY

**"HEY . . . YOU OKAY?" I SAID AS I OPENED THE SCREEN DOOR TO** Will's backyard.

It was just beginning to get dark, and Will stood about twenty feet in front of me with a BB gun in his arms. It had been two days since the game and I hadn't heard anything from him.

"That bad, huh?" I asked, sitting on the porch step.

"Not really, just bored. I haven't used this thing since I was ten," he said, cocking the gun and shooting. A can jumped and rolled away.

"I thought I'd drop by here to see how you were doing. Are your parents going to ease up a little now?"

"Yeah, I think so. You know at first I was really mad at my mom for the whole water boy thing, but then it was fine. It just sucked seeing us lose so badly," Will said, hitting the can again. "You know, my parents went with Coach Mason to meet with all of the other parents. My dad told me he'd never seen my mom that mad. Matt's dad tried to get all up in her face, and my mom just tore him up. So then Dylan's dad suggested that Dylan and Matt do community service through my dad's church, like doing some gardening or something."

"What did your dad say?" I asked, remembering what Luke had said about their past community service.

"My dad took him up on it. He told them they could clean out the bathrooms at the homeless shelter downtown through the summer," Will said, smiling.

"I love your dad!" I said.

"I know. Actually the part I like best is with my mom. It'd have been cool to see her go off on someone else besides me for a change." He put the gun down and stretched out on the lawn.

I walked over and sat down next to him. For a second, he looked just like he did when he was eleven. He propped himself on his elbows. "I sort of forgot to tell you Coach Mason got onto their Facebook pages and saw the pictures from the scavenger hunt and the party."

"How did he see their pages?"

"He might have gotten a little assistance."

"Will, you did that?"

He shrugged. "After my mom and the pictures, that was enough to shut them up."

"Well, I have a confession, too."

Will stared at me and waited.

I took a deep breath. "Okay, this is hard to say, and I don't want you to get mad at me, even though you probably will . . . but I was the one who told Coach Mason."

"What do you mean?"

"I went to him a few weeks ago."

"After I told you not to?"

"Maybe."

Will dropped back onto the ground and didn't say anything.

"Will, I know I said I wouldn't say anything, but I just couldn't let them get away with it! If you want to hate me, I'd sort of understand, although in a way I wouldn't because I think I was right to do it, but at the same time—"

"Charlie, relax! I'm not mad. I'm just sort of surprised. Actually, I shouldn't be surprised. You never listen to me."

"That's not exactly true!"

"No, seriously, it's okay. Now that I've been away from those guys for a while, I'm realizing how messed up everything was. I was just too close to it all to see it."

For a minute, we both stared at the trees and the darkening sky above us.

"Charlie, tell me next year will be easier."

"Well, I don't see how it couldn't be. Unless you decide to join some other group of psychopaths, but I'm betting against it. Hey, look, there's a firefly!" I said, pointing to the trees. It was the first one I'd seen that year. "Wait, I'll get one," I said, getting up. The trees sparkled from all the lights.

I sat back down and opened my hands. "See him? You know they're all male, right?"

"You know, Charlie, I couldn't have gotten through this year without you," he said, putting his hand against mine so the firefly crawled over to him. We both watched it spread its wings and float above us.

"I know, I'm your rock," I teased.

"I'm not joking. I can't imagine being back here without you," he said.

"Okay, me neither, although there were times this year when I really wished you weren't here."

"Can you forgive me?" he said, moving closer, his face inches away from mine.

"Of course. That's what friends are for," I whispered.

Hesitantly, he kissed me lightly on the lips, and I couldn't breathe. I was kissing Will in his backyard. What in the world was happening?

The screen door opened, and we flew apart.

"Will! Where are you?" his mom called out. "Oh, hi, Charlie, I didn't see you all there. You staying for dinner?"

"I don't think so. My mom wanted me home," I said as calmly as I could.

"I'll be in in a minute, Mom. I'm just going to let Charlie out the back way," Will said and grabbed my hand.

At the gate, all of a sudden we were kissing again. "Okay, I'm going to go home now and freak out," I said.

"Why? You didn't like it?" Will said nervously.

"No! I like it, but it's you!"

"I know. I've been wanting to do that for a long time."

"Really?"

"Really." He kissed me again. "Really," he whispered in my ear.

"I'm going home."

He grinned. "Okay, but I'll see you tomorrow, right?"

I nodded and walked out.

# ACKNOWLEDGMENTS

"HOW HARD COULD WRITING A NOVEL BE? I HAVE LOTS OF stories from my experiences working with teens and I'm a writer after all. All I have to do is put it together somehow. . . ."

So, for the record, it was very hard. I have never wanted to give up on a writing project so often and with such vehemence like I did with this book.

But I did it—and I am very glad I did. It is an incredible thing for a nonfiction writer to realize that it's often easier to communicate the truth through fiction. As with all my books, I depended on my students and teens around the country to help me make sure the situations depicted in the novel are as realistic as possible. So everything in this work of fiction is written based on my personal experiences at schools or the experiences of my students.

Now, it's a very humbling experience to have teen editors, because it's not like they spare your feelings, but I wouldn't have it any other way.

First, thanks to all of my 21-and-younger editors. Linus Recht, Catherine Watkins, Molly Seeley (great title, nicely done). To Mr. Jaeger's 2008 creative writing class at Episcopal High School, with special thanks to Wesley Graf and Katrina Brady.

Thanks to Glennis, Allison, and Kristen Henderson, who spent a weekend with me in Washington tearing the book apart. To my next-generation editors: Emily Bartek, who believed I could do it and forced me to keep at it when I really, really didn't think I could or should. You made me laugh as the story came to life and you made sure I kept it true. To Candace Nuzzo, who always keeps the details clear and the waters calm. Much appreciated. To Max Neely-Cohen for taking this project seriously and always being there when the book needed it. You raised it to a higher level when I had no idea how to do that. To Nidhi Berry and Nat Freeman for special inspiration. To Katherine Lehr, whose years as a passionate high school journalist helped bring the *Prowler* to life.

To Gaylord Neely as always. Stacey Barney, who reaffirmed my faith in publishing, gets my sense of humor and went above and beyond what any editor should do. To David Miner and Cary Granat, thanks for being cousins so that I got to do this book with Penguin. Jim Levine for shepherding me through the process; and Kerry Evans at Levine Greenberg, who was a great reader. To Steve Wiseman, my constant, faithful line editor, thank you for seeing Charlie as a hero early on. To my husband, James, who actually needs to thank me this time because I finally wrote something that made him laugh and he didn't mind reading thirty times. To my children, Elijah and Roane, for your excitement that I was writing a "chapter" book.

Finally, to all the teens and kids I work with. I tried my best to write something that would reflect your experiences of what it is like to be your age today—for the good, the bad, and the ugly. I believe what you are dealing with is important and should be respected as such. I hope I did right by you.

TURN THE PAGE FOR AN INTERVIEW WITH

Rosalind Wiseman

# An Interview with Rosalind Wiseman by

## Mavie Cruz of
www.the-bookologist.blogspot.com

### AND

## Regie Cruz of
www.theundercoverbooklover.blogspot.com

**Boys, Girls, and Other Hazardous Materials** **is your first young adult novel. What made you choose to write young adult?**

I didn't choose YA, it chose me. I was asked to write the book by Penguin several years ago, and didn't know at the time if I could do it. But thankfully I ended up with a really amazing editor who comforted me, pushed me, and made me a better writer in the process.

I knew it would be a big challenge. I tell my students to take risks and be uncomfortable all the time, but when I was asked to write this novel I realized it was an opportunity for me to practice what I preach. I have been terrified of failing throughout the whole process, but I pushed through and did it anyway.

**How does it feel being an author?**

It feels cool! All of these funny, interesting, crazy experiences one has have a place to go once you're a writer—especially with regard to fiction. But when it very first happened, I couldn't believe my name was on a book. I would sometimes go to the bookstore just to visit the book—it was so surreal for so long.

**How are you and Charlie alike? How are you different?**

Charlie and I are alike in that we can both be pretty self-conscious at times. We are different in that I think she is more independent-thinking than I was when I was a teenager. She knows herself better than I did, and she isn't as focused on impressing people as I was. But I think that as a writer you often want your main character to be the things you couldn't be. You want them to be real, but push them to do the thing you couldn't have done yourself.

**What was the most difficult aspect of writing *BGOHM*?**

All of it. :-)

**What would you like readers to take from *BGOHM*?**

I've been thinking a lot about that. I wrote a story that is in some ways very typical of a young adult novel, but I tried to weave in a lot of subtle, quiet injustices that kids see every day but never talk about. I am pushing and challenging the reader to see things that are totally normal and dissect them. I want them to be able to realize that even though something is normal, it doesn't make it right.

**What do you see as your strengths and weaknesses as an author?**

I think I'm really good at writing realistic dialogue. The situations that I put my characters in are real—they are experiences I've had working with thousands of kids from across the country over the years. It makes for more confident writing when you know that what you're saying is based on someone's reality.

I think my weakness is describing how a person feels

through their behavior—that has been really challenging for me. Being able to convey in a small gesture how a character feels takes brilliant nuance. I have a really hard time describing the environment in the appropriate amount of detail. I feel like I am always either including too much or too little in my descriptions of a setting in the first few drafts—but I guess that is what editors are for!

**What's the most interesting thing a reader has ever said to you?**

A mom actually recently told me that after reading my book *Queen Bees & Wannabes*, she got divorced because her husband was not treating her with dignity. In the book I say that you have to be honest about the kinds of relationships you have in your life if you're going to ask that of your child. If you have people in your life that treat you like dirt, you won't have any credibility when you tell your kid you don't want the same thing for them. It made me feel sad for a moment that something I wrote would have changed her life so drastically, but ultimately I felt good about having been a catalyst in helping her make a decision that had resulted in her being honest with herself and ultimately being happier for taking the risk.

**How does it feel to have your book turned into a movie (*Mean Girls*)?**

It's complicated. It feels great in many ways, but *Mean Girls* cast such a huge shadow that I don't want to be identified as that being the only successful thing I've ever done in my life. I'm hoping that the novel will be well-received enough to give me a little breathing room from that phenomenon.

**Do you have any "must-have's" while writing?**

Music. It was absolutely critical to the process. I listened to a lot of the stuff that I loved when I was a teenager because it really brought me back to some of those more emotional places. So for me that was a lot of Depeche Mode and The Smiths. But I also love a lot of contemporary stuff and listened to a lot of Rihanna and Three Doors Down and Lily Allen.

**Describe yourself in one word.**

Impatient.

**Books you've faked reading:**

This is honestly one of the best questions I've ever been asked. *War and Peace. Paradise Lost. Brideshead Revisited.* Lots of Shakespeare—I've started a lot of Shakespeare and not finished.

**Books you've bought for the cover:**

*Mists of Avalon.* I actually liked it. But I loved the powerful woman sorceress.

**Books you're an evangelist for:**

*Peace Like a River, Black Swan Green,* the short story "Roman Fever" by Edith Wharton.